SWEET DREAMS

A SUGAR RUSH ROMANCE

NINA LANE

SNOW QUEEN
PUBLISHING

Sweet Dreams
A Sugar Rush Romance

Copyright © 2016 by Nina Lane
2020 edition
All rights reserved.

Published by Snow Queen Publishing

Cover photography: Sara Eirew
Cover design: Perfect Pear Creative Covers

ISBN: 978-1-7360527-5-4

SWEET DREAMS
Nina Lane

&.

Can a sexy bohemian bakery owner teach a rigid CEO how to taste the sweetness of life?

Warning! Contains chocolate eclairs, skinny dipping, hard candy, hammocks, hippie music festivals, and super hot tent sex.

The Sugar Rush books are sexy contemporary romances by New York Times bestselling author Nina Lane. They can be read as standalone novels or enjoyed as a series.

SWEET DREAMS
SWEET ESCAPE
SWEET SURRENDER
SWEET TIME
SWEET LIFE

For Melissa Foster, with immeasurable gratitude.

CHAPTER 1

*a*s it turned out, Cheetos dust incited Polly Lockhart's come-to-Jesus moment.

It wasn't enduring grief over her mother's death ten months earlier, or the agonizing resignation that had preceded it—the diagnosis followed by months of chemo, the hope that both expanded and shrank daily, the pain of watching her mother's body fade into a hollow shell that couldn't contain the warm, vibrant spirit she remained until the end.

No, it was sticky, orange, pseudo-cheese dust that shocked Polly back to her senses.

"Well, hello, stranger!" Mia Davenport sailed across the Indian restaurant, her blond hair spilling down her back and her lithe, sinuous figure clad in a navy sheath dress and heels. "I thought you said it was your three-month anniversary tonight."

"It is," Polly acknowledged, after exchanging hugs with her friend. "I'm just picking up some dinner."

"Oh." Mia glanced at the hostess, who was walking to the kitchen to retrieve Polly's order. "Well, come say hi to the girls. We really wanted you to join us."

"Uh, I'm not really dressed for..." Polly glanced down at her wrinkled paisley skirt and T-shirt, but Mia grabbed her arm and hauled her across the room to a round table where three other young women sat munching on samosas and pakora. The sight of them, all polished and prettied-up for a girls' night on the town, intensified Polly's self-consciousness.

That and the fact that she hadn't seen much of the other girls in the past few years—not with her mother's illness and everything that went along with it. Her friends had always been there, of course, calling and stopping by with food and offers of help, but Polly had been so mired in grief that she hadn't wanted to see or talk to anyone except her mother. And months after Jessie Lockhart's death, Polly was still trying to figure out how to emerge back into the world.

Her older sister, Hannah, hadn't had that problem, Polly thought—not without a twinge of envy over Hannah's ability to keep living, even if that also meant *leaving*. Hannah had taken flight less than a week after their mother died, claiming she needed to "get away."

More like "run away." Sadly, much as Polly wished Hannah had stayed, her sister's flight hadn't surprised her. If it weren't for Hannah's travel blog, she would have little way of knowing where her sister was.

"Happy anniversary, Pols," Emma said. "Three months dating, huh? You know what that means."

Polly didn't, but she smiled anyway as the other women chuckled.

"Sure you can't come with us?" Mia glanced at her watch. "The show starts at eight, and I haven't sold the extra ticket yet."

"No." Polly deflected a pang of regret and glanced back toward the kitchen. "I should go. Brian is waiting."

"So what else are you guys doing to celebrate?" Sarah reached out to pour herself a glass of red wine.

"Um, we're just hanging out."

The other women blinked, as if "hanging out" was a lame way

to spend an anniversary—even a three-month one. Sarah gestured to Polly's face.

"You've got something there, hon."

Polly touched her chin. Oh no, not an unwanted zit. "What?"

Mia peered closer at Polly's face. "Just some crumbs or something."

Polly swiped at her face with her sleeve, then caught Mia looking at her fingers, which were still colored with orange Cheetos dust. Embarrassment flushed over Polly from head to toe. She shoved her hands into her pockets.

"So did Brian get you a gift?" Emma asked.

"I think so." Polly did not, in fact, think so. Brian had never gotten her anything and she had no reason to believe he would do so now, but she couldn't very well admit that to her friends. "We're exchanging gifts later."

"Is he here?" Sarah glanced toward the front doors.

"No, I'm...he's back at the house. I'm just picking up dinner. We're going out later for drinks and...um, dancing." Polly took a step back. "Great seeing you all. Have fun at the concert tonight."

The other women waved, and Mia fell into step beside Polly as she returned to the front counter to pay for the takeout food.

"Really, Pols?" Mia eyed Polly with far more perception than was comfortable. "You're spending your anniversary in the basement, aren't you? What are you doing, helping organize his comic book collection?"

Polly sighed. As one of her oldest friends, Mia had always seen right to the truth, which was both one of her most appealing and most annoying qualities.

"Brian is a homebody," she said defensively. "There's nothing wrong with that."

"For *him*, maybe not." Mia crossed her arms, narrowing her eyes on Polly's face. "But for you? Come on, Pols. You're eating Cheetos and delivering take-out Indian food to your boyfriend on your anniversary? You deserve more, and you know it."

Polly was saved from having to respond—or agree—by the hostess appearing with paper bags filled with fragrant Indian curries and dal. She dug into her patchwork purse for her wallet and handed the hostess her credit card. After she'd paid, she turned back to Mia, who was standing in front of the door.

"Polly." Mia tapped her fingers on her arms. "I am begging you to call Brian and tell him you decided to hang out with your girl-friends tonight."

"I can't do that to him, Mia."

"Why not? It's not like he's doing anything for you. Or *to* you," she added under her breath.

"Hey." Polly frowned, insulted by the implication that she and Brian didn't have a hot and heavy relationship—even if that was, once again, the truth. "You don't know what we're planning."

"I know it can't be anything good, if it started with a junk food appetizer," Mia remarked. "On your anniversary, a guy should take you out to a high-class restaurant, give you flowers and a nice gift, spring for a good bottle of wine, then take you back home and rock your world. He should not be asking if you want barbeque or regular potato chips. And he should most certainly not be sending you out to bring chicken biryani back to his basement so he doesn't have to interrupt his *Deep Space Nine* marathon."

"*Next Generation*," Polly muttered.

"Whatever." Mia sighed and took hold of Polly's shoulders. "Polly, look at me. You are almost twenty-five years old. Twenty. Five. Years. Old. I admire you for your loyalty to Brian, sadly misplaced though it is, but it's past time for you to play the field. Or at least get off the damned bench."

Mia was right. But Polly had spent the past four years living in a shell so dark that even after having emerged ten months ago, her eyes were still adjusting to the light. It was no wonder she'd been drawn to hobbit-like Brian in his basement apartment with the single window, green shag carpet, and walls plastered with geek posters and street signs.

"Don't you dare make birthday plans with Brian." Mia released Polly's shoulders. "I will not allow you to spend your twenty-fifth birthday in his basement, drinking purple soda and watching nerdy TV. I'm taking you out to celebrate, and we're going to have fun. More specifically, *you're* going to have fun. Even more specifically, you're going to remember how good it feels to have fun. And I'd strongly suggest you break up with Brian before next weekend because I'm going on the prowl to find you the kind of man who can show you exactly what you've been missing. In other words, a man who is the opposite of Brian."

"Mia—"

"Nope." Mia shook her head so vigorously her hair flew around her shoulders. "Next Saturday, seven sharp. I'm treating you to the kind of dinner Brian should be buying you tonight, and then we're going out for drinks and dancing. I'll come early to help pick out your outfit. And I'm blocking your texts so you can't cancel. Now I've gotta go. My curry is getting cold. And you still have crumbs on your face."

Before Polly could come up with an excuse to decline, Mia pulled her into a quick, tight hug and flounced back to the table. Polly bent to pick up the paper bags she'd left at her feet. As she straightened, she caught a glimpse of herself in the mirror on the opposite wall.

Her hair was pulled into a messy knot with frizzy tendrils drifting around her forehead, her favorite cotton paisley skirt was wrinkled and sagging at the hem, and there was a grape soda stain on the front of her shirt. Not to mention, a smear of orange dust marred the side of her pale cheek, like a really hideous blusher.

Really, Polliwog? This is what you've come to?

Her mother's voice echoed in her mind. Polly almost winced.

Despite Jessie Lockhart's peace-loving nature, the words felt like a smack right upside Polly's head. Even after she'd gotten sick, Jessie had been all about *living* and having fun, taking risks, following your dreams. Maybe it was time Polly remembered how to do that too.

After scrubbing her sleeve across her cheek, she drove back to Brian's building and walked down the narrow wooden stairs to his basement apartment. The noise of a YouTube video came from his laptop, and an old *Dr. Who* episode played on the TV. The light was a weird yellowish color from the railroad light glowing on the opposite wall.

Brian didn't look up from his sprawled position on the sofa to acknowledge Polly's entrance, but when she marched to stand right in front of the TV, his gaze settled on her with faint irritation.

"You're in my way," he remarked.

"No." Polly put her hands on her hips and summoned her resolve. "Actually, you're in *my* way."

Brian gave a *whatever* shrug and turned back to his computer. Polly reached for the remote and lowered the volume on the TV.

"Brian," she said. "We need to talk."

He sighed gustily and dragged his attention back to her. Polly's nerves tightened. She didn't want to hurt him. They'd met at the local community college where she was taking culinary classes and Brian had been enrolled in a computer science class before dropping out at the beginning of the new semester. He was a good guy, just rather clueless when it came to relationships.

Not that Polly was any more experienced, but Mia was right. She deserved more from her future than sitting in the basement, eating Top Ramen and watching *Mystery Science Theater 3000*. Wasn't that the reason she'd enrolled at Hartford Community College in the first place? To learn how to be a better baker, a smarter business owner, a woman worthy of following in Jessie Lockhart's footsteps?

She looked at Brian with his messy hair and scruffy goatee. How many days in a row had he been wearing that *Futurama* T-shirt?

"Brian, I'm getting the sense that maybe you and I want different things out of a relationship," Polly began gently.

She hoped this news wouldn't make him cry. She'd have a really hard time leaving if he cried.

"Why'd you turn the TV down?" Brian frowned.

"I'm trying to have a serious conversation here. I don't think we're as compatible as I was hoping we were."

He shifted one eye toward his computer screen again.

"Brian."

"Huh?"

"I'm breaking up with you," Polly said firmly.

He didn't respond, his attention on the screen as his fingers moved over the keyboard.

"Brian? Did you hear me?"

"Huh?"

"I'm breaking up with you," she repeated. "Don't blame yourself. It's not you, it's...well, actually it *is* you and not me, and you're welcome to blame yourself, but really, you need to get out of this basement and go do something with your life. It's about time I did too. Brian? Are you listening to me?"

"Yeah." He craned his neck to peer around her at the TV. "Hey, did you remember to order the chicken vindaloo?"

CHAPTER 2

ind your happiness.

Even amidst the noise of the Troll's House bar, the thought zinged around Polly's mind like a pinball. For years, she hadn't had the luxury of thinking about *happiness* in any great detail, but she wasn't going to find it, or her future, in a basement that smelled like old socks.

And frankly she couldn't imagine how she ever thought she might.

Now her future would be about...well, it still involved finding a way to keep her mother's bakery afloat and finishing her spring semester in the culinary arts program, but at least those goals no longer seemed quite so far away.

Polly had promised her mother she would return Wild Child to the warm, homey place it had been before Jessie got so sick, and it was time to fulfill that promise. In her efforts to jumpstart her life, Brian had just been an unfortunate misstep, one she attributed to her weakness for wounded animals and lost causes.

Her *immediate* future, however, involved another birthday cake shot.

"Wow." Polly gestured to the bartender, feeling sort of fizzy and bubbly, like soda pop. "These shots are awesome."

"Agreed." Mia tossed her long blond hair over her shoulder and tilted her head back to down hers. "But I dunno, Pols. This place isn't exactly what I had in mind."

"I know, but thanks for humoring me."

After Mia had treated Polly to a gourmet sushi and teriyaki dinner, she'd wanted to go to an upscale club for drinks and dancing. But Polly had balked at the idea of sophisticated cocktails and gorgeous men and women who actually knew what they were doing. She wanted to be a braver version of herself, but one that was actually attainable.

So she and Mia had ended up at the Troll's House, a dive bar with a rough wood floor, flashing jukebox, neon beer signs, and several pool tables. It was loud, crowded, lots of beer, and nothing fancy. Exactly the kind of place Polly could start to come out of her shell.

Maybe.

"I told you I'd be on the prowl," Mia said unapologetically, scanning the room with her sharp gaze. "And though I was hoping for a Wall Street executive, I can see the appeal of a blue-collar dude."

Polly turned to take the birthday cake shot from the bar.

Live your life. Take risks. Embrace change. Be happy, for God's sake.

Her mother's voice again. The sharp stab of pain Polly had felt at her loss had recently dulled to a soft, perpetual ache around her heart. She'd miss her mother forever, but more and more, Jessie's incessantly positive, you-only-live-once, Polly-I-love-you-but-if-you-don't-move-on-and-be-happy-I-will-come-back-to-haunt-you attitude, was easing Polly's grief.

She licked up another rainbow sprinkle. The alcohol hummed pleasantly in her blood, giving her much-needed courage.

Though Polly had faced a lot of challenges head on, she'd never been confident, much less experienced, in the *Men* category.

Brian aside, she just hadn't been around men that much, especially after her father died when she was nine. Her mother, determined to start a new life, moved out of the Twelve Oaks commune in Santa Cruz where they'd lived all of Polly's life.

Jessie had taken Polly and Hannah to Rainsville, a small farming town south of San Francisco, and opened up the Wild Child Bakery with their father's life insurance money.

Women had always worked at the Wild Child Bakery, and Jessie had been active in feminist groups and women's writer workshops. She had boyfriends every now and then, but they never stuck around. And Polly hadn't had much chance to form her own relationships before her mother got sick.

"They're like a foreign species," Polly muttered to Mia, gesturing toward a group of men crowded around the tables. Even with his comic book obsession and geekiness—or perhaps because of them—at least Brian had been *safe*. "I feel like I'm studying them for research purposes."

"As long as it's sexual research, you're good to go," Mia replied. "I guarantee that great sex will give you the boost you need."

Though the thought of *great sex* made Polly a little nervous, it was past time that she finally got her groove on.

"I'm ready," she said with a firm nod. "I want to experience everything I've been missing, and especially to—" she dropped her voice to a whisper "—get laid."

If she was going to do this, she was going full-force, like turning an egg beater on high speed to get the job done.

"Good girl." Mia gave a nod of satisfaction. "Let's get started."

She spun around on the stool again to face the crowded room.

"What you need first," she continued, "is practice. Look at that guy. Serious, panty-melting hottie alert."

She nodded toward a tall, dark-haired man in his mid-thirties who was playing pool. Polly blinked and focused on him.

Oh, wow. Hottie, indeed. How was it possible she hadn't noticed him before now? He was wearing gray trousers and a white shirt with the sleeves rolled up to reveal his muscular forearms. A striped, silk tie was knotted loosely around his neck, and the collar of his shirt was unbuttoned, displaying a tempting V of tanned skin.

As he leaned over to position a shot, Polly let her gaze travel over the slope of his muscular shoulders and back, down to his very fine ass. She had never been much of a gawker, but this man gave a girl plenty to gawk at.

Then he glanced over his shoulder. Right at Polly.

Their gazes collided with a force that almost knocked her off the barstool. She grabbed the edge of the bar, her heartbeat going from normal to crazy-wild in two seconds flat. The air sizzled with a current of electricity that arced right between them, setting her nerves alight and pooling heat in her core. Her sex actually throbbed, as if he were parting her legs and gliding his fingers right up north to—

He broke their eye contact and returned his attention to the pool table.

Whoa. What the hell just happened?

He shot. And missed.

"Hmm," Mia said. "Maybe you should go console him."

"What?"

"For practice," Mia explained. "You need to learn how to approach a hot guy and talk to him. You have a total opening since he's standing there by himself waiting for his next turn. But if you don't go now, that redhead in the corner booth is going to pounce on him. And she looks like a territorial bitch."

Polly swung her gaze to the busty redhead whose cleavage was about to pop out of her tank top. The redhead was staring at

Mr. Hottie, poised on the edge of her seat as if she were waiting for an opportunity to make a move.

"Go," Mia hissed, grabbing Polly's arm and hustling her off the stool. "I'm right here. If you start to panic, scratch your ear as a signal, and I'll come rescue you."

Polly dug for courage, grabbed her shot from the bar, and approached Mr. Hottie. Thanks to Mia picking out her outfit tonight, she was wearing a black mini-skirt and white, stretchy shirt that gave her a nice hourglass shape without looking trashy. At least, that was what Mia had told her before they'd left for the Japanese restaurant.

Polly stopped beside Mr. Hottie. Just the air around him seemed warmer and charged with energy. A tingle rained down her spine.

He turned his head to look at her. God, he was gorgeous. Strong features shadowed with a delicious-looking dark scruff, black eyebrows arching over thick-lashed eyes, and a sensual mouth that was made for kissing and probably a lot of other dirty things Polly shouldn't know about.

And didn't.

Mr. Hottie surely did, though. He exuded self-confidence, control, and oodles of sexual experience. He could really teach her a thing or two. Or several dozen.

Oh, yes. He was the man she needed and wanted—even though just getting close to him was nerve-racking.

He was still looking at her. Again, her heartbeat jolted into gear, that throb of heat starting right between her legs. She struggled to pull in a breath, frantically trying to think of something to say.

"Hi," she managed.

Amusement flashed in his dark eyes.

"Hi," he replied.

"How…um, how are you?" Polly stammered.

"I'm fine, thanks," he said. "How are you?"

"Peachy."

Oh, God. *Peachy?*

Polly looked desperately at Mia, who was watching from the bar. Mia gave her a nod of encouragement and a discreet thumbs-up. Obviously she had no idea what a ninny Polly was turning out to be.

"Peachy," Mr. Hottie drawled, his beautiful mouth now joining in the amusement with a slight smile. "Good to know."

His voice was like melted dark chocolate. Maybe if Polly just kept her mouth shut, he would forget she was there and she could just stare at him in awe. She'd thought men like him were a myth—the sexy, utterly masculine, controlling kind who made a girl want to drop her panties on the spot.

Mr. Hottie was no myth, though. He was all too real. She could even smell him—a tantalizing combination of soap, scotch, and some purely male scent that must have been testosterone or pheromones or something.

Whatever it was, it was making Polly all hot and damp between her legs. And strongly wishing she could drop her panties.

He nodded toward the shotglass still in her hand. "You like it sweet and strong."

"What?" She looked down at the frothy, creamy shot, the glass rim laced with rainbow sprinkles.

"That's a lot of sugar," he said.

"It's a birthday cake shot."

"A what?"

"Cream, cake-flavored vodka, and chocolate." Polly held up the glass. "Birthday cake shot."

"It's your birthday?"

She nodded. "I'm twenty-five."

"Twenty-five, huh?" He raised an eyebrow. "Still a baby."

A *baby?* She frowned, rankled at the idea that this hot, sexy man didn't see her as a woman.

"Your go, man." The other guy moved back from the pool table.

Mr. Hottie chalked his cue and stepped forward to take his shot. Polly backed away to give him room. He pocketed the yellow ball. Out of the corner of her eye, she saw the redhead and her boobs slither out of the corner booth and start toward him, a predatory gleam in her eyes.

Before Polly could even think of what to do next, the redhead had sidled up to Mr. Hottie and put her hand on his arm. She leaned in to speak close to his ear. Though Polly couldn't hear what she said, she was pretty sure it wasn't *"Hi, how are you?"*

Disappointment stabbed her. She had no idea how to compete with a woman like that, who wore her blatant sexuality like armor.

She turned and shuffled back to Mia, feeling like a whipped dog.

"What?" Mia darted a glance at Mr. Hottie. "What happened?"

"Slutty redhead happened," Polly said morosely. She tilted her head back to down the birthday cake shot, appreciating the sweet burn of alcohol and hoping it would obliterate her disappointment. "Can we go now?"

"Oh, Pols." Mia sighed. "Don't give up so easily. Look, check out that guy over there."

She nodded toward a younger, blond guy at the end of the bar. Polly supposed he was cute, but she couldn't drum up any interest in trying again.

"I promise, we'll find a guy who can rock your world," Mia said. "And your headboard."

The guy beside her, who was in possession of an impressive but fuzzy unibrow that crawled like a caterpillar over his eyes, leaned over and waggled his singular eyebrow at Polly.

"I can help you with that, little lady," he remarked.

The fact that Polly was momentarily tempted was a measure

of how much she'd had to drink, how desperate she was getting, and how bummed out she was over her failure with Mr. Hottie.

"Dream on, dude," Mia told Unibrow Guy, rolling her eyes.

"I'm going to pee, then we can go home," Polly muttered.

She set her empty shotglass on the bar and maneuvered through the crowd leading to the restrooms. After using the toilet, she washed her hands and checked her reflection in the mirror. Aside from being flushed and tipsy, she looked the same as always—curly brown hair falling past her shoulders, ordinary features, nice but nothing fabulous.

At least this time she was free of Cheetos dust and grape-soda stains. But even with Mia's makeup artistry and clothing choices, she still looked like Polly Lockhart.

Not that that was a bad thing. She liked being Polly Lockhart. She just wished she was a more courageous, self-confident version of herself. A girl who was better at navigating the world alone. A girl who didn't find it necessary to hide with a base-ment-dwelling lump because she was too scared to put herself out there.

Polly started back to the bar, reminding herself that she was no longer in a relationship with Brian and, therefore, she was no longer hiding.

A broad, male body was blocking the narrow corridor leading back to the bar. One look—actually, one leap of her silly heart—and she knew it was Mr. Hottie. His back was to her, and he had a cell phone pressed to his ear.

"...yeah, he should have told me but he didn't," he was saying, his voice tense.

Polly stopped. Since she had no idea how long he planned to chat, she reached up and tapped on his shoulder. It was like poking her finger against stone.

He turned with a frown, the phone still at his ear. He looked at her, the crease between his eyebrows easing.

"Excuse me," she mouthed, gesturing toward the bar.

"I'll call you back," he said into the phone. He ended the call and slid the phone into his pocket, his gaze rather unnervingly on her.

"Hello, Peach," he said. "I wondered where you'd run off to."

Peach? Well, that made her feel all warm and tingly in a way that had nothing to do with the alcohol she'd consumed.

Still, Polly scowled at him. A cute endearment wasn't going to make her fall at his feet. Another shot would probably do it, but Mr. Hottie's charm wouldn't.

"Peach, huh?" she said. "What about *baby*?"

A smile tugged at his mouth.

"Happy birthday, baby," he murmured, his deep voice like a rush of heat over her skin.

Polly tried, and failed, to steel herself against his charm.

"What happened to the redhead?" she asked.

"What redhead?"

"The one who had her boobs on you fifteen minutes ago."

"I don't remember any redhead," he said. "I only remember you."

Hottie charm definitely overpowering steel...

He reached out to flick his finger against Polly's lower lip.

A bolt of electricity shot through her. She looked at him in surprise as he held up his finger to show her the pink sprinkle he'd captured from her lip.

"Sprinkle," he said.

Polly flushed. How had she missed that in the mirror? She dashed a hand across her mouth and stepped backward, catching the heel of her shoe on an uneven floorboard. She gasped, feeling herself tilt horrifyingly off-balance. The floor swayed beneath her, and she caught a glimpse of Mr. Hottie's very expensive-looking leather shoes.

"Whoa, Peach." He grabbed her waist and hauled her upright. "Careful."

Polly leaned back against the wall, heat blooming inside her at the sensation of being so close to him, his hands warm and strong on her waist. She could smell him again too, that potent combination of sex and masculinity that sparked a heavy pulsing in her lower body.

"You smell amazing," he murmured, his voice deep and smoky. "Like a ripe peach."

She was ripe, all right. So ripe she was about to fall off the vine. And she wished to heaven she *was* a peach. Then maybe Mr. Hottie would lick her, bite her, eat her...

Oh, lord.

She tilted her head to look up at him. His eyes glittered in the dim light. Though Polly's brain was foggy, one sharp, clear thought shone through.

She wanted this man to kiss her. She wanted to feel the pressure of his lips, his body pressed against hers. She wanted to know what it felt like to be kissed by a man who radiated sexual heat and energy, who smelled like all sorts of manly things like spice and musk, a man who would know exactly how to treat a woman...

His gaze skimmed over her face and lingered on her lips. Her pulse sped up.

Do it, do it! Kiss me.

His hands loosened from her waist. He started to back away.

Without thinking, Polly reached up, grabbed his collar, and yanked his head down to hers. Surprise flashed in his expression the instant before she kissed him.

Or, attempted to kiss him. Because he'd started to move away at the exact same instant, she ended up smashing her lips against his chin. She sucked in a breath and pulled back, staring at his mouth. She took aim and went in for the kill.

Yes!

Her lips crashed against his, hot and damp. She was kissing Mr. Hottie.

Moreover, she was doing it with her mouth open, and holy

God, his tongue swept across hers, and he tasted like salt and scotch, and shivers of pure lust rained through her body, and she wanted to keep kissing him forever and ever...

Resistance suddenly coiled through him. His hands closed around her arms, and he pulled away.

A murmur of protest escaped her. She tightened her grip on him, her back hitting the wall again as she forced him closer. He lifted his head. His mouth broke away from hers, his breath still hot on her lips.

"Honey, I'm not going to..." he started.

"Oh, kiss me some more," Polly breathed, standing on her tiptoes to brush her lips against his. "Please..."

Boldly, she flicked her tongue out to caress his lower lip. He groaned, bracing his hands on the wall behind her as he lowered his head again. Heat exploded through her. His kiss became deeper, more possessive, his arms caging her in and trapping her between the wall and his body.

She gasped in shock at the sensation of his muscled body pressed fully against hers, her breasts crushed to his hard chest, his powerful thigh edging between hers...

Oh God. Was that...?

She whimpered, letting her head fall back as he plundered her mouth with his.

"Christ in heaven, you taste amazing," he whispered, trailing his lips over her cheek and down to her neck. "So fucking sweet..."

Polly's whole body was awash in feelings she'd never felt before, a richness like rum-laced buttercream flowing through her veins. She couldn't believe she was doing this—her, Polly Lockhart, kissing an incredibly sexy man in the back corridor of a dive bar. And loving every minute of it.

Not only did she respond to his kiss with hot fervor of her own, she moaned and wiggled her body against his, even parting her legs to let him get his thigh between them. Her nipples stiffened against her bra, and she rubbed them shamelessly against his chest, sending tingles of heat right to her core.

Mr. Hottie put his hands on the sides of her neck, lifting his head from hers again. Though his eyes were dark with lust, that palpable restraint wound through him.

"It's okay, Mr. Hottie," Polly bleated, unable to bear the thought of him stopping now, despite the fact that her head was starting to reel.

He looked faintly amused. "What did you just call me?"

"Mr. Hottie. You know, because you're so damned smoking hot. And, of course, a *mister*." She reached out and rubbed her hands on his chest, marveling at how freaking hard he was all over. "Wow. How often do you work out?"

"Come on." He grasped her wrist with one hand. "I'm taking you home."

"Oh, yay!" She managed to clap her hands despite his powerful grip. "To your house, right? I'll bet you have a huge fluffy bed. Does it have four posts? Feather pillows? I've always dreamed of getting laid on a four-poster bed with feather pillows."

Mr. Hottie shook his head and pushed away from the wall. "We're not doing this."

"Don't you want me?"

He laughed and grabbed her hand, pressing it to the very hard and impressive bulge in his trousers. Lust zinged through her, even though she couldn't fathom how such a thing could ever fit inside her. But oh Lord, was she ever so willing to try.

"Hell yeah, I want you," he muttered. "But not like this."

"Well, if it's not you, I'm going after that blond guy," Polly warned him. "Or that biker dude over by the jukebox. I just got out of a relationship with a boy who—trust me on this—was more interested in bidding for collectable comic books than having sex with me. And you'd better believe I'm going to make up for lost time."

His brows drew together. "So now you're on a mission to get laid?"

She nodded as the lights dipped and swayed in front of her eyes.

"I'm twenty-five," she said, a stab of self-pity hitting her. "I really want to have sex with a man who knows what to do, so I'd totally be into it. Especially if you have feather pillows."

He breathed out a curse, his eyes darkening. "Be careful what you're asking, Peach."

"I know what I'm asking. I'm asking you to fuck me. And if you won't do it, I'll find someone who will."

"Christ." He clamped his hand around her arm. "I'm taking you home. To *your* home."

Polly didn't want to go to *her* home. She wanted to go to *his* home. Just the thought of him spreading her out naked on his fluffy bed intensified her arousal.

Oh my, she was so incredibly warm. Hot and dizzy. The alcohol and sugar churned thickly in her blood.

"Kiss me again," she pleaded.

"You need water and sleep, not kissing," he said, still holding on to her as she stumbled forward.

"What I *need* is to—"

She jerked to a halt and swayed. He stopped to look at her.

Horrified, Polly stared at him. His handsome features went in and out of focus. She clamped a hand over her mouth. Then she bent double and threw up all over Mr. Hottie's very expensive shoes.

CHAPTER 3

*I*t goes on.

Life, that is. Polly sighed. Even after the most embarrassing experience in the history of the world, life goes on.

And hers did. She didn't remember anything after horking up a bunch of birthday cake shots—well, she didn't *want* to remember anything after that—but Mia apparently dove in to rescue her ("Too late," Polly told her bitterly over the phone the next morning, to which Mia replied, "Well, you weren't scratching your ear.")

Mia then reassured her that Mr. Hottie had been entirely solicitous and helpful in getting her to the car and that he'd appeared far more concerned about her than his ruined shoes.

Polly suspected her friend told her that just to make her feel better, but it didn't work. In no language anywhere in the world could *find your happiness* be defined as "get drunk on birthday cake shots and make an ass out of yourself with the hottest man you've ever seen."

With a groan, she tossed her cell phone on the nightstand and hauled herself out of bed, wincing as sunlight speared through her eyes. Her studio apartment over the bakery—which was old and decrepit, but came with low rent and a fantastic commute to work—was usually a place where she felt happy and peaceful. She'd painted the walls a warm blue, decorated them with posters and paintings of Paris, and furnished it with comfortable, shabby furniture and secondhand bookshelves.

But this morning not even her little nest had the power to make her feel better. Maybe she was just more suited to Cheetos and geeky TV than scotch and sex.

Polly gave herself a mental kick in the pants before she did something stupid like call Brian and ask if he'd won the online bid for *The Amazing Spider-Man 300*. She wasn't going to regress just because of one stupidly drunken night. Besides, people were supposed to get drunk and be stupid on their birthdays. It was a rite of passage.

Okay, so maybe the rite was just for one's twenty-*first* birthday, but as a late bloomer who'd spent her four previous birthdays with her mother, Polly was still entitled to a bit of stupidity. She'd bet dimes to doughnuts that Mr. Hottie had—

Stop. Don't think about him.

Just the memory of how she'd acted with that handsome, utterly sophisticated man made her cringe. So much for hoping he'd see her as a *woman*.

Life, Polly reminded herself firmly, *goes on.*

Despite her mind-numbing hangover and scorching embarrassment, she dragged herself into the shower. After getting dressed, she went down the narrow staircase to the Wild Child Bakery that had once been her mother's dream come true.

Located in an old building that also housed a foreclosed car-parts store and a bail bondsman's office, Wild Child had been in business for fifteen years, but it had started going downhill when Polly's mother got sick and was unable to run the day-to-day operations.

Against Jessie Lockhart's wishes, Polly had dropped out of the San Francisco State history program to return home and take care of both her mother and the bakery, but the ensuing struggles with hospital bills and rent had put Wild Child in a hole that she'd purposely kept hidden from Jessie. If there was one thing Polly had been able to do for her mother, it was ensure that she didn't worry about money.

Not that there had been any of it to worry about. And now Wild Child was so far into a hole that Polly could no longer see the sky above. Trying to lift the bakery out of that hole was proving much more difficult than keeping it solvent.

Her heart sank a little as she stepped inside. The gilt paint lettering on the window was peeling, and her mother's once-fantastic decorations of dream catchers, lava lamps, and mandala tapestries now looked old and shabby. Once upon a time, the mosaic tables and seating area had been filled with easygoing hippies and artists who gathered here to eat, read, talk, and play music.

Several loyal customers still came in regularly, but their patronage wasn't enough to offset operating costs, much less help make a profit.

The bakery's long-time employee Clementine was already behind the counter, putting out trays of fresh-baked cookies. In her mid-sixties with long gray hair and an endless supply of tie-dyed caftans, she had been one of Jessie Lockhart's closest friends.

"Morning, Polly." Clementine nodded toward the espresso maker. "Hate to break it to you, but old Bess has been making some gurgling noises that I don't like."

"Give her some Pepto-Bismol, if we can afford it."

They exchanged wry smiles before Polly went back to the tiny office to tally the week's receipts. She'd had to let their other two employees go because she could no longer afford to pay them, but Clementine had stuck around out of sheer loyalty.

Ignoring her throbbing headache, Polly studied the list of vendor bills she still had to pay and wrote up a priority list. She made a few calls asking for credit and deadline extensions. When she hung up the phone, she glanced toward the door. Clementine stood in the doorway, her brow creased with worry.

"It's okay," Polly assured her. "I'm working on it. I got us some extra time."

Clementine didn't respond, her forehead still furrowed. Unease rose in Polly's chest.

"Clem? What's going on?"

Clementine entered the office and sat down, reaching out to cover Polly's hand with hers. "Polly, you know how much I love you and your mother."

"Why does it sound like you're about to give me bad news?"

"It's not bad news. Just a change."

Polly's heart began to sink. Clementine had been devoutly loyal to her mother and Wild Child for years, and she'd stayed on to help run the bakery so Polly could finish her Culinary Arts certificate. But Clementine was widowed and had to make a living too. And they both knew Wild Child couldn't provide her with one.

"You know my daughter and her husband have been trying to have a baby," Clementine said. "Well, it turns out she's three months pregnant."

"Really? That's wonderful."

"And since they recently moved into a larger house, they asked if I wanted to come and live with them, to help Elaine during the pregnancy and then when the baby is born."

"But they live all the way up in Humboldt County."

Clementine nodded, her hand tightening on Polly's. "I'm sorry, sweetie. You know I want to help you with Wild Child, but I also want to be closer to my family. I need to be, now that I'm going to be a grandmother."

"Of course." Polly swallowed past a lump in her throat. "I understand. You've done so much for me. I can't thank you enough."

"You don't have to." Clementine gave her a sad smile. "Your mother was one of my dearest friends. And I can stay on until summer so you can finish your semester and find a replacement."

Polly managed to smile and nod, even though she had no idea how she was going to afford a replacement. But at least she had until summer to figure out a way.

"I appreciate that," she said. "And congratulations, Grandma-to-be."

They stood and embraced before Clementine went back out to the front. Polly tried to focus on her accounts, though there was a new sense of dread in her stomach at the thought of losing her only employee. On the other hand, it was all the more reason for her to work even harder to turn the bakery around. Or at least try and figure out where things were going so wrong.

She finished up the paperwork, then took her laptop out to the front. Mia was on the other side of the counter, eating a sample of coffee cake.

"You okay, Pols?" Her eyebrows drew together with concern.

"If you can get this hammer out of my skull, I'll survive."

"Sit down. I'll bring you some tea." Mia went around the counter, saying to Clementine, "Polly got her party on a little too hard at the Troll's House last night."

"About time," Clementine remarked.

"Polly, did you try the sage smudging?" Ramona, a dread-locked woman in her fifties with bright tattoos covering most of her exposed skin, was busy threading beads onto a piece of thin wire.

"Yes, but I was also baking cookies at the time." Polly put her laptop beside Ramona's plastic jewelry cases and pulled out a chair. "The resulting smell was not appealing. I wanted to clear out negative energy, not potential customers."

Mia placed a fresh cup of matcha tea in front of Polly and sat down with an éclair. The soft strains of music drifted from a corner, where Jessie's friend Tom sat loosely strumming his guitar.

"You want to have another series of music nights?" he asked. "I know some guys who'd play for free."

"Thanks, Tom, but I can't guarantee any sort of crowd at all, and I'd hate to have people playing to an empty house."

"Polly, your aura is quite damaged." Ramona studied her narrowly.

More like pickled. Polly pressed her fingers to her throbbing temple. She supposed she shouldn't have tried to go from Brian to a man like Mr. Hottie in one fell swoop. Instead she should have tried to find an interim guy, like an organic farmer or an environmentalist.

"What you need," Ramona lifted her tattooed finger in Polly's direction, "is a big *thing*."

"That's exactly what she was looking for last night," Mia remarked.

"About time," Clementine said.

"Clem!" A flush heated Polly's face as the women all grinned.

"Nothing against big things," Ramona said. "But I was talking about something viral. Like a video or sob story to get on one of those 'rescue the restaurant' programs on the Food Network."

"Speaking of sob stories." Mia reached into a bag at her feet and took out a rectangular package wrapped in bright blue paper and tied with a red ribbon. She handed it to Polly with a flourish. "Happy birthday."

"Aww, you shouldn't have." Pleased, Polly accepted the present. "Actually, considering you're the reason my head is about to split open, you totally should have."

She tore the paper off the package to reveal a shiny, hardcover cookbook embellished with a photograph of a handsome, silver-haired man wearing a white chef's jacket. On the table in front of him was a gorgeous array of French desserts—pastel pink maca-roons, glossy strawberry tarts, and chocolate religieuses piled with thick, rich cream. The title read *The Art of French Pastry* by Pierre Lacroix.

"Pierre!" Delighted, Polly reached across the table to hug Mia. "Thank you so much."

Mia gave her a self-satisfied smile. "I knew you'd like it."

"I love it." Polly leafed through the thick pages, her mouth almost watering at the sight of all the pastries.

Pierre Lacroix had been her pastry chef hero for years, ever since she and her mother had religiously watched his weekly program on PBS. *The Art of French Pastry* was his latest book, released only a couple of weeks ago. If she'd had the money, Polly would have run out and bought it on release day, and she had another intense pull of gratitude toward Mia for knowing exactly what she'd love.

"I saw an interview with Pierre in which he talked about his career," Clementine said. "He's part of an exclusive, one-time course being held this fall at the Cordon Bleu in Paris."

"Really?" Polly ran her hand over a photograph of a *mille-feuille*. "That sounds amazing."

"There should be something about it in the book."

Polly turned back to the cover and read the sticker near the title: *Apply for the Art of French Pastry Course.*

"Look it up," Mia suggested.

Polly set the book aside. She pulled Pierre's website up on the laptop and clicked on the pastry course link, which provided the details of the six-month course taught by several renowned chefs. After the course was over, the students would be placed at internships in various patisseries and restaurants throughout Paris, including Pierre Lacroix's Pain du Sucre on the left bank.

"You should apply," Clementine said. "You'd wanted to do a year abroad in Paris when you were in college, right?"

That was true. But Polly had dropped out in her junior year when her mother was diagnosed with leukemia. Jessie Lockhart had been far more important than any trip anywhere would have been, though her mother had also been upset at the thought that Polly had given up her own dreams to come home.

Polly hadn't seen it that way, wanting nothing more than to help Jessie however she could. And she had. But while she would never regret the four years she spent with her mother, difficult as they'd often been, she certainly hadn't expected Wild Child to end up on the verge of bankruptcy.

Her problems ran to the very foundation of the business. She'd lost credibility with her suppliers because of her overdue payments, and as a result, the quality of all her baked goods was dropping. That fact would have horrified Jessie, who prided herself on using only top-level ingredients.

Integrity and *quality* were also part of Pierre Lacroix's professional philosophy.

Polly scrolled through the application, which involved writing an essay and submitting a recipe for an original pastry. She'd never created an original pastry in her life—that had been her mother's domain.

"It would be cool to send my mother's éclair recipe to Pierre Lacroix, or at least to his people," she mused. "Even if I'd never be accepted into the course."

"Do not put that attitude out into the world," Ramona said sternly, opening one of her plastic jewelry cases.

An array of colorful stone pendants sat inside the case. After some examination, Ramona removed a shiny, gray-green stone that flashed with iridescent colors of peacock blue and gold.

"Labradorite." Ramona reached across the table and attached the chain around Polly's neck. "It protects your aura from negative energy and enhances your intuitive powers."

"Thanks, Ramona." Polly admired the shiny stone resting against her skin.

Her intuitive powers could certainly use enhancement—especially if both Brian and her behavior with Mr. Hottie were exam-

ples of how badly those powers had failed her. And certainly her
business intuition had proven to be nonexistent.

For her, at least, the air of Wild Child still echoed with the
sound of folk music, conversation, laughter, and the rhythmic
cadence of beat poetry. And her mother was still in the center of
it all—bringing customers fresh pastries, refilling their coffee for
free, listening to their stories, asking about their families.

Jessie Lockhart had always been so vibrant, so interested in
everyone and everything. She was the reason Wild Child had
thrived. Polly couldn't be the reason it failed.

She *wouldn't* be. And her mother would love the idea of her
éclair recipe winging its way to France and Pierre Lacroix. With
that thought in mind, she pulled up the application and typed in
her name.

After a long day at the bakery, Polly spent the evening writing her
essay for The Art of French Pastry course application. She
contacted her Hartford Community College teachers to request
letters of recommendation, ordered copies of her transcripts, and
came up with a "personal philosophy" of how serving artfully
crafted baked goods was an expression of love and friendship.

She finally managed to get a couple hours of sleep on her
lumpy old mattress before hauling herself up at seven-thirty to
get ready for a visit to the corporate headquarters of The Sugar
Rush Candy Company.

The instructor of her Confectionary Technology course,
which was part of the curriculum for her Culinary Arts certificate, had arranged a class tour of the company's test kitchen and
labs, and they were scheduled to meet in the lobby at nine sharp.

Polly dressed with care in a blue embroidered tunic and skirt,
packed her satchel with a new notebook and pens, and drove half
an hour to Indigo Bay, a wealthy, flourishing town south of the

San Francisco Bay Area that prided itself on its coastal beauty and historic culture.

The downtown square and streets were lined with boutiques, art galleries, and cafés, with the residential neighborhoods stretching into the foothills and toward the rocky coastline. Ivy-covered cottages, cobblestones, and secret courtyards gave Indigo Bay a fairy tale atmosphere, which was somewhat fitting given that the town was ruled over by the family who owned a candy company.

But Polly wasn't fooled by the charming quaintness of Indigo Bay—this was an expensive town where the rich, computer-tech crowd came to eat at gourmet restaurants and taste fancy wines before going to the theater and actually buying paintings at the numerous art galleries.

The sprawling campus of The Sugar Rush Candy Company was on the outskirts of town, a collection of brick buildings perched on a grassy expanse of land overlooking the coastline. The test kitchens and laboratory were housed in a stately warehouse with towers that made it look like a fortress.

Polly checked in at the gate and parked in the designated lot for visitors. She'd never been to the Sugar Rush campus before, but it had been featured in several architecture magazines as a stunning example of the ways in which corporate offices could blend into the environment, with the columned brick buildings also evoking the values and history of the company.

The Sugar Rush Candy Company—originally Stone Confectioners—was founded by Edward Stone in the mid-nineteenth century, and had been the domain of the Stone family for over a hundred and fifty years. Though the name had changed a decade ago, the company was still family-run. The six Stone brothers were a close-knit clan who zealously guarded their privacy and had a reputation for being tough but fair employers.

When the family had moved the Sugar Rush headquarters from San Francisco to Indigo Bay after WWII, the company's presence had turned around the economy of an entire region of the coastline with investments in local businesses, steady employment, and a commitment to sustaining the coastal environment.

Not much had changed about Sugar Rush over the years, including the foundation of their well-loved products like Honeybee Toffee and Swirl Pops, which had been among Polly's favorites as a child.

She went into the lobby where her twelve fellow students and instructor, Gordon Andrews, milled around. The open doors of the gift shop displayed shelves lined with Sugar Rush candy bars, glass cases arranged with chocolate confections, fat jars glistening with taffy, suckers, jawbreakers, licorice, rock candy, and bubblegum.

"Everyone, gather round." Gordon spoke in a hushed tone. "Sugar Rush rarely allows tours into their test kitchens. The only reason we were able to arrange one is that one of the assistant chefs is a former student of mine. So I'm sure I don't need to tell you to please be on your best behavior and exhibit both respect and deference."

"Should we curtsy too?" Cora, a fellow student, muttered beside Polly.

Polly smiled. The Stone brothers were the de facto kings of Indigo Bay, so curtsying in their presence would probably not be out of order. Not that Polly thought any of them would emerge from their lavish offices to talk to a group of community college students.

Gordon introduced them to their tour guide, Henry Peterson, who led them through a door marked "Employees Only." After they put on the required aprons and plastic caps, they followed Henry into one of the test kitchens—a massive, gleaming expanse of granite countertops and stainless steel appliances where the chefs and scientists created different varieties of candy. Two chefs bustled around checking on bubbling pots, as if they were presiding over a modern-day witch's brew.

"For generations, Sugar Rush has prided itself on hand-making all our candies," Henry explained. "Everything from lollipops to sour candies and taffy. Usually there are half a dozen chefs working here, but they've stepped out to allow us time for the tour."

"Is the chocolate tested here too?" Cora asked.

"The chocolate test kitchen is located one floor above." Henry pointed to the ceiling. "This is where we test and create all the other candy. Right now we're working on different varieties of ribbon candy and taffy."

Polly had learned and practiced a lot of the techniques in class, but this was the first time she'd ever been in a real candy kitchen and lab. Henry explained all the different processes as they walked around, and soon her hand began to hurt from scribbling so many notes.

"He's coming!" One of the chefs hurried up to Henry, her whisper loud enough for everyone to hear.

Polly looked up from her notebook, sensing a palpable excitement rippling through the air. Her fellow students shifted and murmured with interest.

"What's going on?" she asked Cora, who shrugged.

"Oh." Henry looked disconcerted. "I wasn't expecting this, but it seems the CEO is about to pay us a visit."

Intakes of breath rose from the culinary students. An excited flutter went through Polly. She'd never even seen one of the Stone brothers, much less met any of them.

"Mr. Stone often stops by to check on our progress," Henry explained, "and you'd better believe we hear about it if something isn't up to speed. Not that that happens often," he hastened to add.

The two chefs hurried to make sure their stations were in order. Anticipation heightened the air. Polly found it rather thrilling. The Stone brothers were legendary, and it felt like everyone was waiting for a rock star to arrive.

Henry started explaining the process of making taffy. Polly scribbled notes about water and glucose, watching out of the corner of her eye as the far door opened.

A tall, dark-haired man clad in a beautifully tailored navy suit and tie strode into the kitchen, a leather binder in one hand. Aside from his strikingly handsome appearance, he had an aura of utter control and self-confidence that made her heart leap in a way that it only had once before.

Polly froze.

No way.

No. Freaking. Way.

Her breath shortened. The excitement in the room intensified. All the women stilled with awe and admiration at the sight of the intimidating Mr. Stone.

Or, as Polly had called him, *Mr. Hottie.*

CHAPTER 4

This couldn't be happening. Two days ago, Polly had not attempted to drunkenly seduce the man who would prove to be the CEO of Sugar Rush. She had not vomited all over his designer Ferragamos or whatever kind of shoes they were. She most certainly had not begged him to fuck her on the feather pillows of his four-poster bed.

Except that she had.

Oh, mother of all that was holy. She wanted to die.

She tried to hide behind Cora and prayed to every god of every religion since the beginning of time that Mr. Luke Stone would not find it necessary to stop and greet her tour group.

Henry was still rambling on about taffy, but Polly had stopped listening. She watched CEO Stone. He took his time walking around the kitchen, stopping to speak to the chefs and examine the contents of two large mixers. His expression was inscrutable, his eyes sharp, his bearing controlled, as if he not only expected deference, but demanded it. He reminded her vaguely of a king who had deigned to visit the peasants.

Then he started toward her tour group.

She glanced at the clock. Could she somehow manage to fake a sudden illness?

"Hello, Mr. Stone." A flash of nervousness crossed Henry's face as he extended a hand. "These are Gordon Andrews's Confectionary Technology students from Hartford Community College in Rainsville."

"Ah." Luke Stone's dark gaze swept over the group. "I like people who are interested in the science of sweet things."

A few of the girls giggled.

Polly's heart raced wildly. She tried to duck farther into the group, keeping her head bent so low her chin smashed into her neck.

Go away, Mr. Hottie. Just go away. Nothing to see here.

"Why don't you introduce yourselves?" Mr. Stone asked. "I'd be interested to know your culinary ambitions."

Polly had to get out of there. She maneuvered backward a few steps, figuring she could dart from the back of the group and make a run for it before anyone noticed she was missing. Her back hit the wall of Gary, a two-hundred-pound soda pop aficionado who was channeling his passion into fizzy candy.

She muttered an apology and tried to scoot around him, but he was standing against the blending table and blocking her emergency exit route.

"Hey, Gary," Polly whispered, poking him gently with her pen. "Could you scoot over just a—"

"Why don't you go first, miss?" Luke Stone's voice swept over her like a hot breeze.

She startled, feeling his gaze land on her with the precision of an arrow. Exactly the way she'd felt it at the Troll's House. Right before she'd—

Okay. She'd put herself out there the other night because she hadn't wanted to hide out in a basement any longer. She wanted to be *brave*. Hiding behind large Gary wasn't exactly brave. Besides, CEO Stone might not even recognize her, given that she was wearing a white apron with her hair hidden beneath an ugly plastic cap.

She took a deep breath and lifted her head to meet his gaze, which was even more penetrating under the bright kitchen lights.

"I'm Polly Lockhart," she said, proud that her voice sounded steady even though she was shaking inwardly.

"Polly," he repeated, his deep voice wrapping around her name as if he could taste it. "And why are you taking Confectionary Technology, Polly?"

"It's a course requirement for the Culinary Arts certificate," she explained. "I own a bakery called Wild Child and want to... um, upgrade it."

More like *keep it from going under completely*, not that he needed to know that.

He held her gaze for an instant longer than was necessary. An electric current passed between them. Her whole body flushed, as if she'd opened a hot oven fragrant with the scent of cinnamon sugar cookies.

"I'm Gary Findley," Gary announced beside her. "And I'm all about—and I mean all about—soda pop, so I'm into learning about how to incorporate soda into candies and maybe even chocolate."

Relieved, Polly listened as her fellow students introduced themselves, and the venerable CEO's attention shifted away from her.

"So have any of you worked at a candy company?" Mr. Stone asked, after all twelve students had introduced themselves.

Most everyone shook their heads in response, except for Ron, who had worked at a chocolatier's.

"Well, then." Mr. Stone set his leather binder on the counter and removed his suit jacket, revealing a beautifully tailored gray shirt that fit his broad chest and shoulders to absolute perfection.

Polly's mouth went dry as she remembered—despite one too

many birthday cake shots—exactly how his chest muscles had felt under her hands. Her palms almost tingled with the urge to touch him again.

"Let's get into the details, shall we?" Mr. Stone rolled up the right sleeve of his shirt.

Every female eye—and a few male eyes—snapped to the revelation of his forearm, lightly dusted with dark hair and corded with muscle. Polly remembered him leaning over the pool table, stretching his forearm out to position the shot...

"Excuse me, sir?" Henry sounded a bit baffled.

"Take them on a tour of the lab," Mr. Stone ordered. "Then when you're finished, they can learn about the manufacturing process."

"Yes, sir." Henry hurried to do his boss's bidding, ushering the group toward the door that led to the adjoining laboratory.

"Miss Lockhart." Mr. Stone pointed with his chin at Polly as he rolled up his left sleeve. "Stay here."

Faint irritation rustled inside her, momentarily quelling her nervousness. Luke Stone was obviously a man accustomed to being obeyed—which, she admitted, might be rather delicious under the right circumstances—but she didn't like his assumption that she would simply do whatever he said.

"I might want to go *there*." She tilted her head toward the taffy-pulling machine.

A smile tugged at his mouth as he approached her, his voice lowering to that deep rumble that felt like a caress.

"Oh, I'll take you there," he murmured.

"Did you require my assistance, Mr. Stone?" A plump chef approached. "I was just getting started on the ribbon candy."

"Thank you, Martha, but I'll take care of it," he replied smoothly. "Why don't you all take a break?"

"Thank you, sir." Martha wasted no time heading toward the locker room.

As her fellow students and the other chefs left the kitchen,

Polly found herself alone with Luke Stone. He took a pair of plastic gloves from a box and handed them to her before pulling on a pair of his own.

"So you want to make candy, Polly," he said.

She wondered if that was a euphemism for *have sex*.

"Um...sure," she replied feebly, unable to prevent a rush of heat at the idea of *making candy* with Mr. Luke Stone.

"This is the mixture for ribbon candy." He turned off the heat beneath a kettle on the stove. "Sugar, water, and glucose boiled together before blending."

He poured the sticky mixture onto a small cooling table beside the stove and added strawberry flavor before starting to roll it. Polly couldn't help glancing at his muscled forearms, the way they flexed and shifted with his movements. They had been the first thing she'd noticed about him the other night.

Well, maybe the second thing. A watch encircled his right wrist, but it was a plain analog kind with a leather strap—not a fancy Rolex like she'd expect a man of his wealth and status to wear.

She stood beside him, unwillingly entranced by the easy grace of his movements as he lifted the heavy mass of candy, folding it back onto itself several times to allow the flavor to penetrate evenly. He explained the technique as he worked, added a layer of vanilla, then sliced the candy and pushed one half toward her.

"Roll it into a log," he said.

As Polly started rolling her section, she watched Mr. Stone surreptitiously. He sure knew what he was doing. He rolled, layered, pinched, and cut with quick, efficient movements. Because he was obviously strong and experienced (well, of course he was), he finished with one batch before she was even rolling hers out for the second time.

"I didn't know the CEO could make candy," she remarked.

"I'd never ask any of my employees to do something I couldn't do."

"You mean you know how to do everything?" she asked.

He arched an eyebrow. "Everything."

A shiver traveled down her spine.

"So where did you learn all these candy-making techniques?" She sounded a little breathless.

"At the company factory in Berkeley," he replied. "My grandfather insisted we all started working on the floor when we were teenagers. I spent three years learning the manufacturing techniques before moving into packaging and sales. Making hard candy was always my favorite part."

"Was it also your favorite to eat?"

"Definitely. My go-to treats were hard candy and Swirl Pops." He rolled out the candy again. "When I was a kid, I once told my father he could pay me for my chores in Swirl Pops. But he wanted me to learn the value of money, so I ended up with a check like everyone else. Which I promptly spent in the gift shop."

Despite his tailored suit and commanding demeanor, it was not difficult for Polly to imagine him as a bright-eyed boy eager for candy.

"Swirl Pops were my favorite when I was a kid too," she said. "Especially strawberry. And Honeybee Toffee. Oh, and those little chocolate bites...what were they called?"

"Nibblers."

"Nibblers! I loved those. Do you still make them?"

"They're one of our top sellers in the chocolate division." He glanced at her, warmth softening his hard features for an instant. "You have good taste."

Polly smiled. After they worked in compatible silence for a few more minutes, she gathered the courage to address the elephant in the candy kitchen.

"So this is weird, huh?" She tried to eke out a casual little laugh. "I'm really sorry, you know, for how I acted at the bar, not to mention pleading with you to...oh, God."

Embarrassment crawled up her neck. She felt him looking at her again and because he really had been nice to her the other night—not to mention an incredible kisser—she held on to her courage and glanced at him.

Zing! Electricity coursed through her the instant their eyes met. He watched her with an inscrutable expression that at least didn't seem to convey reprimand or, worse, disgust.

"What were you doing there anyway?" she asked. "At the Troll's House, I mean. Shouldn't a man like you have been somewhere fancier?"

Amusement flickered in his eyes. "Probably. I like the Troll's House because no one knows I go there." He paused, his gaze narrowing slightly. "People know my name, but they don't know who I am. I'd like to keep it that way."

"Okay." It took her a second to realize the underlying implication of his remark. "You don't think I'd run around telling people, do you?"

He didn't respond. Polly stared at him. She suspected women hit on him all the time, but the whole gorgeous, masculine package of Luke Stone combined with the fact that he was the CEO and owner of a big candy company...well, even she could see why women would go after him like he was the grand prize in the game of *He's Mine*.

Still, Polly wasn't above being insulted by the implication that *she* would ever play that game. She moved closer to him, lifting her head to look him in the eye and trying to ignore the yummy scent of him.

"Frankly, Mr. Stone, I don't care who you are," she said. "Do you really think I'd post all over the Internet about tongue-kissing the CEO of Sugar Rush in the back of a dive bar? For what purpose? To publicly slut-shame myself for drinking too much and hitting on you? Or to *brag* about it? Or to blackmail you into..."

Her voice trailed off as something flashed in Luke Stone's

eyes—something quick and bitter. Though Polly had no idea of its source, something inside her responded with a hard, intense pull of understanding. Because that look was exactly the way she'd felt after her mother died. *Betrayed.*

She stepped away from him, her irritation draining a bit.

"You must be a Capricorn," she remarked.

"A what?" He took off his gloves and tossed them into the trash.

"Capricorns have a tendency to want to control their environment and everyone around them," Polly explained. "That appears to be a very apt description of you."

She didn't tell him that Capricorns were also masters of self-control, which also seemed descriptive of him if their little interlude at the Troll's House was anything to judge by. She, on the other hand, had blatantly exhibited the Sagittarius traits of excessive enthusiasm and bluntness.

Mr. Stone looked at her as if she were the oddest creature to ever cross his path.

"A Capricorn," he repeated.

She peeled off her gloves. "Am I right?"

"Yes, but..." He shook his head, as if something about her astrological knowledge both amused and baffled him. "Look, Miss Lockhart, my point is that I have to protect both myself and our company."

"Well, you have nothing to fear from Polly Lockhart, big bad owner of the Wild Child Bakery," she said dryly, dropping her gloves in the trash. "I'm no danger to you, though I am ready to throw a bunch of doughnuts at you right now."

The darkness faded from Luke Stone's expression, to be replaced with another glimpse of that warm amusement that had Polly tingling from her head to her toes. She put her thumb right at the crease between his eyebrows, pressing to smooth it out.

"You're much better looking when you're not frowning," she said.

Actually, he was dangerously sexy when he was frowning, not that she was about to tell him that.

Before she could pull her hand away, Mr. Stone grabbed her wrist, wrapping his fingers around it like a manacle. He rubbed his thumb slowly across her pulse. The light touch had a devastating effect on her senses, causing her head to spin and her knees to weaken.

She swallowed hard, unable to look away from him. In the brightness of the kitchen lights, his eyes weren't the pitch-black she'd thought they were at the bar. No, they were a rich, golden brown, the color of caramelized sugar and dusted with flecks of gold.

"So how did the CEO of Sugar Rush find the Troll's House?" she asked. "I mean, did you just stumble on it one night and decide to make it your haunt?"

"Pretty much. No one bothers me there."

"Except drunken birthday girls who attack you in the hallway," Polly remarked.

A smile tugged at his mouth. "Guess it was my lucky night."

Pleasure swept over her, shadowed by a twinge of regret. If she'd been at the grocery store and run into "Mr. Hottie from the Troll's House" again, if he were a mechanic or an accountant or a construction worker...well, maybe they could go on a real date and find out if their hot encounter was the start of a lustful kind of destiny.

But given who he was, and who she was...

"Did you mean it?" he asked, his voice low.

"Mean what?"

"That you were at the bar looking to get laid."

Heat rose to her cheeks, but she wasn't about to deny the truth. "Sort of."

His mouth twisted. "*Sort of?*"

Polly glanced uneasily around, though the kitchen was empty.

"I was out with a friend for my birthday," she said. "And I was looking for some fun, yes, not that my motive is any of your business."

"On the contrary." He moved closer to her, his eyes hardening with a distinct sense of possessiveness as his voice took on a rough tone. "It became my business the instant you kissed me. And then it became my business even more when you threatened to hit on another guy if I didn't kiss you again. And then it became *only my business* when you begged me to fuck you."

The words *begged me to fuck you* rumbled through Polly like the trembling build-up of ocean waves. He was still loosely holding her wrist, his fingers at her pulse, and she knew he could feel the quickening of her heartbeat.

"You're not doing it," he said. "You're not going to find some random asshole to hook up with. No way."

"You can't tell me what to do or not do."

"Yes, I can. Because if you're hooking up with *anyone*, Peach, that man is going to be me."

Shock rolled through her. This was a joke, right? The CEO of Sugar Rush staking a claim on her as if she were a territory?

She tried to come up with some sort of indignant response (*"How dare you talk to me like that? I'm a modern woman! I'll hook up with who I want when I want and how I want, and if you think..."*)

Instead what came out was, "What makes you think I still want you?"

His grip on her wrist tightened, his fingers caressing her pulse as if he were igniting it with the sheer power of his touch. Which he rather was. Polly's heartbeat increased, and she flicked out her tongue to lick her lips.

"You can't hide what you want, Peach," Mr. Stone said. "It's one of the many appealing things about you. Have dinner with me."

"What?"

"Dinner," he repeated. "Tomorrow. I'll pick you up at seven."

"Um, is there a *question* in there somewhere?"

"No. But there will be some answers."

The kitchen door clicked open.

"Mr. Stone, it's almost time for your ten-thirty meeting." A young woman who looked like a classic secretary—glasses, brown hair scraped back into a severe bun, sharp-looking suit—approached the stove. "Your brother Evan wanted to speak to you beforehand."

"I'll be there in a minute, Kate."

The woman nodded and walked briskly away. Mr. Stone released Polly and stepped back. She drew in a shaky breath, trembling from the inside out.

"You know, a little politeness goes a long way," she remarked.

"Seven," he said.

He was clearly not a man accustomed to rejection. Polly had a sudden image of him showing up at the door of her apartment above the bakery, with its peeling paint and spider webs. She almost winced.

"I won't be home by seven tomorrow night," she said quickly, pulling her phone out of her pocket.

"Where will you be? I'll pick you up."

God, the man was a bulldozer. "No. But I'll meet you somewhere."

He frowned. "I'm a traditionalist. When I ask a woman out on a date, I pick her up and take her to wherever we're going."

"Well, I'm a progressive who likes to do things my way. So if you want me to go out with you, I'll either meet you somewhere or we won't go at all."

His eyes narrowed. Trepidation fluttered in her as she suspected not many people issued ultimatums to Luke Stone.

"You can come to my place." He gave her an address.

It sounded like he'd conceded to her, but Polly wasn't so sure about that. It felt more like he was luring her onto his turf. And she suspected Luke Stone's *place* was a world away from the badly lit basement where she'd spent much of the past few months.

"Why can't I just meet you at a restaurant?" she asked.

"Because I'm going to drive us there." He folded his arms across his chest. "I'm also going to pay, in case you have any obstinate ideas about that."

Actually, given her financial circumstances, she fully intended for him to pay. She inputted his address into her phone.

"What's your number?" she asked.

He rattled off his number, and she sent him a quick text with hers. A surreal feeling washed over her as she realized she was exchanging numbers and planning a date with the CEO of Sugar Rush, who'd just gotten all possessive about her.

What alternate universe had she just fallen into? Yes, she wanted to be a braver, more confident version of herself, but after the disaster at the Troll's House she'd realized she should start small, like slowly tasting bits of fine chocolate instead of gobbling down a whole bar.

Luke Stone was more like diving headfirst into a rushing, melted chocolate river laced with sexy flavors like amaretto, salted caramel, chili peppers and—

Polly's breathing quickened. She glanced up to find him watching her, and her gaze went unwillingly to his beautifully shaped mouth. Despite his arrogance and *I'm the CEO, obey me* attitude—or perhaps because of it—there was no question the man knew how to kiss. Really, really well. She didn't need to have kissed a dozen boys before him to know that.

Mr. Stone rolled down the sleeves of his shirt and picked up his suit jacket. He stepped past Polly, then paused.

"By the way, Miss Lockhart," he said. "Yes."

"Yes...what?"

"You asked me the other night if I have a huge bed with feather pillows," Mr. Stone said. "The answer is yes."

He turned and walked away.

CHAPTER 5

*L*uke couldn't stop thinking about her. The morning after his impromptu candy-making session with Polly Lockhart, he woke with the unsettling suspicion that she might even have invaded his dreams. Not that that should have surprised him.

She was such a pretty little thing—thick-lashed brown eyes, lips shaped like a bow, brown curly hair spilling to her shoulders. Nice, perky breasts, long legs, round hips. Just the memory of her warm, curvy body pressed against his made him hot.

She'd tasted like whipped cream, chocolate, and rainbow sprinkles. Birthday cake. He'd had to fight not to run his hand up her bare leg and between her thighs to discover how hot and wet she'd been.

He groaned, tilting his head forward to let the water of the shower pound against his neck. After the Troll's House encounter, he'd ensured Polly and her friend were safely in the car and on their way. Then he'd cursed himself for failing to get Polly's last name. Because even then, he'd hated the thought that she'd go off again looking for another guy to artlessly hit on.

Then she'd shown up at the Sugar Rush kitchen yesterday

with her hair all hidden beneath a plastic cap and her brown eyes wide with shock at the sight of him. He'd been shocked at the sight of her too—actually, more like something had slammed into his chest—only he knew how to hide it.

But Polly wasn't a girl who could hide what she was feeling. She was too open, transparent, guileless. He'd known that the instant he'd turned from the pool table and seen her standing there, all flushed, bright-eyed, nervous excitement.

All sweetness.

Tension laced through Luke's shoulders. Despite the fact that he owned a candy company, he didn't do *sweet*. His women were cool, sophisticated, and carefully vetted. Polly was not. Unfortunately, that was exactly what made her so intriguing.

Well, that and the fact that she'd begged him to fuck her. And then snapped at him indignantly about his reputation. And called him a control-freak Capricorn, which was the truth. Not to mention, she was the reason he'd actually made candy, which he hadn't done in more years than he could remember.

Shit. He couldn't do this. He also couldn't *not* do this. He'd made a mistake coming on to Polly and asking her to dinner, but the thought of her with another guy made him want to explode with jealousy and anger—which irritated him to no end considering he barely knew her.

Still. He couldn't let that pretty girl loose on the town, looking for a hook-up. It'd be like sending a lamb into the lion's den. Who knew what kind of dickwad would take advantage of her?

By asking her to dinner, Luke was just keeping an eye on her. He'd have to make sure *he* wasn't the dickwad taking advantage of her, but he could do that. Much as he wanted her, he was nothing if not self-controlled.

So he'd take her to dinner, give her a brotherly lecture about the dangers a girl like her could get into, and drop her back at home with a kiss on the forehead.

Yeah. He could do that. It might kill him, but he'd do it.

He turned off the shower and switched his brain to his agenda for the day. First order of business was to confront his brother, who had been the reason Luke was at the Troll's House at all the other night.

He took ten minutes to shave, another ten to dress, then answered a few emails while eating his usual breakfast of oatmeal and egg whites with spinach.

He got to the office three hours before anyone else, dealt with some overseas issues, put together new project teams, authorized two raises, and worked out a strategy for Sugar Rush to penetrate the "healthy candy" category.

"Morning, sir." His executive assistant Kate Darling came in right at eight with his protein drink, her sharp gray suit and severe haircut signaling the start of his day interacting with employees. "Board meeting at nine."

"Is Evan in yet? He was supposed to be back from San Francisco by seven."

"He just arrived. I believe he's in his office."

Luke stood and shrugged into his suit jacket. "Graphics is sending up a new design for the retro packaging. Bring it into the boardroom when it arrives, please."

"Yes, sir." Kate handed him the meeting agenda.

Luke took it and went down the hall to his brother's office, where the door displayed a plaque reading *Evan Stone, Vice-President of Marketing*.

Evan looked up when Luke entered. Tension thickened the air. A renewed wave of resentment flooded Luke.

"You want to explain why you didn't tell me that Crown Foods approached you to take their chief operating officer position?" he asked, trying to keep his voice even.

Evan's mouth tightened. "When did you find out?"

"Dad told me the other night. I tried calling you, but you didn't answer."

Guilt flashed in Evan's eyes. Luke sat in the chair in front of the desk, his shoulders tight. Not for a second did he think his brother would ever actually leave Sugar Rush, but he hated that Evan hadn't even told him that a competitor had approached him.

"What would you have done if I'd told you?" Evan asked.

"Told the Crown CEO to stop trying to fucking poach from my company."

"Exactly. *Your* company. And you'd have yelled at me that I was betraying Sugar Rush by even thinking about leaving."

Luke stared at his brother. "You *would be* betraying Sugar Rush. How could you even consider working for a competitor?"

"They're not a candy competitor."

"They're a snack foods company, which means they're going after a similar consumer base," Luke snapped. "What did you tell them?"

"You really need to ask me that?"

Luke dragged his hands over his face, hating that he'd even hinted he would ever mistrust his brother. Two years younger than Luke, Evan had been his partner-in-crime for most of their young lives—partly because they'd always gotten along well and partly because of Evan's heart condition, which motivated Luke to take on the role of vigilant, overprotective older brother. Not that Evan had needed protecting, given that he'd always been better than Luke at everything except sports.

Still, they'd become even closer when their parents had more children, with Luke not wanting Evan to be overshadowed by their younger siblings. Evan had never resented Luke's protectiveness, but he'd been such a success—class valedictorian, scholarships, awards—that even without Luke he'd never have been overshadowed by anyone.

"Look, I get it," Evan said. "You know that. But you also need to loosen your grip on *our* company. Your insistence that all ideas go through you is creating a bottleneck, and you won't let anyone else handle the Alpine acquisition. If you don't get back to delegating and trusting people to follow through, then we're going to have another exodus."

Luke was silent. He'd developed an iron-clad hold on Sugar Rush over the past year, but he'd been the reason the company's profits, which had been climbing steadily for twelve years, suddenly nosedived.

He'd been the reason three of their top executives had jumped ship. Worst of all, he'd been the reason his family had been slandered. When the CEO of a venerable family-owned candy company became the center of an ugly, dragged-out paternity scandal, that shit hit the fan like a bullet train.

"I wouldn't doubt that Crown approached me because they heard things are grim around here," Evan continued. "It's only a matter of time before other companies start sniffing around."

Luke grabbed a handful of Sweeties from the bowl on Evan's desk. He tossed a couple into his mouth, the hard-shelled fruit candies making a satisfying crunch with every bite. Hailey's favorite. Funny how he could remember all of his siblings' favorite candy.

"Luke, if you want to change things around here, give me the acquisition of Alpine Chocolate," Evan said. "Prove to the C-suite you still know how to delegate strategically."

Luke hesitated a flash of a second too long. Evan nodded.

"Yeah," he muttered. "That's what I thought."

"Come on, man." Frustration flooded Luke's chest. "They came to me two months ago. With the new facility in Bern getting off the ground, I have to handle Alpine."

"No. You insist on handling Alpine." Evan frowned. "Meanwhile, I'm still spinning my wheels running marketing reports and focus groups and doing the grunt work that David doesn't want to bother with. And you told the board Sam should spearhead the Fair Trade Foundation, so that leaves me out again."

"That's what this is about? You're still mad about the Fair Trade Foundation?"

Evan's frown deepened. "The foundation was my idea."

"And I told you before I went to the board that I can't afford to lose you," Luke said. "To get the foundation structure in place, you'd have to travel to all of our regional centers, probably nine months out of the year. I wanted Sam to do it because I need you here."

"You wanted Sam to do it because you still don't believe I'm capable of that kind of work."

Luke couldn't respond. Because it was the truth. Evan could do the job. He'd always been good at everything. But Luke would not send his brother out on a grueling travel itinerary that involved trekking to remote farms in Africa and South America to inspect processing facilities, set up technical training, and build strategies to improve local infrastructures.

"I'm sorry, man," he said. "I can't. But if you want more responsibilities here, I'll give them to you."

"It's not about responsibilities." Evan turned back to the computer, frustration flashing in his eyes. "It's about making an impact and doing some good. It's about me being part of the company in the way I want, which means without you sidelining me at every turn."

His "sidelining" came partly from Evan's health issues, which had intensified his protective streak. And he would not let Evan run off to remote areas where hospitals were five hundred miles apart, if they existed at all. If Luke had to be the bad guy to ensure his brother's safety, then fine. He'd take the hit.

"Okay," he finally said. "I'll reassess, talk to Carson. Maybe we can get you on board with the China division."

Evan's shoulders slumped, his gaze fixed on the computer screen.

"Remember that you didn't build up Sugar Rush by being a dictator," he said. "You did it through great leadership and a focus on our company heritage. You're losing sight of both those things."

Not wanting to hear any more of the truth, Luke pushed up from the chair. "Board meeting in ten."

He left Evan's office and went to the boardroom. He hadn't been able to shield his family from the bad publicity wrought by the paternity suit. Though they hadn't wavered in their support of him, even when he'd come close to losing his job amidst the scandal, the damage had been done.

And regardless of Evan's warnings, Luke would fix the damage or die trying. His brother was right about corporate headhunting, though it still galled him that Evan hadn't told him about Crown Foods. Maybe because he and Evan didn't hang out together anymore, what with Luke's self-imposed work schedule.

The other night had been the first time in months he'd gone to the Troll's House to grab a drink and shoot pool. After hearing about Crown's attempt at poaching, he'd needed a distraction.

Which had unexpectedly come in the form of Polly Lockhart.

Luke tried not to think about the fact that if Evan had been at the Troll's House with him, he would very likely not have ended up kissing Polly in the back corridor.

And wouldn't that have been a damn shame.

Reminding himself of his resolve to protect Polly the way he did everyone else, he blocked another memory of her as Evan and the other executives came into the room. The meeting began with a finance report, followed by updates on the new vitamin-infused lollipops and edible candy pencils.

After two hours, the meeting ended. Luke returned to his office and tossed his briefcase onto the sofa, turning as his father came in.

"Paula down in HR called me yesterday." Warren closed the door and sat on a chair in front of the desk.

Luke sighed. Paula in HR had been with Sugar Rush for thirty years, which meant she'd known all the brothers since they were kids. Under normal circumstances, that would have been nice for a family-run company, but it also meant that Paula looked a little too closely at employee records and got nosy about things that weren't her business.

"She said you have three months of outstanding vacation time and haven't requested any of it," his father remarked. "I thought you were planning a trip to Hawaii."

"Yeah, uh…" Luke scratched his head. He'd told his father that to get Warren off his case about working too hard. "Hotel was booked."

Warren frowned. "Come on, Luke. You need a vacation."

After his encounter with Evan and the knowledge that other corporations might be sniffing around Sugar Rush again, the last thing Luke wanted or needed was a *vacation*.

"I can't take one right now, Dad. Not with the Alpine Chocolates acquisition about to get off the ground."

"You need a vacation," his father repeated. "A real vacation, not one of those fake ones where you say you're taking time off and you end up in meetings or working from your hotel room."

"I took time off a few months ago."

"You took two days off and worked from home," Warren corrected, frustrated anger hardening his expression. "You haven't taken a single day off since the board agreed to let you stay on as CEO."

"I haven't take—"

Warren held up his hand. Luke fell silent. His father was still the only person in the world who could silence him with one gesture.

"You don't have to punish yourself anymore, son."

"I'm not."

"Then prove it by taking some time off." His father pushed up from the chair, looking at him from beneath his heavy eyebrows. "I want that vacation time used by the end of the year. Your mother would hate to know that you're pushing yourself to breaking point."

Luke's shoulders tensed. "Low blow, Dad."

"So is lying to me about your time off, son."

The intercom on the desk buzzed. Hoping for a way out of this conversation, he turned to answer it.

"Mr. Stone, reception just called to say your aunt is on her way," Kate said from the intercom. "Should I head her off at the pass?"

He groaned. "No, she'll just barrel through. Let her in."

Not that Julia *let* anyone do anything. She swept into his office with a worried-looking Kate at her four-inch heels. In her late forties, tall and elegant with blond hair sweeping to her shoulders in a smooth pageboy, Julia Bennett had a crackling, don't-mess-with-me force field that had served her well since she'd become the self-appointed matriarch of the Stone family after her sister died.

"Thanks, Kate," Luke said. "I can take it from here."

Kate nodded and left, closing the door behind her. Julia put her hands on her hips, her gaze sweeping over Warren before coming to a stop on Luke.

"I'm not an *it*," she said.

"Hello, Aunt Julia." He smiled. "You look lovely, as always."

"Oh, no." She wagged her red-painted fingernail at him. "Put your charm away, Luke Stone. And I strongly suggest you stop using your charisma among the general female population because my friend Barb spent our entire lunch yesterday bemoaning the fact that you dumped her daughter Cindy."

"You mean the Cindy who left an engagement ring ad in my car? After *two* dates that I only agreed to so you'd get off my case?"

"Oh please." Julia threw up her hands and gave Warren a beseeching look. "Warren, tell your son that dreaming about marriage is what women of a certain age *do* when they're dating a rich bachelor."

Luke's jaw clenched. "You know the rules, Julia."

"Maybe it's about time you changed those rules," his father suggested.

"Or at least acknowledged that not all women are out to get you," Julia added. "Not in a bad way, at least."

"Are we done here?" Luke waved his hand toward the papers on his desk. "Because I have more important, and less weird, things to do than discuss vacations and women with my father and my aunt."

Julia arched an eyebrow at Warren. "You got him to take a vacation?"

"I threatened him to take a vacation."

Luke felt the combined forces of Warren's and Julia's penetrating stares.

"You could bring Cindy along," Julia suggested. "She's never been to the Bahamas."

"I'm not taking her there. She'll be expecting a beach proposal."

"Luke." She pinched the bridge of her nose with her fingers and closed her eyes. "Cindy is not a vindictive bitch. In fact, she used to be pathetic. I spent six months reworking that girl's image and personal style. Before me, she had five pashmina shawls. Five. Pashmina. Shawls. And a waterfall cardigan and wedge boots. Seriously."

"Crisis."

"I just don't want her to regress," Julia said. "And I have you and her on the guest list for the Manet exhibition opening at the Fine Arts Museum next month. Couldn't you have waited until after that to dump her? You screwed up my whole seating arrangement."

A headache started pounding at Luke's skull. "So put me at a different table."

"They're all full," Julia said tartly, crossing her arms. "And everyone is paired up, except for you."

"So I won't go."

"The hell you won't go," Julia retorted. "This is for your mother's foundation, Lucas Stone, and you will not start any gossip by not showing up."

Luke didn't bother looking at his father. He wouldn't find an ally there. Though Warren and Julia often clashed, they were united on the fact that everyone would continue to honor Rebecca Stone's memory. Twelve years ago, Warren had lost his beloved wife and Julia had lost her older sister, but they'd pulled together for their family's sake.

And especially for Hailey, the only Stone daughter who had been in the backseat of the car when it careened off the road and overturned in a ditch. Rebecca had died on impact, and Hailey spent months in a hospital bed, wrapped in bandages and attached to enough machines that she'd been almost unrecognizable.

In the wake of the tragedy, larger corporations circled Stone Confectioners like vultures looking for a weak spot to attack. With his father both focused on Hailey and ready to retire, Luke had stepped in to run the company.

He realized now that his drive to protect and improve Stone Confectioners had been his own way of dealing with the tragedy. He overhauled the product line, streamlined production, rebranded the company, modernized manufacturing, and renamed it Sugar Rush.

In the twelve years that Luke had been CEO of Sugar Rush, the company had raked in millions in profits, turned down multiple offers of mergers and acquisitions, established an international presence, and had been on a trajectory leading to the same level as the biggest names in the candy industry. Then the paternity lawsuit had hit the company hard, damaging all his hard work and progress.

But Luke had saved Sugar Rush once. He'd do it again.

"This is important." Julia tapped her finger on his desk. "Call Cindy and tell her you made a mistake."

"No."

"Leave the boy alone, Julia," Warren said. "There are plenty of other women he can ask."

"Like one of his harem harpies?" Julia rolled her eyes. "No, thank you."

Warren slanted her a look as he opened the door. "They're good women from good families."

"So was *she*," Julia replied tartly.

Resentment tightened the air. Luke's teeth clenched.

"And because of *her*," Warren told Julia, "you want Luke to be with a woman you can control."

"I want him to be with a woman we can *trust*."

"Then stay out of his business and let him find one."

Warren strode out of the room. Julia gave an exasperated cluck of her tongue.

"As if *he* knows anything about women," she said. "When you marry your high school sweetheart and spend the rest of your life mourning her loss, you're not exactly an expert on the female species. I, on the other hand, know what I'm talking about."

"Julia." Luke's headache pounded harder. He didn't want to be reminded of how deeply his mother's death had changed Warren. And not for the better. "I'll be at the dinner with a date."

"Not one of the harem."

Luke shook his head. He didn't want one of them. For the past few years, he'd had a select group of women—acquaintances and former girlfriends—whom he called when he needed a date or a fuck, or both, but they'd all lost their appeal. The sex was good because it was sex, but a couple of the women had gotten too clingy lately, culminating in Cindy and her engagement ring ad. Luke wouldn't tolerate that, especially not when he was still putting everything he had into the company. Tenfold.

His commitment to Sugar Rush was just one reason his relationships with women had expiration dates. And when they overstayed their welcome...well, he wasn't such a dick that he'd throw them out, but they went away with a nice severance package.

Of course, none of those possessive, materialistic women were like the artless girl who'd drunkenly smashed her mouth against his and begged him to fuck her.

The image flashed like fire in his brain. Polly's voice echoed in his ears again. *"I really want to have sex with a man who knows what to do…if you won't do it, I'll find someone who will…"*

Luke suppressed a rush of jealous anger, reminding himself of his polite brotherly plan with her. He crossed the room and opened the door pointedly, stepping aside to indicate that he was more than ready for his aunt to leave.

"I'll figure it out," he said. "I will have a date for the sole purpose of keeping your seating chart intact. Now go. I'll call you later."

"Hah." Julia gave him a haughty sneer and swept across the room. "You say that to all the girls."

"But for you, I mean it."

She flipped him off and walked out, slamming the door behind her.

Luke returned to his desk. He let Aunt Julia get away with a great deal because she'd stepped in after his mother died and helped their family. And despite her steamroller approach to his dating life, Julia had never pressured him to get married. She wanted him to date the right women and attend charity events to continue restoring the family reputation in the public eye, but she wasn't marriage-minded.

That was more than Luke could say for his father, who believed fifty-year marriages were still an attainable goal. But his father and mother were the only people he knew who would have reached that goal…if Rebecca Stone hadn't died.

He pushed the memory aside as his phone buzzed. He picked it up.

"Turn on the news," Evan said. "We've got trouble."

CHAPTER 6

"*I* can't believe it," Mia squealed, zipping Polly into a black sheath dress. "I mean, you upchucked all over the guy!"

"Thanks for reminding me," Polly said dryly.

"As if you could forget."

"True."

"And still he asked you out and sent you both flowers and candy."

Also true. Polly glanced at the bouquet of two dozen perfect red roses interspersed with Swirl Pops, Rock 'n' Roll candy sticks, Rainbow lollipops, and several boxes of Nibblers and Honeybee Toffee. It would have been a delightful gift no matter what, but the fact that it included her favorite candies made her feel especially warm inside.

Even so, her head was still spinning from the kaleidoscope she'd just fallen through—the one that had taken her from a basement with a green shag carpet to the back corridor of the Troll's House to a dinner invitation from the hot, insanely wealthy CEO of a major candy company.

"Hair, perfect." Mia walked around Polly, looking her over

assessingly. "Makeup, perfect. Dress, awesome. Shows off your boobs to excellent advantage. Wear the two-inch pumps, though. The three-inch ones are sexier, but if you trip and twist your ankle, the whole effect will be ruined. And I'm sorry to say, my dear, but you can't afford to ruin another effect."

"Tell me about it." Polly smoothed the dress over her hips. "You're sure this dress isn't too short?"

"Pols, it comes halfway down your thighs." Mia fluffed Polly's hair around her shoulders. "God, you are such an old lady sometimes."

And she was so tired of being an old lady at twenty-five years of age.

She looked at herself in the mirror. Still the same Polly Lockhart, just all dressed up and beautified. Except that *this* Polly Lockhart was about to have dinner with the astonishingly handsome, if arrogant, CEO and heir of The Sugar Rush Candy Company.

Panic fluttered in her belly, and she stumbled back.

Mia grabbed her arm. "What's wrong?"

"He's...um, he's really rich."

"I know, right?" Mia patted her shoulder and went over to examine the bouquet of flowers and candy. "You can order lobster and champagne without blinking an eye. Heck, he probably had the lobster flown in from the Arctic Circle. Can I have this?"

She held up a box of multi-flavored Licorice Twirls.

"Go ahead." Polly studied her reflection again and yanked at her skirt. "I don't know anything about rich people."

"Oh, for Pete's sake." Her friend groaned. "What happened to *we are the world*? It's dinner, Polly. Rich people eat like the rest of us, just better food. Enjoy it. Or if you don't want to, I'll go in your place."

"No!"

"See? You really do want to go." Mia smiled with satisfaction as she opened the candy box. "So have *fun*. Kiss him again, but this time please be sober. Maybe do more. In fact, *definitely* do more."

"He's totally out of my league."

"Oh no, girlfriend." Mia shook her head so hard her long blond hair whipped around her shoulders. "We don't do that shit. No man, not even Mr. Richie Rich Hottie Pants, is *out* of your league. If anything, he should be lining up to play on your field. Though I would suggest you do a bit of mowing before he goes up to bat."

Polly laughed. "What do you know about my landscape?"

"Pols, I've known you since we were ten." Mia wagged a purple Licorice Twirl at her. "You didn't let me pluck your eyebrows until we were in college, and when I told you about the Brazilian wax, you gave me a lecture about the anthropological history of hair removal."

"Well, I was taking a women's studies class at the time."

"Really." Mia narrowed her eyes. "Are things at least neat down there?"

"Things are always *neat* down there, thank you. Why are you so interested anyway?"

"I'm just saying you need to be prepared," Mia said. "And you need to stop overthinking this. Have a good time, okay? Live a little."

She gave Polly a quick hug before heading out the door. Polly put on the two-inch pumps and looked at herself again in the mirror. She nodded firmly.

Despite their very different lives and his rather domineering attitude, she liked Luke Stone. He'd been nice to her when she was making a fool out of herself, and he'd been adamant about not taking advantage of her. Not to mention he hadn't been fazed by the fact that she'd upchucked on his shoes.

And he'd actually worked in the Sugar Rush factory and knew how to do all the hands-on stuff, instead of just being ushered into an executive position. He was also clearly protective of his business and family. Fiercely so.

Really, what were the chances of Luke Stone and Polly Lockhart meeting at the Troll's House? And then again at Sugar Rush?

Though Polly wasn't convinced everything happened for a reason—*explain cancer, universe*—she had to admit that Luke Stone had come into her life right when she needed someone like him the most.

She wanted to do more than *live a little*. She wanted to live *a lot*. And if the universe was telling her to get started with Mr. Luke Stone, then Polly would damn well listen.

※

As she drove the bakery delivery van toward Indigo Bay, Polly thought it was a good thing Luke had insisted on driving to the restaurant. She'd had to sell her car after her mother died, and the van was her only means of transport—at least, for as long as it lasted.

The ancient VW sported a noisy, burping engine and a bright exterior decorated with the flower-patterned Wild Child Bakery logo and colorful peace signs and rainbows. Though Polly loved the lurching van, she couldn't imagine pulling it up to the valet parking of some expensive restaurant. The valet would probably tell her that deliveries were around the back.

According to her phone's GPS, Luke lived outside of town on an isolated stretch of land near the shoreline. After three wrong turns, Polly finally found the winding road leading toward his house. The road came to an end at a large gate flanked by two brick posts.

She eased the van up beside an intercom. A security camera on top of one of the towers swiveled in her direction. Her heartbeat increased. What was she getting herself into?

She pressed the button. A few seconds later, the gates slid

open. She started forward again, a thousand second thoughts running through her mind. However "we are the world" she felt inside, it was very weird to rattle her old VW van up the long driveway to where spotlights illuminated the edifice of Luke Stone's...

...ugly, ice-cube mansion.

Polly parked the van and peered through the windshield at the house. Well, good thing it was isolated here on the cliff because she was pretty sure there were zoning laws against this sort of eyesore. It was a massive, blocky structure, all white concrete, steel, and glass walls everywhere.

She'd been expecting something more traditional, like an English-style brick building or a beachfront villa. Not a modern architect's wet dream.

She grabbed her purse and headed up the front steps. The door opened before she could ring the bell.

Luke stood in front of her, holding his cell phone to his ear. He looked deliciously rumpled in torn jeans and an old T-shirt, his jaw unshaven, and his hair messy as if he'd been running his hand through it. But he didn't look like a man about to go on a date.

"Hold on a second," he said into the phone, stepping aside to usher her in. "Polly, I'm sorry, but there's a work thing I'm dealing with. Come in and make yourself at home."

Polly stepped a bit cautiously inside, peering at all the glass and metal. The walls of windows must provide a great view during the day, but right now the curtains were drawn. The furniture was all leather and glass, and aside from some weird abstract paintings, everything was in shades of black, white, and gray.

Futuristic, egg-shaped lights hung from the ceilings, a glass staircase wound to the upper floors, and a stainless steel kitchen with white marble countertops and walls of black cabinets faced the sitting area. It was like walking into a cold, sterile space station.

Except...

Glass jars of Sugar Rush candy sat on the coffee-table and kitchen counters, the glossy Ribbon Twists, sugar-sprinkled Fruities, rainbow lollipops, and Choco-Drops creating little pockets of color against the black-and-white background.

Polly turned to Luke just as he was ending the call.

"So I guess I overdressed," she said wryly.

"No." He sighed and shook his head. "You look great. There's just some stuff going on that I have to deal with...shit."

His phone buzzed again. He looked at the caller ID and back to Polly.

"Go ahead." She waved her hand to indicate she didn't mind him taking the call.

"Help yourself to anything in the kitchen. Or the candy, of course."

He walked away, the phone back at his ear. Polly caught the words "flooding" and "Venezuela."

She took a few Choco-Drops and wandered around a bit as she ate the crispy, chocolaty balls. Aside from the candy, there was no evidence of personal items. Was there a secret room where Luke kept all his books and family pictures, maybe an old quilt and a big, cushy chair he sat in to watch TV?

Nope. Every room on the first floor was all stark, sleek lines and minimalist furniture. A wall of black cabinets housed a massive fireplace, and the bathrooms were all marble and chrome.

The one bright spot was Polly's discovery that the rooms were all organized around an interior courtyard with a swimming pool, but even that was a pristine turquoise rectangle whose water didn't dare to ripple.

When she returned to the main room, she heard Luke's voice through an open door. She peeked inside at a massive glass desk topped with a computer. He was pacing back and forth, still on the phone, but he gestured for her to come in.

Polly stopped in front of the desk, which looked like something out of a catalog—a black blotter, an open planner with appointments and notes written in block handwriting, a leather cup of brand-new pencils, and three Mont Blanc pens resting in a neat row.

"Call me back," Luke ordered whomever he was talking to. Then he tossed the phone onto the desk and looked at Polly. "I'm really sorry. There was a freak storm in Venezuela where—"

He grabbed his ringing phone again and went around to the computer.

"Yeah?" he said into the phone. "Okay, find out if the aid workers are able to reach anyone. No, still nothing from Adam."

The tension in his voice was like wire. He frowned at his computer screen and hit a few keys on the keyboard.

"What've you heard about the airport? I've got thousands of food packages coming down from the warehouse." He listened for a minute and gave a curt, "Okay," before ending the call again.

He sank into his chair and rubbed his eyes. A pang of sympathy shot through Polly.

"Do you want me to leave?" she asked. "We can reschedule for another time."

"No." He dragged his hands down his face. "A storm system just hit northern Venezuela. Torrential rains, hurricane-force winds, the whole thing. We source a lot of our beans from family farms in Venezuela, and there's massive flooding all along the Caribbean coast. I think my brother is down there."

"You don't know for sure?"

"He was supposed to be there, but he didn't call and let us know." Luke frowned at his cell phone and swiped the screen. "We have a disaster response team for situations like this, but the flooding is so bad they can't even get in yet. So we haven't been able to make contact with anyone. Not even Adam."

"Well, if he's *not* there, surely he'd call?"

Luke shrugged as his phone buzzed again. In her business classes, Polly had heard about corporate involvement in disaster relief, but she hadn't known Sugar Rush had a structure in place.

As Luke took the call, she went back to the kitchen. She didn't know much about taking care of business—which was part of the reason she'd enrolled at Hartford—but she knew a lot about taking care of people.

She opened a few of the kitchen cabinets. They were well-stocked with regular stuff like pasta and odd things like buckwheat honey, bone broth, and tins of actual Portuguese octopus. Upon closer inspection, she discovered the boxes and cans were also organized according to category and alphabetized. The contents of the refrigerator would have made Julia Child weep with joy—French artisan butter, organic eggs, fresh vegetables, and a whole drawer of gourmet meats and cheeses.

Polly nibbled on her thumbnail as she stared at the fridge. Despite the plethora of goods, she was a little nervous about cooking anything in the immaculate kitchen, not to mention she had no idea if it was okay to actually use any of this. What if it was all meant for a glamorous dinner party? Not that she'd even know what to do with Portuguese octopus anyway.

Resigning herself, she retrieved her phone and placed a pizza delivery order, hearing Luke still on the phone when the intercom buzzed twenty minutes later. She found pristine white plates in one of the cabinets and loaded one up with three slices of pizza. She poured a glass of carbonated water and carried it into the office.

Luke looked up from his computer, the creases on his brow easing. Polly moved aside a folder and set the plate and glass on his desk.

"I ordered pizza because you still need to eat," she said. "And I wasn't sure if I could use anything in your fridge."

"My brother gets all that stuff," Luke said. "I don't eat here much."

"Well, it's pizza tonight." She nodded toward the plate. "There's more, if you're still hungry."

She returned to the kitchen and picked up a slice of pepperoni for herself. Rather than risk spilling tomato sauce on the furnishings, she ate while standing over the gleaming stainless steel sink.

Afterward, she went to get Luke's empty plate and brought him another bottle of carbonated water. She then found a remote control and pointed it toward the massive TV embedded in the black cabinets.

The fireplace flared on with a *whoosh* that made her squeak in surprise. She fumbled to turn off the flames and found the button for the TV, switching it to a news channel that was running updates on the Venezuela flooding.

She spent the next hour alternating between watching the news and checking on Luke. He also had a news channel streaming on his computer as he talked endlessly on the phone and texted. Polly brought him water, a sliced apple, and had to restrain herself at least twice from rubbing his shoulders, which looked tight enough to break.

Thinking she might be here awhile longer, she went to get her supply bag from her van. The macramé bag was filled with things she took everywhere "just in case"—books, her MP3 player, cracker snack packs, fixings for homemade tea, yarn and needles for a scarf she was badly knitting.

As she was retrieving the bag, a black Mercedes pulled into the circular driveway. Polly stopped when the glare of the headlights hit her. She shaded her eyes, her heart kicking into gear as two tall men emerged from the car, their postures not exactly threatening, but not warm and welcoming either.

"Hello." The man on the driver's side took a few steps toward her. "Are you delivering something?"

"No." Polly slung the bag over her shoulder and closed the van door. "I'm…I'm a friend of Mr. Stone's…I mean, Luke's."

"Oh." The man moved into the illumination of the porch lights, and Polly realized that he had to be one of Luke's brothers. He had the same strong features and thick-lashed dark eyes, except he lacked Luke's hard, unyielding edge. This guy looked *nicer.*

He extended a hand to her. "I'm Evan, Luke's brother."

"Polly Lockhart." She shook his hand, glancing warily past him to where the second man approached. Also tall and broad-shouldered, he had thick, silver hair, handsome features, and the distinguished bearing of the Stone patriarch.

"Warren Stone." He also held out a hand. "Nice to meet you, Polly. Is Luke inside?"

"Yes, I was just getting this." She gestured to her bag. "We, uh, we were supposed to go to dinner but he's been busy with the flooding situation, so I was just hanging out."

The two men looked at each other, then at Polly, almost as if they weren't sure whether or not to believe her. She took a step back toward the van.

"I should probably leave now," she remarked.

"No, it's okay." Evan gestured for her to precede him back into the house. "Luke won't like it if he finds out you left right when we arrived."

Polly glanced at Warren Stone, who only nodded in agreement. She returned to the house with them, and they both disappeared into Luke's office. Their voices filtered through the closed door, their tension and frustration evident in their raised tones and barked orders.

"You're the one who put Sam in charge of the Fair Trade Foundation," Evan snapped. "Send him the hell down there or I'll go myself."

"I'm not sending him into the fucking flood zone," Luke retorted. "And you're not going either."

"That's the whole point of the foundation, to protect the local infrastructure and help with recovery efforts. I have ideas for disaster risk intervention and—"

Warren's deep voice cut in, and Polly went back into the kitchen so she would avoid further eavesdropping. She filled the beautiful teakettle with water, set it to boil, and took three porcelain mugs from the cupboard.

After retrieving cheesecloth teabags and dried flowers from her supply bag, she brewed three cups of tea and arranged the mugs on a sleek tray made of glass and leather. She carried the tray to the office, balancing it on her hip as she knocked.

The voices inside came to a dead stop before Evan Stone opened the door and looked at her as if he'd forgotten she was there.

"Sorry to interrupt." Polly indicated the tray. "But I made you all some tea."

Evan blinked, stepping aside to let her in. She put the tray on a table near the door.

"It's chamomile," she said. "Very soothing. No caffeine. I make it myself with fresh flowers…"

Her voice trailed off as all three men stared at her in bafflement. Anxiety tightened her chest, along with the sudden realization that men of their status very likely did not drink chamomile tea.

No, these were men who sloshed twenty-five-year-old scotch and bourbon into Baccarat glasses, then drank while discussing stock options, liquid assets, and whether to take the Cessna or the Boeing on their holiday to the French Riviera.

Polly took a step back, suddenly wondering if her former boyfriend Brian had drummed up enough money for a ticket to the San Francisco Comic Con. That, at least, was a more familiar world.

"Okay, so…enjoy." She smiled weakly and left the room, pulling the door closed behind her.

Lord. At least she didn't hear them bursting into laughter, but they were probably rolling their eyes at each other.

Time for her to go.

She cleaned the kitchen quickly and put the leftover pizza in the fridge before taking a pen and notepad out of her bag. She scribbled a quick note—*Had to run, hope everything turns out all right*—and left it on the counter before going back out to her van.

As she put the key in the ignition, she tried to ignore the fact that her heart was sinking a little. Or a lot. Because if she acknowledged her disappointment, she'd be forced to admit that she'd been secretly imagining a fairy tale come to life—one involving a bakery girl and the hot, wealthy candy maker who sweeps her off her feet.

Polly groaned. She'd always had her feet firmly planted on the ground. Hannah was the adventurous one, the sister who traveled the world and wrote blog posts about *love*. Polly was the sensible, practical one who stayed at home and was learning how to be business-minded.

She couldn't let herself be romantic—at least, not about a situation where romance was not in the cards.

Giving herself a mental kick, she turned the key. The engine whirred and stalled.

"Come on," Polly muttered, pressing the gas and turning the key again.

The van lurched forward and came to a stop. Two more tries, and she still didn't find herself heading toward the gate at the bottom of the driveway.

She rested her head against the steering wheel with a sigh.

Yeah. Thanks, universe.

CHAPTER 7

*S*he was gone. He didn't want her to be gone.

Luke frowned at the immaculate kitchen, which—aside from the faint smell of pepperoni lingering in the air and her handwritten note—held no evidence that Polly had ever been there.

For whatever reason, he didn't like that. He'd spent the past three hours mired in phone calls, video conferencing, and arguments with Warren and Evan, but part of his mind had always been aware of Polly just outside the office.

The front door clicked open. Luke turned to find her coming back in, and the relief that washed through him at the sight of her felt like a waterfall.

He shook his head. He was being an idiot. He was wiped out. He needed a shower and sleep, and the only reason he wanted to talk to Polly again was to apologize for screwing up their date. Which wasn't supposed to have been a real date anyway.

"Oh, hi. Is everything okay?" She put a macramé bag down on the foyer table.

How the hell did he know it was macramé? Oh yeah, last year

Aunt Julia had made a big deal of announcing that macramé was making a comeback.

Polly approached him, all brown-eyed concern with those freckles sprinkling her nose like cinnamon and her curly hair that he wanted to sink his hands into so he could tilt her head back and...

"Where did you go?" His voice came out sharper than he'd intended.

She blinked. "Well, nowhere obviously. I was going to leave, but my van won't start. I'll call Triple A."

He frowned. "You will not."

"Really, with the ordering me around?" Though her expression gentled as she came closer. "You look exhausted. What's going on with the floods?"

"The rain stopped, at least." He rubbed his hand over the back of his neck. "The farms are all flooded, but the families are safe. As soon as the water drains off, we'll be able to go in and assess the damage. They got medical supplies, food, and fresh water into Caracas, so the aid workers are doing what they can."

"What about your brother?"

"He called from Maracay. He's fine. He's probably heading to the coast now."

Even though Warren had explicitly ordered him not to.

"Well, that's all good news, right?"

Luke looked at her, struck anew by her sweetness. All the other women he knew would have been annoyed by the disruption of their plans, even though they'd have tried to conceal it beneath concern and a remark about his workaholic nature. Then they'd have gone off looking for somewhere else to go so their carefully cultivated beauty wouldn't be wasted.

They would not have stayed to order pizza and brew chamomile tea.

A restless urge simmered beneath Luke's exhaustion, like he needed to somehow compensate for a natural disaster that had prevented him from taking Polly out on the town. Because she looked so damned pretty in that black dress that hugged her figure in all the right places and showed off a half-circle of pale skin leading down to the barest hint of cleavage…

He took a breath and dragged his gaze back to her face. No way would he ever let another guy fulfill Polly's mission to get laid. And despite his knowledge that he shouldn't take this any further than he already had, no way would he let *her* fulfill that mission with anyone except him.

The office door opened, and his father and brother emerged, both carrying the mugs Polly had brought in. She flushed a little at the sight of them. Sensing her anxiety, Luke stepped toward her as if his nearness would be any comfort.

Warren tilted his head back to drain the last of the tea, then lifted the mug to Polly in a silent salute.

"Haven't had chamomile tea since…well, ever." He put the mug in the sink. "But my wife used to drink it sometimes. Not as bad as I always assumed it would be."

"I'm glad you liked it."

"Ancient Egyptians used to worship chamomile for its healing properties," Evan remarked.

"Exactly." Polly smiled. "It was also one of the nine sacred herbs of the Lacnunga, which was an ancient Anglo-Saxon manuscript of medical remedies."

Luke stepped forward, suddenly annoyed by this ridiculous exchange. He didn't want Polly charming his father and brother, especially with folklore about the history of tea. He wanted her all to himself.

Telling himself again he was being an idiot, he indicated that Warren and Evan should leave.

"Nice meeting you, Polly." Evan extended his hand to her again. "Hope we'll see you again some time."

"And thanks again for both the tea and the history lesson," Warren added.

"I'll call you both later," Luke told his father and brother as he walked them to the door.

Evan left without a response, his shoulder still stiff with tension over Luke's refusal to send him to Venezuela. Luke closed the door with a sigh, hating his brother's resentment while at the same time being irritated that Evan couldn't see his reasoning. He had to prove Evan's value to the company in a way that wouldn't drive a wedge between them.

He locked the door and returned to Polly, who was washing the mugs at the sink.

"You don't have to do that," Luke said irritably. "I have a maid."

She laughed. "For what? To pick nonexistent lint off the furniture?"

"What does that mean?"

"Well, it's hard to believe you'd ever leave a *crumb* lying around for anyone to clean up." She waved a soapy hand toward the rest of the house. "I mean, this place is as clean as an operating room."

He tried to be offended by that remark and failed. Because it was the truth.

"This house was designed by the Scandinavian architect Axel Bjork," he said, feeling the urge to defend it in some way.

"Oh, it's very...um, architecturally modern," Polly said. "But I'm guessing the furnishings didn't come from IKEA."

Luke had the feeling she was teasing him, which wasn't an unpleasant feeling at all.

She looked around for a dish drainer or towel. He opened a drawer and handed her a clean linen towel, then watched as she dried the mugs with quick efficiency. She had to reach up to put the mugs back in the cupboard, a movement that made her little skirt rise higher on her legs.

A bolt of lust hit him as he remembered sliding his hand up under her skirt to cup the back of her warm thigh...

He groaned inwardly as his cock twitched.

Shower. Cold.

He jerked a thumb toward the stairs. "I'm going to shower and change. Don't leave."

"I can't. My van, remember?" Polly folded the dishtowel into a perfect square. "So if you won't let me call Triple A, what am I supposed to do?"

"I'll figure it out." Though he wasn't going to try very hard. He didn't want her to leave him right now. "I'll be back soon."

He took a tepid shower that was shorter than he'd intended because he wanted to get back to Polly. Not bothering to shave, he pulled on black drawstring pants and a T-shirt. Feeling marginally more like himself, he returned to where she was sitting at the kitchen counter, checking her phone.

He should take her home. That's what any gentleman would do. Take her home, then get her van repaired tomorrow and have the mechanic drop it off at her bakery.

A vague question crossed his mind. Why did she apparently only own a bakery delivery van? But the thought disappeared half-formed into his fogged brain.

"You look like you're about to fall asleep on your feet," Polly remarked.

"I'm fine."

If he slept, she might not be here when he woke. He suspected she'd call a friend to come and get her because she'd be worried she was inconveniencing him by staying.

"Come on." She slid off the stool and rounded the counter to take his arm. "Lead the way to your bedroom, but rest assured that I'm not going to jump your bones."

"Well, that's a damned shame."

She flashed him a smile. She was so fucking cute.

"You were respectful enough not to take advantage of me when I was in an...um, altered state," Polly said. "So I will extend you the same courtesy."

Luke sure as hell didn't remember being respectful. He remembered shoving his tongue into her mouth and gripping her spread thighs and...

Stop.

"I'm not in an altered state," he said.

"Lack of sleep leads to cognitive dysfunction, including bad judgment."

"Wanting to fu...sleep with you is hardly bad judgment."

Something flashed in her eyes that he didn't like. She didn't quite agree with his statement.

He led the way to his bedroom and pushed open the door. Polly stopped in the doorway, casting her gaze over the room with its linear black Faurschou cabinets and geometric Frank Stella painting above the bed.

"You were lying." Polly gestured to the low, massive bed.

He followed her gaze to the pristine black comforter and black-and-white pillows perfectly arranged against the sleek, black leather headboard.

"Lying about what?" he asked.

"You said you had a huge, fluffy, four-poster bed with feather pillows."

"I said I had a huge bed with feather pillows," Luke corrected. "You were the one who used the words *fluffy* and *four-poster.*"

She crossed her arms, eyeing him suspiciously. "A *huge* bed implies soft, fluffy, and four-poster, not flat, uncomfortable, and Nordic minimalist. Is that even a real mattress?"

"Not only is it real, it's a bespoke Savoir mattress made to my specifications and hand-stitched with chemical-free natural fibers like horsetail and lambs' wool. There is no other mattress like it in the world."

"Really?" Her eyebrows rose. "Well, aren't you fancy."

"More like well-slept." He pulled back the comforter. "And while the mattress may look flat, I guarantee it isn't uncomfortable. Try it."

"Who am I, Goldilocks?" Her look of suspicion deepened. "I'm not *trying* your bed."

"Then you can't prove I was lying."

She narrowed her eyes. Hah. She'd never be able to resist a challenge. He was starting to *know* more and more about her.

Polly approached the bed and sat gingerly on the edge, spreading her hands out over the black sheets. "What's the thread count?"

"Over a thousand. One hundred percent Egyptian cotton."

"Of course." She wiggled backward onto the bed a little more, extending her legs. "Okay, it's really nice. Firm, but not too firm. Soft, but not squishy."

Just like her. Another rush of heat pooled in his groin.

"So it was custom-made for you specifically?" she asked, bouncing a little as if she were testing the springs.

Luke's gaze snapped like a magnet to her breasts, which jiggled in time with her bounces. Christ, she was killing him. He fought the urge to reach down and adjust his growing erection. His loose cotton pants wouldn't conceal it for long.

"Uh, yeah." He cleared his throat when he realized she was expecting an answer. "They tailor their mattresses to a customer's height and weight."

"So what happens when someone else sleeps here?" she asked. "If it was made just for *you*, does a woman get all *Princess and the Pea* about sleeping on it?"

What was it with her and fairy tales? He didn't want to think about any other woman except Polly sleeping in his bed.

He shrugged. "I haven't had any complaints."

"And these are really feather pillows?" She moved farther onto the bed and picked up one of them.

"Down, actually. Siberian white goose."

Polly squeezed the pillow, then lay back on the others and shifted around like she was still testing out the comfort factor.

She looked up at the ceiling and blew a curl of hair out of her eyes.

Then she rolled onto her right side, presenting Luke with an incredible view of her round ass beneath the stretched fabric of her dress. She rolled back to her left. He couldn't take his eyes off her cleavage, which was even deeper with her breasts squeezed together like that.

His dick was starting to tent his pants. He forced his gaze to the painting above the bed, trying to think of spreadsheets and profits. R&D. Product development. Aunt Julia. He let out a breath as his erection began to subside.

"Okay, so it's comfortable," Polly admitted. "I don't know that all your swanky bespoke and goose down makes it any *more* comfortable than my bed, but it's nice."

He approached her. "And what's your bed like, Peach?"

"My bed?" She waved her hand loftily in the air and spoke in a British accent. "My bed is a bargain basement sale mattress with collapsing springs, cheap foam padding, and a deep sag in the middle designed specifically for the shape of my body."

She shot him a grin. Though Luke smiled for her sake, something hard twisted in his chest at the thought that—joking aside —her description was even remotely accurate.

Polly shifted to one side of the bed, as if she were expecting him to lie down. He sat warily on the edge, not wanting to scare her. But she was gazing at the painting on the opposite wall, one hand behind her head and a thoughtful expression on her face.

Luke stretched out on the bed beside her, careful to make sure there was a good distance between them—which wasn't difficult given the size of the mattress.

"I actually like that," Polly remarked.

He looked at the painting, which was a splattering of black, gray, and white paint on a black canvas. Had he ever really looked at it before? After he'd bought the house, Julia had swept in with her Swedish interior designer and furnished the whole place. Luke had left her to it, not caring where he stored his clothes or what kind of table he sat at to eat breakfast.

He had ordered the mattress, though. Eight years ago, after Evan came home from a stay in the hospital, Luke had had one of the custom-made Savoir mattresses waiting in his brother's house. Though Evan had protested the expense, after one night he'd lauded the bed's comfort to such a degree that Luke hadn't been able to resist ordering one for himself.

Evan had been right, too. The mattress, and resulting quality of sleep, was a luxury Luke didn't regret.

Especially now that Polly Lockhart was lying next to him on it.

"It's kind of *free*." She spread her hand out to indicate the painting. "All the other art in this house is so geometric and symmetrical. But that one looks like the artist actually had some fun splashing paint on the canvas and maybe even going a little wild. It's like a bunch of spun sugar strings all tangled together."

When Luke didn't respond, he sensed her look at him.

"Don't you think?" she asked.

"Yeah, sure."

She shifted onto her side, facing him. Against his better judgment—because looking at Polly in his bed while lying beside her would be a monumental test of his self-control—Luke turned onto his side to face her too.

She looked good. He suspected she'd look good doing anything, but lying in his bed with her hair fanned out over her shoulders, her hands tucked beneath the goose-down pillow, and her brown eyes fixed on him with all that curious innocence... yeah, she looked *edible* good.

"Hi," he said.

Polly smiled. "Hi. This is weird."

"Yes, it is."

"If you'd asked me three days ago if I thought I'd ever find myself in the fancy bespoke bed of the Sugar Rush CEO, I'd have said you were nuts."

"And yet here you are."

"Here I am."

His for the taking.

She didn't have to say it.

Luke had been around. A lot. He knew what women liked, what they wanted, what they needed. All he had to do was reach over and sink his hand into Polly's soft hair, curl his palm around the back of her neck, and pull her gently toward him.

All he had to do was press his mouth against hers, tease the seam of her lips open with his tongue, and delve inside to taste her sugar sweetness. All he had to do was slide one hand over her bare leg, up under her little skirt to find whatever scrap of lace she was wearing beneath.

She'd squirm and sigh, breathe whispers into his mouth, tentatively put her hand on his chest. He'd tighten his grip on the back of her neck, drawing her closer so she'd press her breasts against him.

All he had to do was tug her stretchy dress over her head to reveal the curves of her luscious body in her bra and panties— white lace, maybe, something she'd picked out because she was dressing up for their date. Nothing designer, no La Perla on her, just simple, sweet lingerie. Her nipples would be hard already, the outline of her areolae visible through the thin fabric, and she'd push her breasts toward him as if begging him to touch them.

And he would. He'd unclasp her bra and fondle her pretty breasts, lowering his head to lick her nipples and make her gasp. She'd watch him with a stunned kind of pleasure, as if she couldn't believe what they were doing. Then he'd take her hand and guide it to his hard cock, closing her fingers around the bulge under his pants so there'd be no doubt as to where this was going.

That was all he had to do. He could hear her panting, the little moans that would stream from her throat as she slipped her trembling hand into his pants to grasp his erection. Her touch would be cool and light, sending a shocking bolt of lust through him. He'd ease her back onto the pillows and slide his fingers between her legs, where he'd find her already damp and ready.

She was ready *now*. He could have her for the rest of the night, for as long as he wanted. All he had to do was reach out with one hand.

He cupped the side of Polly's face. Her breath caught, her lips parting slightly. He brushed his thumb across her lower lip, thinking he would probably hate himself for this in the morning.

"Go to sleep, Peach," he said.

She blinked. Luke pulled away from her and turned off the lamp beside the bed. His heart was hammering. He lay down, his back to Polly, and closed his eyes.

Damned if it wasn't the worst sleep of his life.

CHAPTER 8

ow. Wasn't *that* the best sleep of her life?

Polly looked at the ceiling, enjoying the sensation of the mattress embracing her. The foggy dawn light filtered through the white curtains along the wall, but she had no desire to leave the bed to open them.

She stretched, and her muscles lengthened gloriously like smooth, pulled taffy. Her sleep had been deep and untroubled, the kind she'd had as a child when she hadn't been worried about adult things like paying her rent and bills on time. The goose-down—*Scandinavian* goose down—pillows cradled her head like a cloud, and she swore there was some new zesty energy coursing through her veins.

Not to mention, even on a subconscious level she'd been deliciously aware of Luke's strong body beside her, the soapy scent of him drifting into her dreams.

She turned to glance at him. He faced away from her, in the same position he'd been in when they'd gone to sleep. His shoulder muscles still looked strained beneath his navy T-shirt, the tendons in his neck still tight.

Polly lifted herself onto her elbow, her lovely relaxation

fading a bit. She reached out and put her hand on his shoulder. Sure enough, his muscles were all bunched up and tense.

He twitched. She pressed her fingers into his shoulder a little more to see if his muscles would loosen up at all. Hard as a rock.

Luke shifted, peering over his shoulder at her. His messy hair fell over his forehead and his face was set with irritation. He was all scruffy, dark-eyed male. She swallowed hard. Oh, he was so handsome.

"What're you doing?" His voice was rough.

"Good morning to you too, sunshine," she said. "Did you sleep well?"

"I did not."

"Oh. I slept like a baby."

Polly had never heard a man actually growl before, but she was pretty sure that was what Luke did.

He stabbed his finger at the door. "Guest bathroom down the hall has soap, towels, and toothbrushes."

He threw the sheets aside and stalked into the bathroom, shutting the door hard behind him.

Okay, so he wasn't a morning person.

His mention of a bathroom made Polly aware of her bladder, so she hurried down the hall to wash up and brush her teeth. She wiggled out of her too-tight pantyhose and rolled it into a ball. She even *looked* well-rested, she thought, studying herself in the mirror as she tugged a silver comb through her tangled hair.

She went downstairs to put her pantyhose in her purse. She retrieved her cell phone and checked in with Clementine, who had insisted on opening the bakery this morning after hearing about Polly's date.

"Just in case the date goes long," Clementine had said cheerfully.

Polly texted her that the date had, indeed, gone *long*, but due to the broken-down van and not other long…things.

Whatever you say, dear, Clementine texted back.

Polly rolled her eyes and headed back upstairs to talk to Luke about dealing with the van and getting home. He was sitting on the edge of the bed, his elbows on his knees and his head in his hands.

"Luke?" Alarmed, she hurried to his side. "Are you all right?"

He looked up, his features still lined with fatigue. His hair was damp, and water trickled down his temples, like he'd dunked his head under the faucet.

"Did something happen in Venezuela?" Polly asked.

"Vene..." He shook his head. "No. Everything's okay."

"I'm sorry you didn't sleep well." She brushed a drop of water off his neck. "It must have been because I was here."

"Yeah." He sighed heavily and dragged a hand down his face. "It was because you were here."

Polly tried to deflect a stab of hurt, along with the question of whether he slept badly when he was with *any* woman or if it had just been her. She didn't actually want the answer to either question, hating the reminder that he had lots of other women, not wanting to believe he could be uncomfortable with her.

But if it *was* because of her...

She stepped back and gestured to the bed. "Lie down on your stomach."

"What?"

"Come on." She pressed on his shoulder to get him to do her bidding. "Face down."

His eyes narrowed with suspicion, but he didn't appear to have the energy to resist. He stretched out on the bed and pulled a pillow beneath his head.

Polly's nerves suddenly tightened as she tracked her gaze over his broad shoulders and back, the material of his T-shirt fitting him like a second skin, and down to his very firm rear.

She took a breath, experiencing a sudden visceral memory of pressing herself against the front of his hard body. What would it feel like to press herself against the *back* of his hard body?

Come on, Polly. Focus.

Luke had been very generous—and again, respectful—by letting her sleep in his bed and not once trying to touch her.

Wait a second. Aside from the caress on her cheek, why hadn't he touched her? He obviously knew she still wanted him. Any woman would. And Polly could only partially blame the alcohol for how she'd acted at the Troll's House because on a deep, primal level she'd just *desired* the man. She'd known the second she saw him again at Sugar Rush that her attraction to him was still hot and electric.

And given what he'd said about her hooking up with anyone but him…

She shook her head to dislodge her musings. The past forty-eight hours had been very odd indeed, so it would be best if she stepped back and reexamined this whole situation later—like on a day when she hadn't woken up in a bed that probably cost more than the whole Wild Child building.

"Am I supposed to take a nap?" Luke turned his head on the pillow and opened one eye to peer at her. "Because I'm constitutionally incapable of sleeping past five in the morning."

Polly glanced at the clock, which told her it was five thirty. Funny that both she and Luke Stone were naturally early risers.

"No." She knelt on the bed beside him. "You're just supposed to relax."

"I'm constitutionally incapable of relaxing."

"Not true. You're a cardinal sign. Cardinal signs govern the seasons and have the power to change."

He gave a faint laugh into the pillow. "All right, Peach. Prove I can relax."

Polly's heart sped up as she settled her hands on his shoulders. He tensed, a reaction that was neither reassuring nor flattering, but she tightened her grip and started to massage his rock-hard muscles. He was knotted up like a badly tied shoelace. After a few minutes of tentative rubbing, she got to her knees and put more force into her strokes.

Luke let out his breath. His muscles loosened a little, allowing her to slide her fingers to the back of his neck. The warmth of his skin flowed up her arms, and another sigh from him emboldened her further. She pushed her fingers into his hair, the thickness of it tickling her palms as she massaged his scalp, around his ears, then back down to his shoulders and his upper back, using slow even strokes.

There! His body began to slacken, his muscles becoming more pliable. She pressed her weight into her palms, making circular motions around his upper shoulders and digging her thumbs along the ridge of his spine.

He groaned. *Groaned.* A husky, masculine rumble whose effect on Polly's nerves was in no way lost by the fact that it was muffled by a goose-down pillow.

"Where in the name of everything holy did you learn how to do this?" Luke asked, his voice thick.

"I grew up on a commune," Polly said. "And one—"

"A commune?" Luke interrupted. "Like a hippie farm?"

"They're called *communes.*" She deliberately pinched the back of his neck a little too hard. "Or intentional communities. Twelve Oaks is a lovely place near Santa Cruz. I lived there until I was nine. One of the residents was a massage therapist who would give free treatments to anyone who lived there. I'd help her set up and sometimes stay and watch. Then I'd practice massages on the cats and dogs that lived on the property. I was sort of like the local animal whisperer."

"Well, now you're the CEO Whisperer. Or a witch casting her spell. You could make a fortune with those hands."

Polly thought that was what she was trying to do, but with baking rather than massages. She'd always liked helping people feel better, whether with massages, cookies, or home-brewed tea.

But helping *Luke Stone* feel better was a whole new level of exceptional, and not because he was the CEO of Sugar Rush.

Because he was the hot, pool-playing guy from the Troll's House who'd smiled at her and kissed her and made her feel *alive* again.

"Massages should be part of a holistic approach to total well-being." She scooted back to run her hands over his shoulder blades. "The harmony of your body, mind, and soul. When those three areas are in balance, you can achieve your full life's potential."

"I'm all about full potential," Luke mumbled.

He shifted and pushed up to his elbows. Polly took her hands off him.

"Are you okay?" she asked. "Did I do something wrong?"

He gave a short laugh. "Hell no, Peach. You're doing everything right."

He grabbed the back collar of his T-shirt and hitched it over his head, then tossed the shirt to the floor before lying back down.

Oh my.

Polly swallowed hard as she stared at the landscape of his naked back, his straight spine bisecting the smooth muscles on either side. The strong curves of his shoulders sloped down to the insanely impressive bulges of his biceps and corded forearms. His skin was smooth, golden-brown, and so mouth-wateringly tempting that she ached to trail her lips over the ridge of his spine.

Her heart was racing. She reminded herself what she'd set out to *prove* to him, as well as the fact that he was obviously still expecting her to return to the massage.

I'm going full force, she'd told herself at the Troll's House.

She pulled in a heavy breath, gathered her courage, and straddled Luke's lower back. The movement caused her skirt to ride higher on her thighs—not that he could see that, but the position allowed her to press weight evenly on both sides of his back. It also allowed her to feel the sheer strength of him right between her legs, but she tried to push that out of her mind and focus on her task.

Touching his bare skin was heaven, the friction against her palms warming her all the way down to her toes. When he groaned again, she pressed harder, kneading his lower back—where his drawstring pants were starting to ride dangerously low—and along his sides. Her breathing grew faster and sweat trickled between her breasts, but she held on to her composure and focused all her energy on helping Luke relax.

His muscles loosened slowly, molding like pliable dough beneath her hands. His own breathing slowed, his body sinking against the mattress. She slackened the pace of her massage, switching from short kneads to long, easy strokes designed to increase the flow of blood. She ended with a light rubbing of his lower back.

He was breathing deeply and evenly, his head turned to the side and his eyes closed. Polly eased away from straddling his thighs to sit beside him on the bed again. She leaned in closer to his ear.

"Luke," she whispered. "Are you asleep?"

"No," he mumbled.

"You can turn around now."

"No, I can't."

"Why not?"

"Because I have a boner the size of a redwood tree."

A giggle escaped Polly at the same time that arousal poured through her veins. She let her gaze stroke over his body again. His muscles were still loose and relaxed, but there was a new kind of tension coiling through him. Sexual tension.

And if Polly rephrased his remark in her mind, which she absolutely did, she thought that what Luke *had* was a "big, throbbing cock."

She almost moaned aloud, squeezing her thighs together to assuage the ache that had burgeoned since she'd first started touching him. She'd been wet since then, too, her sex so slippery that he'd probably be able to slide his big, throbbing cock into her with no resistance whatsoever...

She closed her eyes, unable to stop herself from pressing her hand between her legs. Need sparked through her body, a flame that had been kindled the instant she'd looked up and met his gaze across the crowded bar.

She opened her eyes and looked at him again. He pushed to his elbows and turned his head. A hot, electric current sizzled between them.

There were a lot of things Polly didn't know, or at least that she was still learning. But if she focused and paid attention to her instincts, she knew what she wanted. As long as she didn't get swept up in silly thoughts of romance, then Luke Stone was exactly what she both wanted and needed.

She leaned closer and gazed into his lust-dark eyes.

"Turn around," she whispered.

"You don't know what you're asking, Peach."

"Yes, I do." She pushed gently on his shoulder. "Turn around."

With a slight grimace, he turned and flopped back against the pillows, his breath expelling on a long rush. Shivers raced through Polly as she drank in the sight of his bare chest, all beautiful, sculpted muscles and six-pack abdomen leading right down to...

Holy mother of...

She stared in shocked fascination at the massive bulge tenting the loose cotton of his pants. Her body responded with a surge of lust so sharp she almost gasped.

"You should walk away right now," Luke muttered hoarsely, his voice infused with both urgency and warning.

She dragged her eyes away from his erection and back up to his face.

"Why?" she asked.

He blinked. "What?"

"Why should I walk away?"

He gave a humorless laugh and shook his head. "I'm not the right guy for you, Peach. Yeah, we could have a great time together, but you're the kind of girl who deserves something long-lasting, and I can't give that to you."

"I'm not asking you to."

"I always put my work first."

"So do I."

He frowned. "I'm too old for you."

"I'm not too young for you."

"I'm tedious and boring."

"Yeah." Polly poked him gently in the chest and gave him a wry look. "That's exactly what I thought when I was grinding up against you at the Troll's House."

"I can't make you any promises."

"I'm not asking for promises."

"I come with a crapload of baggage."

She shrugged. "Don't we all?"

Luke studied her for a minute, as if she were a puzzle he couldn't quite solve.

"Do you ever let anyone have the last word?" he asked.

"When it's warranted." She leaned closer to him, resting her hand on the pillow beside his head. "But right now, I think it would be a good idea if you just stopped talking."

She lowered her head and kissed him. A thousand fireworks exploded inside her at the touch of his warm lips against hers. She put her other hand on his chest. His heartbeat pulsed beneath her palm as she increased the pressure of the kiss.

Luke muttered a noise low in his throat. He grasped the back of her neck and pulled her closer, his tongue flicking out to slide across her lower lip. Heat bloomed in Polly, intensifying her simmering arousal and emboldening her to slip her hand down his chest, past the washboard ridges of his abs, and down to...

Oh God.

Her fingers trembled as she cupped his erection, feeling the warmth of his shaft burning clear through his pants. She broke her mouth away from his and turned her attention to his lower body.

Her courage faltered for a second before she reminded herself that she was the one who'd been pushing for things to go further. So she had to be the one to take them there, even if she didn't have nearly his level of experience. She glanced at Luke, who was watching her with heavy-lidded eyes, his chest rising and falling with every hard breath.

"Maybe we can just fool around first," she said breathlessly. "Not go...you know. All the way. Yet."

He continued looking at her, faint amusement glimmering in his eyes.

"We don't have to go *all the way*," he agreed gravely.

"Is that lame? I mean, I'm sorry if I—"

"Polly, if you don't take my cock out right now, I'm going to come in my pants and we won't even get halfway to *all the way*."

Her heart kicked up another notch. She hooked her fingers into the waistband of his pants and slowly tugged them over his hips. His cock sprang free, rising upward like a living thing, so big and hard that Polly's sex clenched with anticipation.

She sat back on her heels and licked her lips. "Um...wow."

Luke groaned, reaching down to wrap his hand around his shaft. "If you lick your lips one more time, you'd better do it closer to my dick."

"Oh. Do you want me to..."

A faint chuckle rumbled through his chest. "Not yet, Peach, or this will be over before we even get started."

He stroked his cock. She couldn't take her eyes off the sinuous movement, the way he slid his palm with such natural ease from base to tip. He nodded to her dress.

"Take it off."

Anxiety twisted in her stomach. She grasped the stretchy fabric and pulled it over her head to reveal her bra and panties, both plain white and bordered by a lace trim dotted with tiny rosebuds.

His breath hissed out as he raked his gaze over her full breasts and round hips. A rush of self-consciousness hit Polly as she briefly compared herself to the sleek, bone-thin women who probably frequented his circle, but he was looking at her with such desire that her concerns quickly faded.

"Come here." Luke pushed himself to a sitting position and tugged her toward him so insistently that she fell against his chest with a gasp.

And then he was kissing her again, hot and deep, and her whole body arched toward him in surrender. She drove her hand into his hair, reveling in the exquisite pressure of his mouth, the solid strength of his body against hers.

"Fuck, you're sweet," he muttered, pressing a line of kisses over her neck as he slid his hand up her bare leg. "You taste like cherries. Bet you're juicy like one too."

Polly's breath caught as he nudged his hand between her legs, urging her to part them. He shifted, lowering her back onto the pillows and coming over her to brace one hand beside her head. He flicked open the front clasp of her bra and her breasts popped free, her nipples so stiff she was almost embarrassed by the evidence of her arousal.

He whispered another curse, lowering his head to capture one of her nipples between his teeth. Electric sparks shot all the way down to her core.

"Oh." She wiggled beneath him, stunned by the combination of pleasure and light pain as he tugged gently at her nipple, then soothed the ache with a sweep of his tongue. "Oh, that feels good."

She became faintly aware that, although she had been the one to instigate this encounter, she was absolutely not in charge. Nor did she want to be. She watched Luke in a daze as he caressed her body in all the right places, the friction of his palms leaving paths of warmth over her skin.

He kissed his way down her soft belly, his scruff rubbing her like the finest sandpaper. She tensed when he reached her tight cotton panties and twisted his fingers in the waistband. She was soaking down there—she'd been hot since she first started rubbing his shoulders—and again her arousal was a little embarrassing.

Luke pulled her panties off with a flick of his hand, yanking them down her legs and tossing them to the floor. Then they were both naked, his cock nudging against her hip, their breathing so hard it almost drowned out the sound of her heartbeat.

"You're incredible." He ran his hand up and down her body, his touch warm and smooth. "Perfect."

Polly had never felt perfect, but in that moment, she absolutely did.

"Luke!" she gasped, thrusting her hips involuntarily upward as his fingers slipped between her thighs and found her damp cleft.

"Ah, shit, you're so wet already." He pressed his mouth against hers. "Open up for me, Peach."

A flush swept over her. She parted her legs and opened her mouth. Then he was inside her in both places, his tongue sliding against hers and his forefinger moving back and forth in her sex.

Past the fog of lust, she dimly thought she didn't want to come quite so soon, but she couldn't stop her whole body from simply yielding to him. A hot melting sensation filled her veins, the swirl of thick cream into dark French roast coffee, the slow dissolve of sugar into boiling water, the softening of bittersweet chocolate on your tongue.

Luke lifted his head away from her, a flush cresting his sharp cheekbones and his eyes glittering. He slipped his fingers up to her clit and slowly massaged it.

She moaned, wiggling her hips to encourage him to rub harder. "I'm...I'm getting close."

"Good." His hot breath caressed her cheek. "I'll take you over the edge."

He increased the pressure just a little, spreading two fingers on either side of her clit. The tension broke. Polly came with a shriek, bucking her hips upward as vibrations trembled and rocked through her body. Luke's voice was a low stream of pleasure and encouragement in her ear as she fell back against the pillows.

"Oh my God," she gasped. "And that was just from you touching me."

He chuckled and rubbed his lips across her collarbone. "I plan to do a hell of a lot more than that, Peach. But not just yet."

She lifted herself onto her elbows. His erection was still rock-hard.

Her heart thumped against her ribs. "Can I touch you now?"

"Not until we agree on a rule." He slid his hand down her body again. "Never *ask* if you can touch me. You can always just do it."

"Agreed," she breathed, closing her fist around his warm shaft.

His sharp intake of breath bolstered both her confidence and her fascination. Wanting to find out if she could take him over the edge the way he'd done to her, she began stroking his cock slowly.

"Ah, fuck..." He groaned and lay back against the pillows, one arm behind his head and his eyes half-closed. "Jesus, that's good."

Polly sat up, sharply aware of her nakedness and the fact that Luke was watching the sway of her breasts as she knelt beside him. A sudden urge seized her to straddle the *front* of his body this time and position his cock right at her opening before slowly lowering herself onto his shaft...

She shivered. As much as she wanted him to actually fuck her, she was almost relieved that they weren't going quite that far *yet*. It was intimidating enough just touching his very hard, male body, so she was more than happy to start by dipping her toes into the river of hot masculinity that was Luke Stone. And his cock.

She rubbed her hand up and down his erection, letting her fingers drift lower. A thick vein pulsed along the underside of his shaft. Curious as she was to know what he tasted like, she couldn't work up the courage to lick him like an ice-cream cone.

Yet.

Another groan rumbled through him. She glanced up, rather thrilled to see that he'd broken into a sweat and his chest was heaving, the muscles flexing and rippling beneath his taut skin.

"Polly..." A lust-edged warning laced his voice.

"Come on, Luke," she whispered, staring at the movement of her hand on his slick shaft. "I want to see you come. Give it to me."

She tightened her grip and massaged him with faster, harder strokes. His body tensed suddenly, and he gave a rough shout at the exact instant that he came, his seed splashing over his abdomen and onto Polly's breasts. She drew in a ragged breath, her whole body quivering with excitement and fresh longing.

Luke sagged back against the pillows, exhaling a long breath as she gently urged the final sensations from his body. He grasped her wrist and pulled her toward him.

He slid his hand to her nape and held her in place, his gaze oddly intent on her face. Something about that look twisted through her, as if he were still questioning the wisdom of getting involved with her.

Then she remembered his expression of relief when she'd

come back into the house after having been unable to start her van. How he'd ordered all the chefs and her entire culinary class out of the test kitchen so he could be alone with her. How fiercely possessive he'd been about her not hooking up with another man.

From the instant she'd seen Luke Stone, she hadn't wanted any another man. She only wanted him.

A strange feeling fluttered inside her, pleasure mixed with the unease of realizing that not only did she want him, she also liked him. A lot. He was straightforward, hard-working, dedicated, and caring. Yes, he had control issues, but frankly so did she or she wouldn't still be holding so tightly to Wild Child.

But surely her growing fondness for Luke was a good thing, an emotion that would only enhance their hot sexual relationship. It was like indulging in a bag of her favorite candy while knowing she'd run out eventually. The limited quantity made her enjoyment all the sweeter and more satisfying.

With that resolved, she leaned over and pressed her lips against his. He tightened his grip on the back of her neck and deepened the kiss. Her blood warmed all over again, faint dizziness sweeping through her head.

"Forget the candy, Mr. Stone," she whispered, sliding her hand down his chest. "You're the one who gives me a sugar rush."

He smiled and pulled her closer. She sank into the kiss, trying not to think about the fact that a rush was usually followed by a *crash.*

CHAPTER 9

She was gone again. Luke knew it the instant he opened his eyes.

Except this time, the evidence of her presence was everywhere—in the sex-drenched smell of the sheets, the indentation of her head on the pillow, the rumpled comforter, even the fact that the first thing he saw was the painting Polly had admired on the opposite wall. He could still feel her hands on his body, her cherry taste in his mouth, her scent on his skin.

He pushed up and swung his legs over the side of the bed. Twin emotions rolled through him—a strange combination of deep satisfaction and disappointment. Satisfaction because the night he'd spent with Polly had been unlike any he'd ever spent with a woman—which he'd known it would be with her—and disappointment over the discovery that she was gone.

A note sat on the bedside table, written in her curly handwriting:

Called a cab, but will be in touch later about the van. Thanks for a lovely night and an amazing sleep.

*P.S. I took some of those fruit gummies from the jar in the
kitchen. Are they new? They're delicious!*

A shaft of sunlight fell over the note. Luke lifted a hand to
block it, then realized with dawning shock what he was doing.
He looked at the clock, blinking as if the numbers 9:34 were
somehow a visual lie.

What the...?

He shoved his legs into his pants, hitching them around his
hips as he went downstairs to find his cell phone—which he'd left
in his office. He never left his cell phone in his office at night. He
always kept it on the nightstand.

Sure enough, the phone was filled with texts and voice mails.
He called Kate, who sounded breathless with concern.

"Mr. Stone, everyone has been so worried," she said. "Are you
all right? Were you in an accident? I've been checking the traffic
reports, but—"

"Kate," Luke interrupted. "I'm fine. I overslept."

She was silent for a moment. "I'm sorry, sir? You overslept?"

"It was a shock to me too," he admitted wryly. "But you can
send out a news flash that I'm fine and will be into the office
soon."

"Yes, sir. Would you like me to order you some breakfast or...
er, brunch?"

"No, thanks. I'll see you within the hour."

He ended the call, answered a bunch of others, and checked in
on the flooding situation in Venezuela. The relief organizations
had gotten in and were distributing fresh water, food, and
medical supplies. His brother Adam reported that the waters
were receding and they had crews out to assess the damage.

There was no text from Polly, no matter how many times
Luke scrolled through the messages in the hopes that he'd
missed one.

Seemed he was still an idiot, even in the light of day.

He walked into the kitchen and opened the refrigerator to take out the eggs, seeing the pizza box sitting on the middle shelf. With a shrug, he took out a piece of cold pepperoni and ate it while walking around and opening the curtains.

The glass house afforded majestic views of the California shoreline—cypress trees dotting the rocky cliffs, white-capped ocean waters, soaring seagulls, and breaking waves. The scenery had sold Luke on the house, and he was further irritated that Polly had spent the night but hadn't even seen the view.

Polly, all softness and light with the incongruity of her shy smile, who had worked him to an orgasm as if she'd known exactly what he liked.

Hell. *She* was what he liked. All of his good, protective intentions aside.

He polished off the pizza and removed the lid from a jar of Puffles, multi-colored gummy candies sprinkled with silver sugar crystals. He took a few out and popped them into his mouth, unaccountably pleased that Polly had liked them since they were a new product in the Sugar Rush line of bite-sized treats.

His gaze landed on the macramé bag she had left on the counter. Deflecting a pang of guilt that he shouldn't do this, Luke opened the bag and spilled the contents onto the counter. Then he rifled through them as if he were an archeologist digging for clues.

There were the usual girl things—hairbrush, lipstick, tampons, mirror—and a little plastic first-aid kit. Paperback books, a romance novel, a "live your best life" self-help book, and one about using an accounting software program. A half-knit scarf, chewing gum, incense, hard candies (not Sugar Rush, he noted with displeasure), sunglasses, hand sanitizer, and a notebook filled with scrawled lists. At the bottom of the bag, there was a silver elephant charm with a loop for a necklace.

As Luke studied the little charm, his cell phone buzzed again with a call from Kate.

"Mr. Wyatt from Godson and Wyatt called and asked if he could see you this afternoon instead of tomorrow," she said. "You have a one o'clock opening, but will you be here by then?"

"Of course I'll be there by one." He glanced down at his half-naked body. "I'm practically on my way right now."

"Very good, sir. I'll schedule the appointment then."

Luke put his phone down and headed upstairs to shower, still holding the elephant charm in his fist.

§

After a day at work during which Luke had to keep pushing Polly out of his head and reminding himself to *"focus, dammit,"* he inputted the Wild Child address into his GPS and headed toward Rainsville.

When he exited the interstate, he realized he was nowhere near downtown Rainsville—where he'd assumed the bakery was located. Instead he was on the outskirts of town, an area filled with old, clapboard buildings, overgrown lots, and junkyards.

He navigated a dead-end street, turned, and circled the block three times before finding himself in front of an abandoned warehouse. With a frown, he checked the address again and peered across the street at an old stucco building that had several boarded up windows, a bail bondsman's office, a closed auto parts store, and...Wild Child.

An old awning sat above the door with the name Wild Child written in faded blue. The windows were decorated with flowers and peace signs that might have been bright and cheerful ages ago, but now just looked faded and sad. A Closed sign hung crookedly on the door.

Shit. Polly had said she was trying to upgrade her bakery. She'd need a wrecking ball to upgrade this hole in the wall.

Luke shoved his car into gear and headed back to the interstate.

Don't get involved.

Since college, he'd been rigidly focused on Sugar Rush, and never more so than over the past year. Though there had been a time when he'd thought he'd fit marriage and kids into his well-organized life, he'd soon realized there was no room for that. He'd always been wary of people—aware they usually wanted something from him—but the lawsuit had made him downright suspicious of almost everyone.

He couldn't let his guard down with a cute bakery girl, even if he could still feel her hand circling his dick, still see the naked curves of her breasts, still feel her body shudder as she came. He'd meant it when he said he couldn't give her anything long-lasting, and it didn't matter that she hadn't seemed to mind.

From his experience, women always eventually *minded* his lack of desire and ability to commit. So despite his determination to prevent Polly from hooking up with anyone else, he couldn't start an affair with her. He *wouldn't*.

Having come to that conclusion, he pulled through the gates of his mansion. Polly's old van still sat in the driveway. The painted peace signs and flowing Wild Child Bakery logo looked incongruous against the backdrop of minimalist Scandinavian architecture. By contrast, Polly had *fit* both in his house and in his bed.

Luke suppressed that realization. He would get the van fixed and returned to her tomorrow. Then he'd walk away and get back to his real life.

CHAPTER 10

$\mathcal{P}$olly finished icing a tray of éclairs and stepped back to admire her handiwork. Of all the Wild Child products, her mother's éclairs were still the bakery's top seller—not that that was saying much these days.

But at least they were the one pastry Polly still held to Jessie's standards with fresh vanilla cream, *pâte à choux* pastry made with real butter, and dark chocolate ganache. Every time she made the éclairs, she knew she was being true to her mother's legacy.

She started setting them into fluted cups when the wind chimes over the door jingled. Polly glanced at the mirror behind the counter, her heart crashing against her ribs as the glass reflected a tall, dark-haired man.

"Hello, Polly."

Luke Stone's deep, resonant voice flowed right into her blood, eliciting a rush of happy warmth that intensified when she turned to face him. He looked striking and incredibly masculine in a tailored suit and tie, his dark hair brushed back from his strong features, but Polly's mind filled with a memory of him wearing only his drawstring pants, his gorgeous chest bare for both her visual and tactile pleasure.

But at the moment, he was all powerful CEO. As he approached the counter, Polly's whole body tingled with an awareness that was both sweet and spicy, like chocolate truffles spiked with cayenne pepper.

"What can I get for you, Mr. Stone?" she asked primly, hoping he would respond by leaning across the counter, planting a nice, hot kiss against her lips, and growling, *"This."*

"Your van is outside," he said instead, handing her the keys and the macramé supply bag she'd left at his house. "New starter, fan belt, and fluid check. The bill is on me."

He held up his hand when she opened her mouth to protest.

"I'm paying," he said. "Don't argue."

Despite his imperious, no-nonsense tone of voice, gratitude welled up inside Polly with unexpected force. She needed the van and she didn't have the money for repairs. So the fact that Luke was insisting on taking care of it…

It was the first time in a long time that a man had taken care of something for her. Or just taken care of *her.*

"Thank you." She stowed her bag and keys underneath the counter. "That's generous of you, and I'm very grateful."

Luke gave a short nod and folded his arms across his chest. He looked cross. Polly hoped his attitude didn't have anything to do with their sexy encounter two nights ago.

"I have to go now," he said, like it was somehow her fault.

"Okay. Would you like a pastry to take with you?"

He glanced at the displays. "Which is your favorite?"

"Oh, the éclairs, definitely." She took a fresh one off the tray and put it on the plate for him. "I've had to…um, revamp some of the recipes, but this one has always stayed the same. I still use Valrhona's cocoa powder, Madagascar vanilla, and the best quality organic milk and farm-fresh eggs. I also make some with liqueurs or chocolate cream."

"Looks delicious." He reached into his pocket for his wallet.

"It's on the house," Polly said.

Luke gave her a frown of mild disapproval and put a ten-dollar bill on the counter. "Only give food away if it's a sample or a donation."

He picked up the glossy éclair to take a bite, his eyebrows lifting slightly. A drop of cream clung to his lower lip, and the urge to reach up and lick it off seized Polly.

He took another bite. A sudden anxiety tightened her belly. Did he like it? Then she told herself not to care. She knew the éclairs were incredible.

"All of the bakery items are my mother's original recipes," she said.

He studied the éclair as if he were examining it under a microscope. "She must have been quite the baker."

"She was."

Polly turned away and started making a fresh pot of coffee. Her mother had invented all the Wild Child recipes in the kitchen of the little two-bedroom apartment where she, Hannah, and Polly had moved after they left Twelve Oaks. Every day when Polly and Hannah came home from school, their mother had glasses of milk and a new kind of fresh-baked cookie or cupcake waiting at the table.

And the treats were always mouth-wateringly delicious, baked with hand-chopped bittersweet chocolate, real, organic butter, and an immense amount of maternal love. At the time, Polly needed nothing else in life.

"This might be the best éclair I've ever had." Luke took another bite.

Warm pleasure flowed through her. "Thank you. My mother was very proud of them."

"So why is it that you sell so many other breads and pastries?"

"Because this is a bakery?"

"I mean, how many products do you sell?" He indicated the display cases, which had baskets and signs for dozens of baked goods—cakes, muffins, doughnuts, croissants, tarts, cupcakes, danishes, and more. Jessie Lockhart had been a master of experimenting with recipes, and if something came out good, it ended up on the bakery shelves.

"A lot," Polly admitted. "I mean, I can't afford to bake them all every day, but I freeze most of the dough and bring it out on a rotating basis. So on Mondays, we have doughnuts, muffins, and danishes, and on Tuesdays we have croissants and brioche, and so on and so forth."

"And the éclairs?"

"Oh, we always have the éclairs."

"Polly, I need to leave early tomorrow." Clementine came in from the kitchen, pulling on her sweater. "Dentist appointment at three. Will you be back from class by then?"

"Yes, I'll be here around one thirty. Thanks."

Clementine tugged her long, gray ponytail out of the collar of her sweater, her gaze going to Luke and his fish-out-of-water corporate appearance in the middle of Wild Child.

Luke extended his hand to her. "Luke Stone."

"Oh!" A curious sparkle appeared in Clementine's eyes as she shook his hand. "Welcome to Wild Child. Polly is doing great things here."

Not quite true, but Polly appreciated the props.

"It's a nice place." Luke's gaze tracked over the dusty mandala tapestries.

Clementine squeezed Polly's arm and gave her a "well done, girl" look before taking her keys out of her purse.

"Must get home to feed the cat." She headed toward the door. "I'll see you tomorrow, Polly. Pleasure meeting you, Mr. Stone."

"Likewise."

After Clementine had gone, Luke focused on Polly again. He had a tense set to his shoulders that intensified the sinking feeling in the pit of her stomach. Not only was he all knotted up again, he was being reserved and distant, as if maybe he regretted taking up with her. Whereas she'd been floating two feet above the ground for the past forty-eight hours. Until now.

He did warn you. He was honest. Nothing long-lasting. No promises. And you were fine with all of that, remember? In fact, it's what you wanted from the very start.

"How long have you owned this place?" he asked.

"My mother opened it when I was ten." Polly deflected a stab of pain as she added, "She passed away last year."

"I'm sorry."

"She was sick for a long time, so..." She waved a hand, not wanting to get into it. "Anyway, I've been running Wild Child ever since."

"Do you have brothers or sisters?"

"I have a sister. She's a few years older than me. She travels a lot."

"For work?"

"She writes a travel blog," Polly explained. "She left home right after high school, so after that, it was just me and my mother."

He was quiet for a minute. "So you're alone."

The word *alone* actually hurt, like the accidental prick of a knife point. Even after Hannah left, Polly hadn't felt alone before her mother got sick because they still had each other, and Wild Child was always filled with people and lively activity.

But when the leukemia took hold of Jessie Lockhart, their lives were overrun with treatments, medical bills, and struggles with the bakery. In the months that followed the diagnosis, Polly hadn't been able to stop the *alone* feeling that crept over her like a shadow. Even Hannah's visits hadn't assuaged the loneliness because her sister had come and gone so quickly.

"I'm not alone." She scrubbed at a smudge on the glass counter. "I have Clementine and plenty of good friends."

He studied her, his hands in the pockets of his trousers. "You're running this place and going to school."

"I've had Clementine's help with Wild Child, so it hasn't been that big a deal."

A skeptical look flashed across his face, even if she'd told the truth. Her mother's suffering through countless rounds of chemo and then a bone-marrow transplant had been a *big deal*. Working hard was just...working hard.

Of course, things would change yet again when Clementine moved this summer. Polly needed to find a replacement by September, but she couldn't do that until the bakery started turning a profit. She wouldn't be able to return to Hartford Community in the fall if she didn't have someone to staff the bakery while she went to class.

She pushed aside the fear and discouragement that hovered like smoke at the edges of her mind. She would find a way. Eventually.

"Did you want anything else?" She gestured to the display cases.

"After the éclairs, what's the next bestseller?"

"Doughnuts." Polly took a chocolate-glazed doughnut from the case and put it on the plate. "I don't do a lot of varieties just because they're too time-consuming, so it's a basic recipe with different glazes."

Luke took a few bites, nodding with appreciation.

"And what happens to the unsold inventory?" he asked.

"I donate it to a food kitchen at the end of the day."

"Then you start over in the morning?"

She nodded. Why was he asking so many questions with that pensive look on his face, as if he were doing calculations in his head? He took another walk around the bakery, studying the art prints on the "consignment gallery" wall and the three flyers pinned to the community bulletin board.

Polly refused to be ashamed of Wild Child, but seeing Luke Stone—shimmering with the aura of his accomplishments and success—standing in the middle of the old, faded hippie décor made her sharply aware of their differences.

He turned away from a sparkly pink lava lamp and approached her again. His brown eyes glittered, as if he were waiting for the answer to a question that hadn't been asked out loud.

But they both knew what it was.

"Polly Peach," he said.

Oh, damn. The endearing nickname made her go all soft and mushy inside. Not to mention how her blood warmed at the sound of his deep voice, which was like chocolate-caramel sauce melting over a butter cake.

"You're in trouble," he said.

That was the truth, though for once she wasn't thinking about overdue rent and unpaid bills.

Since she couldn't very well deny it, she just nodded. "I've been trying to save Wild Child ever since my mother died, but I'm failing. And I don't know why."

"For one thing, the location is lousy. Not to mention potentially dangerous."

Polly didn't bother agreeing with that because then she'd have to tell him she'd had two break-ins and an incident of vandalism in the months since the bakery's alarm system had broken.

"We've been at this location since the beginning." A hollow ache formed in her chest. "And Wild Child was successful before my mother got sick."

"Did she do something differently?"

"She always found ways to encourage people to congregate here," Polly said. "She hosted guitar concerts, art collectives and shows, writers' groups. I tried to keep all that going after she died, but no one seemed interested anymore. That's partly why the bakery ended up in a hole."

"What kind of profits did your mother have?"

"Enough to stay on top of bills and rent." Polly didn't want to admit that her mother's bookkeeping and accounting skills had been awful. Wild Child's success had been in the customers and atmosphere, not in their profits. Still, the bakery had been solvent.

Until Polly took over.

"Have you applied for business loans?" Luke asked.

"Yes, but I always get turned down because of bad credit. And honestly, even if I did get a loan, I wouldn't know how to use the money correctly. I've never learned how to properly run a business, much less save one from going under. That's just one of the reasons I'm taking classes."

"It's tough to salvage a business when the location is so bad," Luke said. "And this part of town is getting worse. You should consider closing down, maybe starting somewhere else."

"No way. This bakery was my mother's dream. I'm not going to let it die."

"You might not have a choice," he said. "People can't even get here without navigating that dead-end detour. The parking is lousy, and there are very few other businesses in the near vicinity to help draw customers. Not to mention that abandoned warehouse across the street looks condemned, and the whole area isn't safe. You'd better not work here alone."

Polly ignored that remark.

"Look," she said. "When I get my culinary certificate, I'll have more leverage with suppliers. I'm also taking business and tax preparation classes so I can improve the accounting practices. I'm going to get it together if it kills me."

"How much help do you have?"

"Just Clementine. I had to let most of the employees go, but Clementine refused to be fired. She's more of a…volunteer than an employee, though."

Luke studied her for a minute, and Polly could almost see the wheels and gears turning and clicking in his strategy-sharp brain.

"I can help you fix this," he said.

"The bakery?"

He nodded. "The location is a hurdle, but I can help you with supply costs, P&L, branding, marketing. You need to streamline your products, fix your pricing and volume estimates, and get your business plan under control."

Polly Lockhart was no fool. It was a massively huge thing to have the CEO of Sugar Rush offering to help her. This was a man who commanded hundreds of thousands of dollars for his consulting and lecture services, the man who had single-handedly transformed his family business into an internationally expanding conglomerate.

And while it was true that Polly's first instinct about him had centered on his sexual expertise, she could learn more about business in one hour with Luke Stone than she could in a full year of community college business courses.

But...

"I...I can't ask you to help me," she said. "I certainly couldn't afford to pay you for your consulting services."

"I don't want compensation," he replied. "I'm offering pro bono."

"But I have nothing to give you in return."

Silence descended between them. Their eyes met. A current of electricity sizzled in the air before Polly broke her gaze from his.

"Well, let's not go there," she muttered. "My mother firmly believed people should live however they choose, but she would come back to haunt me if she thought for one second that my payment to you involved taking off my clothes."

Luke shook his head, his mouth compressing. "This isn't an exchange for sex. You know that. So do I. I'm offering to help you because I like you, you need a lot of help, and I know what I'm doing."

Though Polly warmed at the phrase *"I like you,"* she still didn't want to feel like she had nothing to give him but her body.

"Luke," she said gently. "I can't tell you how much I appreciate the offer, but honestly, it would just feel *weird*. The fact is you're offering me a service for free that would normally cost a fortune, and neither one of us can pretend that doesn't have something to do with the fact that I was buck naked in your bed the other night."

"Maybe it has something to do with the fact that you got *me* naked," he replied, his tone faintly irritated. "Maybe you have me under some sort of pagan witch's spell."

Polly couldn't help grinning at the thought of Luke Stone being under anyone's control but his own. With his sterile house, obsessively ordered refrigerator and cabinets, and three Mont Blanc pens lined up to the millimeter, he was a man ruled by order and control.

He paced to the windows and back. The line of his shoulders was tense, his spine straight as metal. She couldn't help comparing the rigid CEO of today with the warm, sexy man who had surrendered to her massage two nights ago.

"How do you have fun?" she asked.

A deep crease formed in his brow. "Fun?"

"I mean, besides shoot pool every now and then," Polly said. "What do you do that makes you happy?"

"I travel." Luke shrugged. "Work out."

"What about dating?"

"I don't date. There are certain women I take to social events, but they aren't dates."

"What are they then?"

"Women I take to social events."

"Do you have fun?" Polly asked.

He was silent for a moment. "Not really," he finally said.

"Why don't you think of the women as dates?"

"Because I don't want to lead them on. I'll never marry any one of them, and as my aunt Julia will tell you in her pit viper way, some women *of a certain age* are out to land a rich bachelor.

So I have agreements with those women that our relationships have parameters and deadlines."

"Parameters and deadlines," Polly repeated dryly, even as an odd stab of sorrow hit her. "How fun."

Faint irritation sparked in his golden-brown eyes. "Why are you asking me all this anyway?"

Find your happiness.

She had made progress with her quest recently, but finding an intangible emotion wasn't nearly as easy as finding a missing sock.

And yet it also meant looking in new places. That was just one of the things she'd learned at Twelve Oaks. Though her family had left the commune when Polly was nine, she still believed in its basic principles of helping others, working hard, and giving back.

But until this moment, she'd lost sight of the other values imparted by the commune life. And standing there looking at CEO Stone with his stiff shoulders and perfectly knotted tie, imagining him at a gala dinner with a beautiful woman at his side, remembering the wistfulness in his voice when he talked about his love for Swirl Pops, reliving the sensation of his pliable muscles and warm, taut skin under her hands...

"My mother used to tell me it was important to find your happiness," she explained.

"Okay."

"When was the last time you napped in a hammock under the trees?"

Luke blinked. "Uh...never?"

"Played a board game?"

"I used to play games with my brothers. I think."

"Listened to music? Juggled? Painted a picture?"

"I don't have time for that kind of thing."

"Neither do I. And I think that's the problem. Luke, thank you so much for your offer. I would love to have your help getting Wild Child back on track."

Bafflement appeared in his expression. "So you accept?"

"Yes. But in exchange, I'd like to take you out on a few dates," she said, then added, "*Fun* dates."

Luke scratched his head. "Okay."

She smiled. "Good."

"Why do you want us to go on dates?"

"Because I like you too," Polly said. "And because maybe the best way to find happiness is to look for it with someone you like."

CHAPTER 11

As Luke drove back to the Sugar Rush offices, he believed his head was spinning. That never happened to him. He always thought with clarity and logic.

But ever since Polly Lockhart had crashed into his life, he'd been...*off-balance*. Unable to stop himself from kissing her, then getting possessive about her and asking—okay, ordering—her out on a date. Then he had some thorn in his side about not wanting her to leave his house, and then they'd made each other come so hard the bed shook, and then he'd slept until nine-fucking-thirty-four...

And now he was offering her pro bono consulting services and wondering how she'd managed to get under his skin so fast that *his head was spinning*.

Not good. Bad, in fact. Really goddamned bad.

But he couldn't just let her bakery go under when he, of all people in the world, knew how to fix it. Polly was standing in quicksand, and he had the rope to haul her out. He couldn't walk away from her now. He *wouldn't*.

He turned off the highway to the Sugar Rush campus. After parking in his assigned spot, he stalked into the building, nodded a curt greeting at the receptionist, and took the mirrored elevator up to his seventh-floor office.

"Mr. Stone, you have some papers to sign." Kate rose from her chair as he approached. "I left them on your desk."

"Thank you." He handed her the box of éclairs and doughnuts Polly had packed up for him. "Get someone to take these around to the others."

"Yes, sir." She took the box and peered inside with a murmur of delight. "Also, there's a call from Miss Peterson asking if you were still planning on attending her yacht party tomorrow night. It's leaving from Pier 40 at nine."

Luke groaned. There was only one place he intended to be tomorrow night, and it was not on Miss Peterson's yacht.

"I'll tell her you have an unexpected work meeting," Kate said quickly.

Kate was the best hire he'd made in the past two years. After his former assistant retired, he'd intended to hire someone with years of experience. At twenty-six, Kate had had almost no experience, but she'd so impressed Luke during her interview that he'd hired her on the spot.

That time, his instincts had proven correct. He thanked Kate again and went into his office, forcing his brain to the multiple tasks at hand. He first did a crime report check for the neighborhood where Wild Child was located.

Though he wasn't surprised by the multiple reports of robbery, theft, weapons violations, and drug investigations in the area, his jaw clenched harder the more he read. Because the public incident reports were incomplete, Luke called the Indigo Bay police chief to ask for more details.

"I'll have to get back to you since that's not my jurisdiction," Brad said. "Give me a couple of hours, okay?"

"Sure. Thanks."

After ending the call, Luke reminded himself of his main priority and turned his attention to company business. He reviewed several budgets, allocated funds to the retro product development, returned five calls, then checked his email. A message from Polly appeared on the screen.

TO: Luke Stone, Megalomaniac Willy Wonka
(l.stone@sugarrush.com)

FROM: Polly Lockhart, Tea Brewer Extraordinaire
(polly@wildchildbakery.com)

Mr. Stone:

Attached are the password-secured Important Financial Documents you requested. I will be at my desk until five p.m., should you have any questions. If not, I will be at your office at two p.m. tomorrow for our meeting.

Sincerely,
Polly Lockhart

Luke hit the reply button.

TO: Polly Lockhart, Pagan Witch
(polly@wildchildbakery.com)

FROM: Luke Stone, Master of the Universe
(l.stone@sugarrush.com)

Miss Lockhart:

Received and noted. You have a great ass.

L. Stone

He printed out the documents and logged out of email. He'd been expecting that the bakery's finances would be a mess, but he hadn't expected this level of disorganization. Polly's business assets were nonexistent, and her profits on a steady decline. She had no cost of sales or even a list of expenses.

He wrote up a preliminary business plan, studied other bakeries in the nearby area, looked into the suppliers Polly had been working with, and redid her projected cash flow and balance sheet. By mid-afternoon, he started to think he had some solid ways for her to get a handle on her business before it dropped out from under her.

He nodded with satisfaction. That was all he had to do. Go on a few dates, help her get the bakery back on track, and teach her how to run it properly. She was a smart girl. Once she had the tools in place and knew how to use them, she'd be fine.

And *then* he could walk away.

The intercom buzzed. "Mr. Stone, your...shit."

Kate's voice dropped off just as the door opened and Julia strode into his office, looking like she'd just stepped out of the pages of *Vogue* in a gray tweed Chanel suit.

Kate followed, her expression both worried and irritated. "I'm sorry, sir. I didn't realize she would take the stairs."

"Thanks, Kate," Luke said. "I've got this."

His assistant left, closing the door behind her. Julia approached his desk with her usual predatory "give me intel or I will crush you" look.

"Who is she?" Julia asked. "Evan said she was there the other night when he and your father arrived."

Luke made a mental note to have a *talk* with his little brother. "Evan needs to stop gossiping."

"Well, when I threatened to turn my matchmaking efforts

onto him rather than you, he sang like a canary." Julia arched an eyebrow. "Do I know her?"

"No. You've never met her. In fact, we just started seeing each other."

Julia looked at him skeptically. "Since when?"

"Uh, last week."

"You started seeing her *last week* and you had her at the house?"

"*My* house," Luke corrected.

"And is there a reason you didn't tell me this the other day?"

"Yeah. It's none of your damned business."

Unfazed by the sharp retort, Julia stepped closer to the desk. "So where did you meet her?"

"While I was out."

"What does she do?"

"She owns a bakery. And she's in the culinary program at Hartford Community."

"What bakery?"

"Just a hole in the wall. I'm helping her sort out the business end."

Julia frowned. "Why?"

"Because I can." Luke sighed. "Julia, if it'll make you happy, I'll ask Polly to the museum dinner. You can meet her then, and your seating chart will be intact."

She tapped her fingers against her arms, her eyebrows high, still looking as if she wasn't sure whether or not to believe him.

"Now go away," Luke said.

"She doesn't sound as if she'd quite fit," Julia remarked.

"I'm not doing that soap opera crap with you. Either I bring her, or I don't go. That's it."

"All right." She held up her hands in a placating gesture. "I trust your judgment."

The comment twisted inside Luke. Because they both knew his judgment had failed in the past.

Once. Only once. He had no intention of it failing again.

After Julia finally left, Luke turned his attention back to Polly's paperwork. Close to six, he checked his email and opened a message from the Indigo Bay police chief. Brad had attached a PDF of crime incidents in the vicinity of Wild Child over the past year.

Luke opened the file and scrolled through it. More drug investigations, weapons violations, robberies. Then his gaze landed on the line *non-residential burglary*, followed by the address of Wild Child.

His jaw clenched. According to the police report, one break-in had occurred last May at eleven p.m. and the other in mid-October after midnight. The suspects had gotten away with petty cash in both incidents, having gained entry through a picked lock and broken window.

Luke picked up the phone and placed an urgent call to the head of the security company who'd worked with Sugar Rush for years. He issued Gavin a set of instructions as he tossed folders into his briefcase and shrugged into his suit jacket. Dusk was already starting to fall. By the time Polly closed the bakery at seven, it would be close to dark and she'd be alone.

He drove to Rainsville and parked in the shadow of the warehouse across from Wild Child, thinking his car might not be there when he returned but seeing no other option. The only light in the building was the one in the bakery window.

He crossed the street and pushed open the door. Polly looked up from cleaning the cold case, her curly hair pulled back into a messy knot and her apron streaked with chocolate.

A smile bloomed on her face. A strange feeling tightened his chest in response. She actually looked happy to see him again. Not many people were.

"Hi there," Polly said. "What are you doing back here? I thought we weren't meeting until tomorrow."

Luke shook off the odd feeling, reminding himself why he

was here. "Why didn't you tell me you've had two break-ins in the past year?"

She winced. "How did you find out?"

"Police report. Why didn't you tell me?"

"It wasn't a big deal. Besides, the burglars didn't get much. I keep everything important in the safe."

"I don't care what they got," Luke snapped. "I care that they *broke in*. How many times has that happened over the years?"

"We've had some issues, but no one has ever gotten hurt," Polly said. "And the alarm system has been a good deterrent, but it went out a few months ago and I haven't been able to afford a new one."

"I'm buying you a new one," he said. "That's not negotiable."

"They're terribly expensive. I've shopped around." She scrubbed at the counter and shook her head. "I can't let you buy me a whole new system."

"Well, you're going to," he retorted. "Because I'm not helping you improve a business that doesn't even have a decent security system. By the look of it, you also need new locks and deadbolts. Loss prevention is Business 101. I've already called the head of a security company and told him to put together a team to do a risk assessment of Wild Child, both the physical structure and your computer system."

She pressed her lips together and looked up. "I do want your help, but I don't want you to pay for everything I need. However, if we agree this is a loan and that I'll pay you back when the bakery starts turning a profit, then I accept. And thank you."

Luke nodded, still not entirely satisfied with the agreement but understanding her desire not to take a handout from him. He'd have felt the same way. And he liked her belief that the bakery *would* start turning a profit one day soon. Failure wasn't an option.

"I looked over your paperwork," he said. "How about I go through your files to see if there's anything we missed?"

"Sure, go ahead." She gestured to the back office. "The key for the desk is under the flour sack."

He went into her tiny office and compiled old bank statements, tax returns, and lists of suppliers. He put them all in the trunk of his car and returned to help Polly finish clearing out the display cases and mop the floor. She closed out the register and got her things together.

As Polly locked the front door, Luke stared at her features, the dusting of freckles on her nose, the bow shape of her lips. The curve of her throat, the V-neckline of her T-shirt that exposed a tempting expanse of white skin. He remembered how her breasts had felt, her hard nipples pressing against his chest, her mouth open against his…

It was dangerous the way he couldn't stop thinking about her. Couldn't stop wanting her. She was crowding into places in his mind that he'd always reserved for either his family or his business.

"Where do you live?" he asked.

She hesitated. "Upstairs."

He frowned. "Upstairs?"

Polly ducked her head and took a set of keys from her bag. "Come on."

They walked to the narrow alley behind the bakery. Luke followed her up a rickety staircase to a front door with an old, rusted lock.

Was she fucking kidding him?

"You *live* here?" he asked.

She nodded. "I've been here for about a year. My mother, sister, and I used to live in an apartment downtown, but I couldn't afford the rent after she died. So the landlord said I could move into the studio. The commute is fantastic."

She smiled. Luke didn't. He hated the thought of her struggling to pay the rent after her mother's death. And it made him batshit crazy to know that she'd probably been sleeping here when a couple of thugs were breaking in downstairs. What if they'd taken the narrow stairs leading to her apartment? What if they'd *hurt her*?

Anger and apprehension flooded his chest. A bakery in trouble was one thing. *His girl* in trouble was something else entirely.

"Home sweet home." She opened the door and spread her arm out.

Luke shook his head to dislodge his thoughts, especially the one about Polly being *his girl*. He forced his fists to unclench as he followed her into the studio apartment.

One room with a bathroom and tiny kitchen, the place had secondhand furniture, a dining nook with a white painted table, and framed prints on the walls. There was a little vase of flowers on the coffee-table and a patchwork quilt tossed over the bed.

The wall plaster was cracking, the kitchen appliances were rusty, and the window was small and dingy, but somehow Polly had made the apartment look…nice. Really nice. *Put your feet up and take a deep breath* nice.

"You did a great job with this place," he admitted, not that the décor made it any more okay that she was living here.

"Thanks." She tossed her bag onto a chair. "If you're nice to the tenant, she'll give you free cookies."

"It's not cookies I'm after." Luke couldn't help smiling when her cheeks got pink.

"Be good, Mr. Stone."

"You sure you want me to be?"

"No."

Polly winked at him and headed toward the bathroom. He let his gaze stroke over the curve of her ass in her worn jeans. Her sweet, spicy scent of oranges and cloves wafted over him.

He took a breath, battling the urge to have it out about her living conditions. Though he'd known Polly for less than two weeks, he already knew she'd bite back if he went on the offensive.

He circled the room. A copy of Pierre Lacroix's *The Art of French Pastry* sat on the coffee table. A corkboard hung on the wall, layered with photos and cut-out magazine articles of Paris. The bookshelves were stacked with novels, chef's biographies, and cookbooks, and a CD set of "Learning French." A bunch of classic movie musicals—*The Sound of Music, An American in Paris* —sat beside the small TV.

Luke found himself putting all those pieces together to form a full picture of Polly Lockhart. He didn't do that with other women. Come to think of it, he also didn't go to women's homes or apartments. They always came to him.

He opened the kitchen cabinets and the refrigerator, neither of which contained much except for mac and cheese, yogurt, and canned pasta. Probably all she could afford.

Tension tightened his neck. He needed to get her back to his place. Hell, he needed to *keep* her there so he didn't have to think about her living alone in this dump, waking at four to open her failing bakery before trudging to a community college for culinary arts classes.

Polly emerged from the bathroom, her flour-dusted jeans exchanged for black yoga pants and a Grateful Dead T-shirt, and her hair a tangle of shiny curls around her shoulders.

"Get a jacket or sweater." Luke could come up with a plan later, as long as he didn't let her out of his sight. "We're going to dinner."

She rolled her eyes, crossing her arms over her chest. "How about...*Polly, will you please have dinner with me tonight?* Go on, try it."

He smothered a rush of irritation. "Polly, will you have dinner with me?"

"No."

"What the..."

She held up a hand to stop his imminent tirade. "I don't have time tonight. Yes, we're going to go on dates soon, but tomorrow morning I have a test on aerated confections and nougat."

"What about the bakery?"

"Clementine is opening tomorrow. I'm taking the afternoon shift."

He took his phone out of his pocket and hit the search button.

"What are you doing?" Polly asked.

"Ordering Chinese food."

"I told you, I don't have time to—"

"You need to study, right?"

"Yes."

"Well, Peach, today is your lucky day." Luke spread his arms out. "Because I know a hell of a lot about aerated confections and nougat."

CHAPTER 12

*L*uke Stone knew a lot about...*a lot*. Polly was pretty sure of that.

And she had no doubt he was an expert on seducing women with champagne and expensive dinners, but as he sat across from her at the worn kitchen table, Polly imagined she was probably the only woman in the world who could get weak in the knees over his explanation of batch process nougat-making.

"It requires an eight percent moisture content before the whipping agent is added to the syrup." He wrote on her scribbled notepad. "The whipping agent is usually egg albumen, gelatin, or milk protein."

When she didn't respond, he glanced up to catch her staring at him. Her heart jumped. His jaw was dusted with five o'clock stubble, giving his strong features a very sexy and dangerous look. She liked him that way. Heck, she liked him ten ways from Sunday.

"Did you learn all this just from making candy?" she asked.

He nodded. "In addition to our branding overhaul, we had to

revamp and streamline a lot of the processes when I took over the company. Made everything more efficient."

His cell buzzed again, as it had at least half a dozen times in the past hour. With an apology, he checked it and responded to an email.

"Do you ever take time off?" Polly asked.

"Sometimes."

"You don't sound very convincing."

He didn't look up from his phone. "I travel often for work."

"Where?"

"Europe. Switzerland, Germany, and France mostly."

"How many times have you been to Paris?"

"I don't know." He swiped the screen on the phone. "I go a couple times a year for business. We consult with several chocolate and candy makers in Paris."

"Really? Like who?"

He rattled off the names of the chefs who ran Fouquet, La Maison du Chocolat, and Alain Ducasse. Polly had read their books, visited their websites, learned where they were educated and trained, watched their TV shows.

And Luke Stone personally consulted with them.

"What about Pierre Lacroix?" she asked.

"We worked with him last year to develop a candy version of macaroons."

Awestruck, Polly sat back. She pictured Luke visiting the kitchens of such renowned chocolatiers and patisseries—the air filled with sweet scents and the lyrical cadence of French, watching chefs create towering, sugar-glass confections and tiny, perfect candies of almond paste. Miniature apples and pears, hand-painted animals and *sucettes*. Caramels, pralines, bon-bons.

She looked down at her textbook. The Hartford course in candy technology was required for the Culinary Arts certificate, and though she was enjoying the class, it was nothing compared to what she could learn in Paris.

She reached for the open bag of Jelly Rolls, which was one of several packages of candy Luke had produced from his briefcase, and plucked out a few red ones. The Sugar Rush version of jelly beans, Jelly Rolls were soft, round candies encased in a smooth icing shell. He'd also brought a bag of Puffles, the gummy candy she had liked, and Chocolate Crackles, crispy nut-and-puffed rice nuggets coated with bittersweet chocolate.

"These were my sister Hannah's favorite when we were kids." Polly indicated the Jelly Rolls. "She was never really into desserts, but she liked these."

"They're based on a French fruit candy called *calissons*."

"Where do you stay when you visit Paris?" She popped the red Jelly Roll into her mouth, enjoying the burst of sweet cherry.

"One hotel or another," Luke said. "Wherever the secretary books a room."

He made it sound like he was visiting Podunk, Nowhereville, and staying at the Motel 6. Polly had thought she had missed out on a lot of youthful adventures, but she was only twenty-five years old. She had a lot of time left to see the world and have new experiences—at least the possibility was there even if she didn't have the resources to do any of that anytime soon.

Luke hammered out another text or email on his phone. A crease furrowed the space between his dark eyebrows, and a slight frown curved his mouth.

He needed to nap in a hammock under the trees, to feel the sunlight filtering through the leaves and a breeze drifting over his skin. She needed that too.

He glanced up, as if sensing her gaze on him. "What?"

"When you were a kid," Polly said, "what did you want to be when you grew up?"

Luke gave a humorless laugh. "I can't remember that far back."

"Sure you can." She poked his leg under the table with her foot. "At various times, I wanted to be a firefighter, a magician, a veterinarian, and queen of the sky island of Cerulia. Not necessarily in that order."

"So which one took precedence?"

"Well, I ended up majoring in history in college. But mostly so I could have an excuse to do a year abroad in Paris."

"And did you?"

She shook her head. "I was going to, but then my mother got sick, and I came back to Rainsville to be with her."

Something flickered in his eyes. "So you left college."

"I had to. I wasn't going to leave my mother to face cancer alone. But when I'm finished at Hartford, I'll be a certified pastry chef. If I have better qualifications and can get Wild Child back on its feet, I hope to expand into catering and wedding cakes. Maybe even open an online shop."

Maybe even go to Paris one day.

No one ever said dreams had deadlines, though Luke might not understand that. Even his romantic relationships had deadlines.

"So what did you want to be when you grew up?" she asked again.

He was silent for a moment as he leafed through one of her textbooks. "I wanted to pitch for the San Francisco Giants."

"Really?"

He nodded. "I actually got into Stanford on a partial baseball scholarship. Played for three years until I had to leave."

"You left Stanford?"

"My mother died." A shadow crossed his face. "She was killed in a car accident, and my sister was badly injured. Our family was a mess after that. And when other corporations heard what had happened, they thought Stone Confectioners would weaken. They started rumors of a takeover after we rejected their sales offers. And my father was focused on my sister's recovery, so I dropped out of Stanford and moved back to Indigo Bay to take over as CEO."

"What did your dad say about you leaving?"

"He didn't find out until it was already done. And then it was too late."

Silence fell, edged with a faint sadness over dreams about baseball and sky islands that never had a chance to take root.

"We both left college because of things that happened to our mothers," Polly said, struck by both the coincidence and the realization that perhaps it was just one of the reasons she'd been so drawn to him. She'd seen herself—the responsible, hard-working sibling who'd put her family first—reflected in him.

"Yeah." Luke gazed at her, and it almost seemed as if the same recognition appeared in his eyes. "Strange, huh?"

"There's a belief that our souls guide us to certain people because something in them reminds us of ourselves or because there's something we have to learn from them," Polly said. "It's an attraction of energies, the seeking of fulfillment. Sometimes opposites attract, but sometimes *likes* attract. We like each other, and we're also alike. So, on one level it's not so strange after all."

Faint bemusement tightened his features. "You're very different from me, Peach."

"How?"

"You're warm. Trusting. Open. Friendly."

"So are you. You're just a little more guarded, that's all."

He shook his head with a laugh. "A little more, huh?"

"We have some differences, of course," Polly said. "But on a fundamental level, we're…"

She paused, realizing she was about to say *the same.* But that would be like telling him they were soul mates, which they couldn't be given the fact that he could make no promises to her.

"We're similar," she finally said, handing him a blank piece of paper. "I'll prove it. Write down your favorite Jelly Roll flavor."

Still baffled, he picked up a pen. Polly took another piece of paper and shielded it with her arm as she wrote down her favorite flavor.

"On the count of three, we reveal our answers," she said. "One two three."

They both put their papers in the middle of the table. Side by side, written in his scrawled handwriting and her curly letters, were the words: *Cherry vanilla.*

She gave him a triumphant grin. "See?"

"Well," Luke said, his voice deep with amusement, "far be it from me to deny the proof of candy."

He reached over to take a few cherry vanilla Jelly Rolls, then picked up her open confectionary textbook.

"Speaking of candy," he said. "If you're going to ace this test, you'd better keep studying. I'll quiz you."

He went over to flop on the sofa, stretching out with one bare foot on the coffee table. His sheer size and masculinity were a striking contrast to the floral sofa, but he looked relaxed in her little apartment. Like he was at home. And given their similarities, it made sense that he would feel comfortable in the surroundings that she'd created.

"What is the approximate density of a marshmallow?" He popped the Jelly Rolls into his mouth.

"Between point two five and point seven grams per milliliter."

"What are the basic ingredients of nougat?"

"Lecithin, DMG, and sugar ester," Polly said. "Which helps stabilize the emulsion."

Luke tossed out more questions, leafing through the book and a few of the papers Polly's teacher had assigned. Finally he put them all on the coffee table and sat up.

"You'll be top of the class, Peach." He lifted his arms above his head for a stretch. "You'll have to come work for me after you graduate."

"Why, Mr. Stone, are you offering me a job?" Polly pushed up from the table and approached him.

She let her gaze slide admiringly over his body, lingering on his shirt stretched across his broad chest and shoulders. His tie hung loosely around his neck, and the first few buttons of his shirt were undone, revealing a tempting V of tanned skin.

"Sure." Luke grabbed her around the waist, tugging her down onto his lap. "You can be my personal assistant."

A rush of warmth filled Polly. She settled herself on his thighs. "You already have an assistant."

"Not a *personal* assistant." Luke's hand slid up her leg. "You can be in charge of walking around my office half-naked and occasionally bending over to pick something up off the floor."

She gave him a light smack on the cheek. "Pig."

"What? I'll give you all the candy you want."

"Hmm. Sounds like you'll want the same thing from me."

"And who could blame me?" His eyes crinkled with a smile.

He lowered his lips to hers. Pleasure filled Polly as their mouths sealed together in a warm, lovely kiss that held the promise of more. Luke lifted his hand to cradle the side of her face before trailing his lips down to the hollow of her throat.

She eased back into the strong circle of his arm and gave herself up to the heat flaring like quick-fire between them. Already her nipples were budding up against her bra, and she nestled closer to nudge her breasts against his chest.

He made a noise low in his throat as he brought his mouth to hers again. He tasted all sweet and sugary, like cherry jellybeans, but the tension radiating from him was anything but sweet. It was all hard male urgency and increasing sexual heat.

Polly wiggled against his groin and parted her lips under his, letting him sweep his tongue into her mouth. She threaded her fingers into his thick, dark hair and held him against her as he stroked his hand up her leg and between her thighs. A breathless moan escaped her when his fingers pressed lightly against her, rubbing the material of her panties into her cleft.

"Ah, you're hot already," he muttered, moving his other hand around to cup her breast. "Stand up and strip for me."

Polly's heart crashed into her ribs. She pulled back to stare at him. "Strip for you?"

"Take your clothes off."

"I know what *strip* means."

"So do it." His mouth curved with a faint smile of challenge.

She narrowed her eyes. She had never stripped for a man in her life, but she'd recently learned a little something about negotiating.

"I'll strip for you if you strip for me."

"You strip for me, and then you can strip me," he countered.

"Is this a prelude to *all the way*?"

"I sure as hell hope so."

"Deal."

She eased off his lap, deflecting a twist of nervousness. It would be easier if she set the mood. She dimmed the lights and found "Lady Marmalade" on her media player. Then she told herself to pretend she was at the Moulin Rouge as she started doing a little bump and grind. Too late, she remembered she was wearing yoga pants and a torn T-shirt, not to mention her everyday underwear.

But from the hot, anticipatory glow in Luke's eyes, he wouldn't have cared if she was wearing overalls as long as she intended to take them off. The music started to pulse in rhythm with her increasing heartbeat. She tugged the band out of her hair and shook it out over her shoulders, swiveling her hips as the music launched into the chorus. *Voulez-vouz couchez avec moi ce soir?*

She already knew Luke's answer to that question, and the knowledge that he *wanted* her was enough to bolster her confidence. She pulled off her T-shirt and tossed it to the side. His gaze fixed on the curves of her breasts cupped by a beige cotton bra.

Polly strutted around, swiveling her hips and shoulders. She moved closer to him, holding his gaze as she hooked her fingers into her pants and wiggled them down her legs and off. Now clad only in her bra and panties, she grabbed Luke's loose necktie and unfastened it, pulling it off with one tug. She draped it around her neck and backed away, still dancing.

Oh, she was getting hot. The combination of the heady beat and the intensity of Luke's gaze made her blood rush like hot cream through her veins.

He made a circling gesture with his forefinger. Polly turned, shaking her rear a little in what she hoped was a close approximation to twerking. She turned back around, her heart leaping. He was grasping his erection through his trousers, his eyes dark with lust.

"C'mere, pretty girl," he ordered gruffly.

She strutted her way toward him, her breath catching when he grabbed her hips and hauled her closer to straddle his lap. He urged her to sit back on his thighs, his warm hands sliding over her curves and to her back. With a flick of his fingers, he twisted the clasp of her bra and divested her of it in one movement.

Polly shivered. Although she was supposed to be the one taking off her clothes, she did find his gesture rather masterful. And sitting on his lap with her breasts bare, stiff nipples quivering, and wearing only her panties...her pulse pounded so hard she barely realized the music had stopped.

Luke muttered something under his breath and palmed her full breasts, his tanned hands a striking contrast to her pale skin. He twisted her nipples, sending a shock of electricity right to her core. She stifled the urge to writhe against his strong thigh.

"That was one hot number, Peach," he murmured, running his forefinger along the edge of her panties. "How wet did that make you?"

"Very," she breathed, unable to stop herself from shifting closer to press against the bulge in his trousers. "But I'm supposed to..."

"Oh, you will," he assured her, sliding his hand right down into her panties.

His fingers found her damp cleft, moving over her clit in that expert way he'd done before. No question that Luke Stone knew what he was doing. She pushed against the pressure of his hand, aching for more. He slid one finger inside her and eased it back and forth.

"So tight," he whispered. "Can't wait to sink my cock into you."

She couldn't wait either. Going *all the way* no longer provoked anxiety, only hot anticipation. She submitted to the pressure of his hands and leaned forward as he brought her mouth to his. His tongue flickered out to stroke deliciously across the seam of her lips, his hands moving up to caress her breasts.

She moaned against his mouth. Through the fog of lust, she dimly remembered their agreement about the striptease, and she forced herself to pull back so she could work the mother-of-pearl buttons on his shirt.

She didn't know much—okay, anything—about men's clothing, but even she could tell that his shirt was made of the finest textured cotton, with the cut fitting his chest and shoulders to such perfection that it had to have been custom-tailored just for him.

And yet no matter how beautiful the shirt was, there was no comparison to the sight and feel of his body beneath—his smooth, muscular shoulders, the gorgeous slopes of his pecs leading down to his rigid abdomen and that trail of hair Polly wanted to follow with her tongue right down into the forbidden zone.

She bit her lower lip, gazing at the movement of her hands over his chest, her fingers tracing his washboard abs. She shifted on his lap again, pulling in a breath as her clit throbbed.

Lord. She was going to come just from touching him.

She slithered off his lap and got to her knees in front of him, her naked breasts swaying. After working the buckle of his belt, she pulled it off and unzipped his trousers. She felt his gaze burning into her as she tugged his trousers and boxer briefs off. The sight of his thick cock—and the somewhat unnerving thought of how it would fit inside her—sparked her with a renewed rush of both anticipation and heat.

She curled her hand around his shaft and tentatively licked the tip.

"Ah, fuck." Luke rested his head against the back of the sofa and speared one hand into her hair. "Take it in as far as you can, Peach. Fuck me with your mouth."

His raw command sent sparks bursting through her blood. She lowered her head, taking him in inch by delicious inch. Then she closed her lips around his shaft and sucked him like a Swirl Pop.

His groan of appreciation emboldened her to keep going. If she'd thought that sitting almost naked on his lap was sexy, this was beyond anything she could have imagined. Crouching between his legs, sucking on his erection with his hand gripping her head possessively, her body so ripe for more...

"Stop." His hand twisted and tightened in her hair.

She pulled away and sat back, drawing a hand across her lips as she looked up at him. His chest was heaving, his eyes burning. He sat up, fumbling to get a condom from his wallet before he hauled her back into his lap.

In one movement, he stood, gripping her ass to hold her against him. Polly wrapped her legs around his waist.

"Quick," she whispered, unable to stop the plea in her voice. "I want you so badly."

He strode across the living room to the bed in the corner. He lowered them both to the mattress, his eyes smoldering as his mouth crashed down on hers.

Polly arched upward, wanting every part of her body to touch his. She wound her arms around his shoulders and opened her mouth as her breasts rubbed against his chest and her legs twined with his. Luke pressed his lips across her cheek and down to her neck. He licked a drop of sweat at the hollow of her throat before moving lower to her breasts.

"Oh my God," she gasped, driving her hands into his thick hair. "That feels so good."

His laugh was muffled against her skin.

"*You* feel so good," he murmured. "Soft and sweet, and you smell like a damned flower garden..."

He stroked his hands down her sides and captured one of her nipples between his teeth. His fingers tangled in the waistband of her panties as he stripped them swiftly off her legs. He sat up, his hot gaze raking down her naked body.

Polly squirmed, yearning for him to fill her, to ease the empty ache.

"Please," she begged.

He tore open the foil packet and rolled a condom over his erection before edging between her legs. Her heart raced with both arousal and faint apprehension. He moved over her again, bracing his hands on the mattress.

"Lift your knees," he said, his jaw tight with self-restraint. "I'll go slow."

She brought her knees up, fire flaring over her nerves as he pushed slowly inside her. And even though she was already intimately acquainted with his cock, her nerves tensed as her body sought to accommodate him.

He paused, sliding his hand between them to find her swollen clit. The pressure of his fingers uncoiled streams of pleasure in her nerves, and she felt herself softening.

"Okay," she whispered.

He pressed forward, but still slowly, as if he were afraid of hurting her. And oh, God, the easy, slick immersion was the sweetest torture. She moaned, writhing underneath him. Then he was fully inside her, his head lowered and his breathing hard against the side of her neck.

"Oh, shit, you're so tight," he muttered roughly. "Christ, the things I could do to a sweet girl like you..."

"Then do them," Polly breathed, bucking her hips upward in invitation. "I want you to. God, Luke, I've waited so long for a man like you. Show me what I've been missing."

He paused, his gaze searing right through her. Then he pulled back, sliding halfway out of her before easing in again. The second time, Polly matched the movement, and then he started thrusting inside her with rhythmic, slow strokes, creating a delicious friction that fired her urgency higher.

"More." She dug her fingers into his shoulders. "I want it. I want *you*."

A groan rumbled through his chest. He plunged into her deeper. Their bodies collided again and again. Streams of pleasure washed over Polly.

"I feel it," she gasped, stretching her arms over her head as her breasts bounced in time with his thrusts. "I'm going to come..."

"Do it," he ordered through clenched teeth. "Come on my cock, honey. Give it to me."

"I'm almost there." She gripped his biceps, her arousal climbing to the breaking point. "I'm going to...now...*now!*"

A cry tore from her throat when bliss exploded over her nerves. She quivered and shook, clenching around his shaft as he continued thrusting inside her. He lowered his mouth to hers, his muscles tightening. He surged inside her and stilled with a rough groan, his own body shuddering with release.

Luke collapsed on top of her, their breathing hard and their bodies damp with sweat. Polly wrapped her arms around him. She tingled all over with lingering pleasure.

With a muffled grunt of satisfaction, he rolled off her, reaching out for her with one arm. She shifted to her side and landed right up against his body—which was lovely but also a little embarrassing since gravity invariably rolled all sleepers into the deep sag curving the middle of the mattress. Not that Luke seemed to mind, considering the way he pulled her right into the sag with him.

"It's not your Savoir bed," she felt compelled to remark apologetically.

"As long as you're in it, I'll sleep in any bed."

With a smile, she curled up against him and rested her head on his chest. As she drifted into sleep, she had the vague thought that she was going to have to come up with something spectacular to beat this particular exercise in *fun.*

CHAPTER 13

*P*olly woke when dawn light threaded through the curtains. Luke was gone, but the scent of him still clung to the sheets and pillow. She absorbed the delicious warmth sliding through her veins before she rolled over to grab her T-shirt and panties off the floor.

After pulling them on, she used the bathroom and emerged to find Luke sitting at the kitchen table, his attention on his phone.

She leaned her shoulder against the doorjamb and took a minute to admire the way he looked, his hair sleep-tousled and his gorgeous body clad only in his white shirt, all the buttons unfastened to reveal a tantalizing glimpse of his bronzed, sculpted chest.

He glanced up and met her gaze. Heat sizzled through the air.

"Really?" Polly asked dryly. "Other people are actually up at this hour to take your calls?"

"They don't take *my* calls," he replied. "I take theirs. They wait for mine."

"So is that what I should do?" She stalked slowly toward him. "Wait breathlessly by the phone for a call from the eminent Luke Stone?"

"It would be advisable." He slanted a glance at her as she approached.

She took his phone and set it aside before pushing her way between him and the table to straddle his lap. He was wearing his trousers, and the sensation of the expensive material felt rather delicious against her bare thighs.

After wiggling a little to get comfortable, earning herself a muffled groan from Luke, she draped her arms over his shoulders and looked him in the eye.

"If I told you to clear your schedule for Saturday night because I plan to take you out on a date, would you do it?" she asked.

He hesitated for an instant. Polly poked him in his rock-hard abdomen.

"Would you do it?" she repeated.

"I'll have to see what's on the calendar," he said. "But I'll make every effort."

"You'd better do more than make an effort. Because I'll be at your house Saturday night whether you want me to be or not."

"I can make you no promises," he said.

Polly tried to ignore the sense that that remark was a reminder of something more serious than a night out.

"Promise me Saturday night," she said.

He reached around her to grab his phone from the table.

"You're kind of a pain in the ass," he muttered, scrolling over the screen. "I have a meeting at four to look over a downtown building for a retail site, but I can clear my schedule after six."

"Give me that." She took the phone from him and pulled up his calendar for Saturday night. In the six o'clock slot, she typed *"Go on a date with Polly and hope I get lucky."*

She handed him the phone back. He looked at the screen, his eyes crinkling with amusement.

"I don't hope I get lucky with you," he said.

"You don't?"

"Nope." He rubbed his nose against hers. "I'm already lucky with you."

Polly smiled. She eased back and threaded her fingers through his hair, brushing it away from his face. His gaze slipped down to the pendant she still wore on a silver chain around her neck. His fingers grazed her skin as he lifted the pendant into his palm and studied the flashes of blue, green, and gray embedded in the stone.

"It's a Labradorite crystal," she explained. "The Inuit people believe it fell from the fires of the Northern Lights. It's meant to protect my aura from negative energies."

"Your aura, huh?"

"Everyone has an aura. It's the energy field that surrounds all living creatures and contains their essence. My friend Ramona said mine is damaged, so she gave me this stone as protection."

"And you think it works?" He let the stone fall back against her chest.

"I'd be foolish to claim it didn't," she replied. "My mother always said not to deny something exists just because you can't see it or it can't be proven scientifically. There are too many mysteries in the world. Things you can't explain by science or logic."

"Like what?" He sat back and studied her, running his hands up and down her thighs.

"Grace," Polly said. "Mercy. Faith in a divinity that no one has ever seen. Hope even when a situation seems hopeless. Love."

Luke shook his head, his expression skeptical. "There's no mystery to love."

"How would you know? Have you ever been in love?"

"No. It's all just pheromones and endorphins."

"Oh, my *God.*" Polly laughed and draped her arms around his shoulders again. "You are such a cynic. You're going to be one of those old curmudgeons sitting on your front porch, shaking your fist and yelling at the neighborhood kids to get off your lawn."

"Good thing I met you first then, huh?" He brushed his thumb rhythmically across her collarbone. "Maybe you can save me from that fate."

"As long as I'm on your schedule," she murmured, "I'll save you."

She leaned forward and pressed her lips to his. As they indulged in another long kiss, she felt as if she were spiraling upward into sugar-laced clouds, her whole being filling with sweetness, rainbow sprinkles, and an emotion that felt remarkably close to happiness.

CHAPTER 14

*D*espite the fact that Polly hadn't gotten much sleep the night before, she sailed right through her test on aerated confections and nougat, successfully completed a pectin jelly exercise in her Jellies and Gummies lab, and learned about two new tax exemptions she could claim in her tax preparation class.

By the time she arrived at Wild Child to take over the afternoon shift from Clementine, she was feeling both productive and still all loosely warm from her night with Luke. She was sore in an entirely pleasant way, and it seemed as if thick, rich honey had replaced the blood in her veins. Not to mention her mind kept drifting off to replay the taste of his hot cherry-vanilla kisses, the glide of his big hands over her skin—

"You could take him to the Renaissance Fair." Mia held up her phone triumphantly, waving it at Polly from a table where she was sitting with Ramona and Tom. "Now that is a man I'd love to see decked out in velvet breeches and a waistcoat."

Polly tried to picture it and failed. The images of Luke in her head were all about crisp, tailored suits or just his long, muscular body stretched out above her...

She shivered, pressing her legs together and trying to focus on filling éclair shells with chocolate cream. Though she would happily jump right back into bed with him for the rest of the weekend, she did want them to have some fun that wasn't sex-related.

"There's a UFO meet-up and watch in Davis next Monday," Tom offered.

"Or you could bring him to my fortune-telling group on Friday." Ramona flicked one of her dreadlocks over her shoulder.

"Maybe you could get his-and-her massages," Mia suggested. "Or take him for a spa day. Soothe in Indigo Bay gives detoxification baths using mud from a volcano in Cartagena."

"Luke could just fly to Cartagena and go skinny-dipping in the volcano, if he wanted to." Polly spooned more cream into the pastry bag. "Besides, I have to do things that don't cost too much since I don't want him to both advise me about the bakery and pay for dates, especially since *dating* was my idea. I thought I'd take him to the Snowflake Club for the Riders concert on Saturday night."

Mia looked doubtful. "Snowflake skews a little young for him, doesn't it?"

"He's thirty-four, not fifty-four," Polly said, vaguely insulted on Luke's behalf.

"I'm just saying you might want to consider something more sophisticated." Mia approached the display cases, peering at the rather sparse offerings.

"He's the sophisticated one, remember? I'll bet he hasn't been to a dance club in ages."

"Neither have you," Mia reminded her.

True. But this whole thing with Luke had started as a way for her to get back out into the world, and she was doing exactly that. So good for her.

Her phone buzzed, and she took it out of her apron pocket. A text lit up the screen:

L. STONE: How did the CEO feel without his peach?

POLLY: Hungry?

L. STONE: PIT-iful.

POLLY: I have to break up with you now.

L. STONE: I'd never sign off on that request.

POLLY: Are you at work?

L. STONE: In a board meeting.

POLLY: And you're texting me?

L. STONE: Under the table.

POLLY: Omg. I've made it to the boardroom under the table. Maybe next time I'll make it into your lap.

L. STONE: Any time you want. My lap is reserved for you.

"Earth to Pols." Mia waved her hand in front of Polly's face. "You're out of doughnut holes."

"Oh, sorry." Polly slipped her phone back into her pocket. "I'll fry you up a batch. Can you watch the counter?"

Mia went around the counter to wait for non-existent customers while Polly returned to the kitchen. She grabbed a bowl of dough and dropped spoonfuls into the fryer. As she waited for the dough to crisp, she indulged in a memory of Luke's fingers trailing down her spine, as if he were memorizing each of her vertebrae while he pressed his lips to the hot hollow of her throat and...

She jerked herself back to attention and fished the doughnut holes out of the fryer. After draining them and sprinkling them with powdered sugar, she brought them out to Mia.

"Yum, thanks." Mia plucked a doughnut hole out of the basket and bit into it. Her eyebrows rose. "Wow. What did you do differently?"

"What do you mean?" Polly put a few on a plate and brought it over to Ramona and Tom.

"New recipe?" Mia indicated the doughnut hole as she chewed.

"No." Polly frowned. "Why? Do they taste different?"

"Yeah, they're better, actually. Lighter."

"It's just the regular batter." She selected one for herself and took a bite.

A crisp, sweet flavor flooded over her tongue alongside a light airiness that reminded her of the *pâte à choux* dough for éclairs rather than doughnut batter.

"Wait a second." Polly went into the kitchen and peered into the stainless steel bowl sitting beside the deep fryer.

Well, that explained it. How had she not noticed she was frying the wrong dough?

Because you were too busy remembering Luke Stone ravishing your body.

Any girl in the world was entitled to a free pass for making a mistake while thinking about getting hot and heavy with CEO Stone.

"I used the wrong dough," she explained, returning to the front counter. "That was the *pâte à choux* I fried, not the doughnut batter."

"Happy accident." Ramona reached for another one. "You should sell these too."

"I've used similar dough for French crullers," Polly said, "but those are ring-shaped like actual doughnuts."

She put the bowl on the counter next to the pastry bag and the tray of éclairs she'd been filling. Out of curiosity, she picked up one of the fried éclair balls and piped a bit of custard into the center before popping it into her mouth.

Wow. Her senses exploded with the taste of rich, creamy chocolate combined with the crisp airiness of the pastry.

"Try this." She filled more of the fried éclairs with custard and handed them to Mia, Ramona, and Tom.

All three ate the confections, their eyes growing wide with appreciation and surprise.

"Delicious."

"Amazing."

"A little eggy," Mia remarked. "But if you tweak the recipe, you'll be on to something."

The wind chimes over the door jingled. Polly's heart gave a little leap at the thought that Luke might be coming to pay her a visit. Instead what looked like a geeky special ops force entered.

The five men were dressed in black trousers and black polo shirts bearing an insignia on the breast, and one of them—a tall, square-jawed guy with glasses who wore an impassive expression —was carrying a tablet and a briefcase.

"Polly Lockhart?" He extended a business card. "Gavin Knight, Knight Security. Luke Stone asked us to conduct a security risk assessment of your establishment."

The men behind him were already skulking around, checking the door locks and windows and muttering to each other.

"Go ahead." Polly took the card with a slight sigh.

She really didn't want to be indebted to Luke any more than she already was, but damn the man for being *right*. Wild Child had needed a security upgrade for months now. Heck, it had needed *security*.

"We'll need access to your computer later today." Gavin Knight removed his glasses to peer at her with penetrating blue eyes. "We'll start with the physical assessment."

"Sounds fun," Mia remarked.

Gavin Knight regarded her blankly. "Are you an employee here, ma'am?"

"No, sir." Mia slid her gaze over the security guy's rather broad shoulders. "But I am a *miss*, not a ma'am."

Polly threw her friend a "really with the flirting?" look.

Mia shrugged and mouthed, *"I'm bored."*

Gavin returned his expressionless gaze to Polly. "Ms. Lockhart, we'd also like a list of your employees to assess staffing security levels."

"I only have one employee," she said. "I assure you she possesses a *zero threat* security level."

"We still need her information, ma'am."

"She'll be in tomorrow morning, if you want to talk to her yourself."

"Yes, ma'am."

Gavin Knight gave Polly a short nod before setting his briefcase on a table and opening it to reveal a high-tech laptop.

"Can I offer any of you some coffee?" Polly asked.

"No, thank you, ma'am. We're here to work."

She left them to it. Mia, Tom, and Ramona polished off the rest of the fried éclair balls and gave Polly their opinions on what the pastry needed to make the launch from *delicious* to *out of this world.*

As the security team continued to work, Polly went back to the kitchen to experiment with the *pâte à choux* she normally used for the éclairs. She tested and fried several recipes, then put each batch on a separate plate and filled them with the chocolate custard.

She brought the plates to the front counter. Tom had left, but Ramona was conducting a tarot card reading for Mia.

"Attention, please, gentlemen," Polly called to the security guys who were still prowling around the bakery, writing on their notepads, inputting things into the laptop, and still doing a great deal of muttering. "Since you're all experts on assessment, I'd like you to assess these different pastry recipes, please."

The men looked up, glancing from her to their leader, Gavin. He frowned.

"We don't offer pastry assessments, ma'am."

"You can start now." Polly nudged one of the plates toward a blond man who was crouched beneath the cash register, fiddling with the wires. "Just taste them and tell me which one you like best."

With an audible sigh, Gavin nodded at his team. The men approached the counter and sampled the different offerings, making noises in their throats and looking up at the ceiling as they chewed, swallowed, and assessed.

"This one." The blond guy pointed at the first plate. "Light, airy, and rich without being overly sweet."

"Agreed," another dark-haired man said. "Nice chocolate flavor too."

"Two is a little saltier," a third man remarked. "The extra salt pairs well with the chocolate, but the first one is crisper. I'd go with one too."

Polly marked three votes for the first plate as Mia and Ramona came over to sample and offer their opinions. After more discussion, they agreed that number one was the winner.

"Mr. Knight?" Polly gestured to the plates.

Looking faintly irritated, Gavin stood up from the laptop and came to taste the different pastries. Unlike the other men, he wasn't quite as methodical, eating them in swift succession before nodding at the now-empty plate number one.

"Agreed," he said. "Number one. Back to work, men."

The security team dispersed and resumed their tasks. Gavin picked up a napkin to wipe the chocolate off his mouth.

"Are they cream puffs?" he asked.

"They look like hot security guys to me," Mia remarked, eyeing the blond man.

Polly grinned. Gavin Knight did not.

"I mean these." He gestured to the remaining pastries.

"They're a combined doughnut and éclair," Polly explained. "I invented them by mistake."

"Do you sell them?"

"Not yet."

"Best cream puff I've had in a while," Gavin remarked, before adding in a deadpan tone, "I do declare."

Mia swung her gaze to him. "You did not just say that."

"I believe I did."

"Are you from the South?" Polly asked, though she hadn't detected an accent.

Mia gave her a pointed look. "Pols, he just named your new creation."

Polly grabbed a piece of paper and wrote down the word *Declare*, then crossed it out and changed it to *Declair*.

As she looked at the word, she realized it was the first time she'd ever created an original recipe. Her mother had been a master of recipe creation, unafraid of mixing and matching ingredients to come up with the perfect confection. And Polly had always been a willing taste-tester, but she'd left the actual inventing up to her mother.

Until now.

Before she forgot all the ingredients and proportions, she scribbled down the recipe, then returned to the office and pulled up the website for The Art of French Pastry class.

She'd sent in her mother's éclair recipe with her application, and though she still didn't think much of her chances of acceptance—it would be like winning the golden ticket for Willy Wonka's chocolate factory—she also wasn't very happy about the idea of passing her mother's recipe off as her own.

Dear M. Lacroix (not that Himself would be reading this, but what the heck...)

Enclosed please find my original recipe for a hybrid pastry known as The Declair, a cross between a doughnut and an éclair. I would like to add the Declair to my application, as submitted earlier, to fulfill the original recipe requirement.

Thank you for your time.

Sincerely,
Polly Lockhart

She hit the send button and returned to the kitchen to make up
another batch of Declairs.

CHAPTER 15

$\mathcal{A}$fter their pastry assessment, the Knight Security special ops force returned over the next few days to purchase Declairs during their off-duty hours. Their appreciation for the pastry seemed to spread the word among their friends and family, as several people came in specifically to ask for it, often buying muffins and croissants as well.

Polly was both surprised and pleased by the small but increasing profits at the end of the day, and she emailed the total sales to Luke to keep him apprised. But if she had thought the hot consummation of their relationship—not to mention his texting her during a board meeting—would have turned him into a marshmallow, she was proven sorely wrong. When it came to the business of Wild Child, CEO Stone was as demanding a taskmaster as ever.

For the rest of the week, he came to the bakery every day. In between making his own calls and responding to emails, he sat with her in the office and instructed her on how to use a new accounting program, where she needed to cut expenses, and how to calculate business ratios. He advised her on tax preparation, her leasing contract, health insurance, and employee management.

Polly absorbed so much information that she might soon be qualified to run Microsoft with all she was learning. She completed the somewhat painful task of choosing which products to take off sale and which to keep, negotiated with suppliers, and changed the pricing list. Luke contacted a financial services company on her behalf, and the manager agreed to give Polly a small business loan, which she could use for remodeling the interior.

Gavin Knight and his security guys also returned to install the security system at both Wild Child and Polly's apartment. She always had plenty of Declairs waiting for them, and by the time they were finished with the installation, she was pretty sure not even Houdini himself would be able to break in.

Gavin spent an inordinate amount of time explaining the system, assuring her she was connected to a twenty-four-hour manned control center, inputting passwords and security codes, and using terms like *biometric access* and *encrypted communication paths.*

Despite the fact that Polly thought it was all a bit of overkill, there was no question she felt more at ease both at the bakery and at home. And knowing she would pay Luke back for the cost, she plunged even more determinedly into shoring up the bakery's business plan.

The following Saturday, after Polly dressed in a Mia-approved, drinks-and-dancing outfit consisting of a blue stretchy top ("makes your boobs look spectacular") and a short, pleated skirt ("flirty and cute"), she and Luke drove to the Snowflake Club, which was housed in a somewhat run-down building on the other side of town.

A sense of misgiving rushed through Polly as they went into the jam-packed room that was vibrating with ear-splitting music and noise. She didn't remember it being quite this crowded and loud. But now that they were here, finally on a real live date, she couldn't falter.

"Isn't this great?" she yelled, squeezing into a chair between the wall and a table which Luke had miraculously discovered was unoccupied. "It's one of the hippest joints on the alternative music scene!"

Luke responded, but Polly only knew that because she saw his mouth move. Since she couldn't hear what he said, she smiled and nodded.

He folded his body into the chair beside her. His gaze moved over the crowd, which was packed wall-to-wall with sweaty, T-shirt-clad college students bopping and jumping in time to the beat of the Riders playing on stage.

Mia had been right about the Snowflake Club skewing too young for Luke. In his tailored white shirt and gray wool trousers, he looked like a professor or chaperone rather than a guy out to have a good time.

He spoke again, though she couldn't hear him over the noise.

"Excuse me?" she shouted, leaning closer to indicate he should speak into her ear.

"I'll get us some drinks!"

"Great!"

He patted her knee beneath the table, eased out of the chair, and started making his way toward the narrow bar, which was five tipsy college kids deep and seven across. Luke didn't stand much of a chance of coming back with a drink, but Polly appreciated him for trying.

She settled her elbows on the table, wincing as something greasy and sticky clung to her bare arms. She dug in her purse for a tissue and tried to scrub the tabletop. Had the Snowflake Club always smelled so richly of body odor or had the Riders brought out the "too much wrath for a bath" crowd?

"I'm guessing beer is the safest bet here." Luke squeezed back into the chair beside her, depositing two glasses of watery-looking ale on the table.

"How did you manage to get these?" Polly yelled.

"All that football with my brothers must have paid off."

"You played football a lot?"

"What?"

"Nothing!"

Luke sat back, reaching up to wipe a trickle of sweat off his temple. He reached into his pocket for his phone and started scrolling. Polly couldn't blame him for being bored and restless—this clearly wasn't his kind of place.

She started to suggest they leave when her cell phone vibrated. She took it out and glanced at the screen to find a text.

LUKE: Are you a magician?
POLLY: Uh…no. Why?
LUKE: Because every time I look at you, everyone else disappears.

Pleasure fluttered through Polly, and she nudged him with her elbow. He continued typing on his phone without looking up.

LUKE: Are you a parking ticket? Because you have *fine* written all over you.
POLLY: Oh my god. Don't tell me CEO Stone is really just a cheesy pick-up artist in disguise.
LUKE: Okay, I won't tell you that.
POLLY: For the record, you don't need pick-up lines with me.
LUKE: For the record, you had me at "Hi."

They both looked up at the same time, their gazes meeting with a current of hot tenderness. A slow grin spread across Luke's face as he put his phone back into his pocket. He leaned over and brushed his lips across her cheek to her ear. His breath tickled her skin, sending a shiver down her spine.

"Dance with me," he said.

"Really?" Polly looked at the writhing mass of people. "You sure?"

Luke again maneuvered out of the chair as the dance crowd undulated wildly. He grabbed her hand and tugged her to her feet. She followed him through the crush of sweaty, damp bodies. Because he was so tall and broad-shouldered, people automatically moved aside to make room for him. Within seconds, they were in the middle of the floor, the hot air compressing around them.

This *had* been her idea. Polly started bumping around as best she could considering there were thrashing bodies closing in on her from all sides. The music pounded inside her head, hurting her ears, eyes, and even her nose.

But she couldn't let Luke know that this craziness wasn't exactly what she'd planned when she'd decided to take him out for a night of drinks and dancing. Polly hadn't been to the club in well over a year, but now that the universe had put Luke Stone right in front of her, she had to keep her promise to show him a good time.

"Woo hoo!" She swiveled her hips and turned in a circle, narrowly missing colliding with the girl to her right. "This place rocks!"

Luke put his hands out three times to stop other people from crashing into them. Polly spun around again just as a guy bumped her from behind.

Luke caught her around the waist, and for an instant the world receded as she remembered him catching her that night at the Troll's House. Except this time, she was in full possession of her senses, and the solid strength of his body came right up against hers. He tightened his hands around her.

"Okay?" he shouted.

Polly nodded, a flush of embarrassment crawling up her neck. What was she thinking bringing CEO Stone to a club like this? He was a man accustomed to going to the opera or the theater, not a hole in the wall so crowded it was probably a fire hazard.

"Maybe we should go—" she began, but then he settled her hips against his and started to dance with her.

Polly drew in a breath, surprised and flustered by the sensation of his strong body moving to the noise that passed for music. The lead singer screeched something into the mic, and a piercing feedback rattled her ears.

The crowd surged and yelled. Luke's grip tightened. Sweat dripped down her neck. She slipped her arms around his waist and rested her head on his chest. The fact that they were both getting hot and sticky intensified the throbbing sensation in her blood.

The world receded farther. Luke spread his hands over her rear, moving them in slow circles. Even past the noise, she heard his heavy heartbeat. And then it was just the two of them, their bodies sealed together and rocking slowly in a rhythm of their own making. He pressed his lips against her temple. She breathed in his scent of soap, shaving cream, and heat.

"Mosh pit!" someone yelled.

Luke lifted his head, his eyes crinkling with wry amusement. "A mosh pit might be a little too much fun for me."

"Me too." Polly curled her fingers around his as they made their way back to the table and squeezed into their chairs. She grabbed the beer, which was stale and flat, but still cold.

An agonized scream from the Riders caused the crowd to surge joyfully. Luke shot to his feet, getting in front of Polly as a boy started to stumble into their table. Next thing she knew, the boy was crashing into Luke, who then grabbed him to keep him from going down. The table tipped. The beer splashed all over both the floor and Luke's shirtfront.

"Sorry, man!" the boy yelled.

Luke said something in response as he steadied the kid back on his feet. The boy ran off into the mosh pit again.

"Your shirt." Polly fumbled for the tissues in her pocket and began wiping down Luke's wet shirt. Greasy streaks appeared over the beer stains, and she realized she was trying to clean him up with the same tissues she'd used to scrub the gunk off the table.

"Oh no." She grimaced at the realization that his very expensive shirt had been ruined. "I'm so sorry."

Luke straightened an overturned chair. "You okay?"

"I'm fine." Though her head was starting to throb anew.

"Let's get some air." He helped her out of her chair and guided her through the crush to the door.

Once outside, she gulped in the fresh, night air and sagged against the building. "Well, that was interesting."

Luke brushed a lock of hair off her sweaty forehead. "And fun."

She looked at him dubiously, though her heart warmed with gratitude toward him for making the most of what could have been a disastrous evening. "Thank you."

"Thank *you*." He nodded toward the street. "Come on. Let's go get cleaned up."

Polly hadn't even realized the beer had also splashed onto her, despite Luke's heroic attempt to protect her. They walked back to his car, which miraculously hadn't been stolen in the somewhat dodgy neighborhood, and headed back to his house.

"Since we both need showers, you should stay here tonight." He ushered her inside.

"I don't have any extra clothes."

"There's some in the guest bedroom."

Of course there were. Luke's bachelor pad was outfitted for... a bachelor pad.

Ignoring the reminder that she was not part of his usual strata of high-class women, who would have taken him to the opera instead of a sweaty, overloud club, Polly followed him up the stairs. Her gaze fixated on the row of windows that overlooked the inner courtyard and shimmering pool.

"Do you ever swim?" she asked.

"I do laps sometimes. Why?"

"The pool just doesn't look like it's ever been used."

"My brother Evan comes over to swim every now and then." He paused to look at her. "You can use it, if you want."

"Will you swim with me?"

"Now?"

"Sure." She poked him in the side. "It'll be fun."

He shrugged. "Okay. You can probably find a suit in the dresser in the guest bedroom."

Polly didn't love the idea of wearing a swimsuit that might have been worn by another woman, but she walked into the guest bedroom to riffle through the drawers. The lowest one contained several brand-new swimsuits in different styles and a stack of ridiculously plush towels.

She stripped off her clothes and glimpsed herself in the mirror. Then, not sure if she was exercising bad judgment or being outrageously flirtatious—there seemed to be a fine line between the two—she wrapped her naked body in a towel and headed out of the room.

She went down to the pool, astonished at how stepping into the courtyard was like entering a private oasis—plants and trees lined the walls, a small waterfall cascaded from a rock garden at one end, and cushy seating areas were arranged near a fireplace. Spotlights glowed on the water, and overhead the sky blazed with stars through the glass roof.

Polly sat on the edge of the pool and dangled her feet in the water. She turned her head when the door opened and Luke approached. He was breathtakingly masculine in navy swimming trunks and nothing else, his muscular chest with all its smooth lines and planes crafted with the precision of a sugar sculpture.

His gaze skimmed appreciatively over her and lingered on the valley of her cleavage where she had knotted the towel.

"Do I get to see?" he asked, his voice a deep caress over her skin.

A touch of nervousness wound through her. "Maybe later."

He lowered himself alongside her, his thigh brushing hers. She shifted, making sure her towel was still secure.

"Speaking of fun," Luke put his feet in the water beside hers, "or in this case, a complete lack thereof...I wanted to ask if you'd go to the opening of a museum exhibition with me on the twenty-first."

"Really?" Polly did a quick calculation. That was three weeks away. She guessed that meant he intended for their relationship to continue at least that long. "That sounds fancy."

"It is." His breath expelled on a sigh. "It's a fundraising dinner for my mother's foundation, and my aunt Julia is the one organizing it. She's expecting me to bring a date or she'll unleash her ninja match-making skills on me."

"I take it that's a bad thing?"

"With her, it is. Besides, I don't want to be match-made with anyone except you."

Polly tried not to let that little remark nestle right in the middle of her heart.

"Will the rest of your family be there?"

"Some of them. If that's a deal-breaker, I get it."

"It's not." She paused, then confessed, "I don't think there are any deal-breakers here."

He glanced at her. "None?"

"Well, if you turn out to be a secret ultra-villain, I might have some reservations," Polly said, "or if your favorite band is Black Sabbath, then we're done. But other than that, no."

"Does that mean you'll come to the exhibition opening?"

"That depends. Are you asking me as a *date* or just a woman you take to social events?"

"Definitely a date."

"Then I accept. Thank you for asking me."

They exchanged smiles. Curious though Polly was about everything—Luke's family, his mother, the foundation, even his match-making aunt—she suppressed the questions bubbling in her mind. The deeper she delved into Luke's life, the more difficult it would be to extricate herself when the time came.

Whenever that might be.

She nudged her hip against his. "So you've never been in love, huh?"

"Why do you ask?"

"You said love was just about pheromones or whatever. So I assume you've never actually been in love, or you decided the feeling was like a post-workout endorphin rush."

Luke shrugged. "I've had that rush for a woman, yeah. But it doesn't last."

Because by definition, a *rush* didn't last. Especially a sugar rush. Sure, you enjoyed the bag of candy while you were wolfing it down, but eventually you ended up with plunging glucose levels and a stomachache.

Polly flicked her toes in the water, creating a series of ripples.

I can't make you any promises.

You deserve something long-lasting and I can't give that to you.

His words echoed in her mind, even though she wasn't supposed to want anything long-lasting. At least, not from him. She'd just wanted a good time, some *fun*, as she jumpstarted her life again. No, she hadn't thought about what would come *after* the jumpstart, but that was the point, right? Live in the moment. Eat the whole bag of candy.

She pulled her feet out of the water and stood, clutching the towel around her. She walked around to the far end of the pool, her feet making wet footprints on the travertine patio. She stopped at the edge of the deep end and looked into the water, seeing only lingering ripples and the hazy blur of her own reflection.

Her heart kicked against her ribs. She glanced up at Luke, almost feeling the burn of his gaze as he watched her. Gathering her courage, she took hold of the knot in the towel.

In one motion, she yanked it off and tossed the towel behind her. The cooler air brushed against her naked body for an instant before she dove headfirst into the pool. The water enveloped her in a wave, as cool and refreshing as lemonade spilling down her throat on a sweltering day. She swam deeper until her lungs protested, and then she shot upward and broke through the surface with a gasp.

She swiped the water off her face. Luke was still watching her, only his expression was hotter, his body lined with erotic tension. Polly flipped her wet hair away from her forehead.

"You coming in?" she called.

"Actually I might want to watch you swimming like a mermaid," he replied. "I heartily approve of your choice of bathing suit."

She swam closer to him, deliberately looking at his swim trunks.

"Have you ever skinny dipped before?" she asked.

"If I have, it wasn't memorable."

"Come on in, then." She paused, treading water. "I'll make it memorable for you."

"Peach." Luke slowly got to his feet, his gaze never leaving her. "You make everything memorable."

He hitched his fingers into the waistband of his trunks. Polly's breath caught as he slid the trunks slowly off. He kicked them to the side and stood there with his hands on his hips, as if he knew quite well that just the sight of his naked body had a devastating effect on her senses.

After walking to the deep end, he dove into the pool, his body splitting through the water like a knife and disappearing beneath the surface. The sight of his long, muscular form coming right toward her sparked a pleasurable rush of apprehension. She turned in the other direction, wondering if she could outswim him. He came up beside her with the speed and grace of a shark.

With a breathless laugh, she swam faster. Luke's hand clamped around her ankle. Flailing, she tried to yank herself away, but his grip was inexorable, and he grabbed her other leg and pulled her toward him. She surrendered quicker than she would have liked. They both stilled at the same time.

Polly was breathing fast, even though she hadn't even gone the length of the pool. Water drops cascaded down the hard planes of his face and made his eyelashes all spiky. His gaze tracked over her neck to where her breasts bobbed just above the surface of the water.

She splashed him suddenly, letting out a shriek of laughter as his eyes widened. She bolted away, but only made it a few feet before his arms clamped around her waist and hauled her back against his solid naked body.

All the breath escaped her lungs as Luke moved her over to the side of the pool, his hands coming around to caress her breasts. His lips, cold with water, pressed against the side of her neck.

Polly turned. She looked up into his face, his strong features that had become so familiar and dear to her. A warm, rich feeling flooded her heart.

"Tell me you believe in love," she whispered.

His eyes flickered with an indefinable emotion. "I believe in you."

And then he was kissing her before she even realized he'd moved closer. His mouth crushed against hers, hot and demanding. She gasped, her arms going up of their own volition to twine around his shoulders as she sank under the onslaught of his kiss.

He hauled her against him so forcefully that the water surged around them. Her breasts pressed against his hard, wet chest, her fingers curling into the sleek muscles of his shoulders.

Faint dizziness spun through her head as the kiss deepened. She opened her mouth and slid her tongue across his. He gripped her ass, and she wrapped her legs around his hips. He moved them both through the water before lifting her onto the travertine patio.

Water streamed from Polly's hair down her face and body. She stared at him, struck by the feral glint in his eyes, his damp hair casting his features into sharp relief. Divested of corporate trappings, he exuded a primitive sex appeal, one that made her feel sinuous and free, like a wild strawberry plant flourishing in a sun-drenched field.

She pressed her hands to the sides of his jaw and brought her lips to his again. The kiss lasted for seconds, it lasted for hours. He pulled away from her only to trail his mouth over her bare shoulder and down to her breasts.

Polly moaned, wiggling on the stone floor as her sex began pulsing in response to the warm, delicious sensation of his mouth.

"Wait," she murmured, pressing his shoulders.

He lifted himself off her. "What?"

"Remember when I told you I've always dreamed of getting laid on a huge bed with feather pillows?" she asked breathlessly.

Luke gave a choked laugh. "I believe you said a *four-poster* bed with feather pillows."

"Whatever. And remember that last time, we didn't go all the way." She put her hand on the back of his head and pulled him down to her.

"Let's do it now," she whispered.

He gave her another long deep kiss before hauling himself out of the water. He picked her up effortlessly and strode toward his bedroom. And though the water quickly cooled on Polly's skin and left her cold and clammy, the unbearable sexiness of being masterfully carried to Luke's bedroom heated her from the inside out.

He lowered her onto the gorgeous bed and straddled her body, his gaze raking hotly over her bare breasts. He was almost fully erect, and the sight of his hardening shaft elicited a surge of arousal in her blood.

"Hurry," she whispered.

He shook his head, his eyes gleaming. He palmed her breasts, his long fingers tweaking her nipples. He moved lower, pressing kisses over her breasts and belly before gently parting her thighs. Before she could grasp a semblance of thought, he'd already spread her open with his fingers and stroked his tongue over her folds.

"Luke!"

He gave a muffled noise in response, shifting to hitch her legs over his shoulders as he began licking and sucking her with exquisite precision. Polly fisted the bedcovers, shocked arousal flooding her in a wave.

"I'm…." she panted, sweat breaking out on her skin. "Oh my god, that's so…so good…I'm going to…"

"Come on, Peach," he murmured.

She squirmed, unable to stop herself from pushing her lower body toward him, wordlessly begging for more.

"Luke." She tightened her grip on the bedcovers. "Please, please…*Luke!*"

With a cry, she bucked up against him when sensations suffused her body. He continued licking and stroking her until the vibrations ebbed, and then he pulled away to sit up slowly. Deep, dark satisfaction filled his eyes.

"You're so fucking sexy." He lowered his mouth to hers.

With a moan, she eased her hand between them, sliding her palm over the ridges of his chest and down to his cock.

"I need you," she whispered.

He moved away from her only long enough to grab a condom and roll it onto his erection. The mattress dipped a little with his weight as he returned to her, his eyes smoldering and his muscles tense.

Polly thought they were both ready to get right down to the main event, but instead Luke covered her body with his and pressed light kisses across her face. He stroked his hands through her damp hair and kissed her forehead, her eyelids, her nose, her lips, all the way down to her neck.

Then he urged her thighs farther apart, moving between them to position himself right at her opening. Even with her body still throbbing from an orgasm, the sensation of his cock right there —hard, hot, big—made her tense a little.

He slipped his fingers down to rub her sensitive clit before slowly pushing into her. She inhaled sharply, every nerve heightened as her body opened to accept the slow, heavy glide of his shaft.

She wiggled her hips to encourage him to go deeper. His jaw clenched as he eased into her another couple of inches, leaning over her to brace his hands on the bed.

"Fuck, you feel so good," he whispered, his hot breath stirring the locks of hair on her forehead. "Open up wider, Peach. Let me in."

Hadn't she done that already? In a daze, she lifted her legs and hooked them around the backs of his thighs. Let him into her life, her body, even into her heart...?

He groaned, sinking into her like a key fitting into a well-oiled lock. He clutched her hips, pulling back partway before thrusting into her again. Back and forth. Back and forth, the increasing rhythm pulsing through Polly's blood in time with the beat of her heart.

She surrendered, falling into the swirl of lust as they moved together. One more stroke of his fingers and she came again with a cry, her body lifting off the bed. And then Luke plunged inside her with a groan, hard shudders wracking him as he succumbed to his own pleasure.

They collapsed on the bed together. He wrapped his arm around her, hauling her against his side. Their breathing slowed, and Polly resisted the urge to sink into the pull of sleep.

As much as she wanted to spend the night curled into him as if she belonged there, she couldn't give in to the allure of actually sleeping with Luke Stone again. It would be far too easy to get used to such a pleasure.

"I should get home," she murmured. "Now that my apartment is like living in Fort Knox."

"You're not leaving tonight."

A retort pushed up into her throat over his implacable tone, but she swallowed it back down. Hidden in Luke's order was the unspoken reason he was making the demand in the first place. He didn't want her to leave because he wanted her to *stay*. That filled her heart with both cautious hope and unease.

She rubbed her cheek on his chest. A little silver object resting on his nightstand caught her eye, and she reached over to pick it up. It took her a second to realize it was an elephant charm, exactly like the one she always carried in her macramé bag.

"Where did you get this?" She held it out.

"From your bag."

Polly arched an eyebrow. "Seriously? You stole it from me?"

"I borrowed it," he corrected, running his hand over her hip.

"What's it doing next to your bed?"

He shrugged. "Whenever I see it, it reminds me of you."

It sounded like a casual remark, but Polly sensed the meaning beneath, like a perfectly ripe, red cherry hidden inside a chocolate shell. Luke liked thinking about her. And being reminded of her.

"It's a good luck charm." She set the elephant charm back on the nightstand.

"Then it's already worked for me because you're here."

Polly smiled. She trailed her fingers down the hard, hair-roughened length of his forearm to where his hand rested on her hip. She traced the outline of his knuckles and his long, beautiful fingers that touched her with such delicious expertise.

After taking hold of his wrist, Polly turned his hand so his palm faced upward.

"This is your life line." She slid her finger over the curved line near his thumb. "Yours is quite strong and clear, which doesn't surprise me. And you have a secondary line running parallel to it, which indicates great vitality."

She pulled his hand closer and touched the small lines beneath his pinkie finger. "These are your money lines, which show that you're intelligent and good with finances and invest-ments. Your head line, here, is straight and extends to your pinkie. That means you have a very practical, analytical mind, but sometimes you think too much before making a decision instead of trusting your instincts. And your fate line indicates a strong, successful career and social status."

She ran her fingertips lightly over his palm again. His hand twitched slightly in reaction to the tickling touch. She felt his gaze on her face.

"What about my heart line?" he asked.

"How do you know there's a heart line?"

"Logic. If there's a fate, head, and life line there has to be a heart line."

She pretended to study his hand intently, though his heart line was the first thing she'd noticed about the pattern criss-crossing his palm.

"Your heart line is deep and clear." She glided her finger over the curved line. "That shows you have a good love life and strong, secure emotions. But it's also somewhat high on your palm, which means you're cautious about commitment. And see how it straightens out here? That indicates you can be ruled by intellect rather than emotion. But it curves toward this finger and shows you're a very passionate and intense lover."

"Hmm." His voice rumbled in his chest. "All that from a line on my palm?"

"Well, I could have told you some of it without seeing it." She curled his fingers into his palm and cupped her hands around his fist.

"Another mystery of life that can't be seen or proven?" Luke asked.

Maybe. Polly's intuition certainly told her she was falling for him in ways that had nothing to do with logic and everything to do with her heart.

And she could read the signs, both in his palm and his actions—his overprotectiveness, his desire for her to stay, his "borrowing" a reminder of her, the way he touched her, his confession that he *believed* in her. All of those things spun together like feathery, sweet cotton candy right in the center of Polly's heart, creating a truth that both thrilled and scared her.

Despite his talk about not making promises, Luke Stone was starting to fall for her too, at least a little bit. She tucked herself against him again and closed her eyes.

Where would they both land?

CHAPTER 16

*P*olly put a chicken pot pie in the microwave and returned to the kitchen table, which was covered with a pile of textbooks and papers. She sat down and opened her confectionary sciences book, but instead of focusing on studying the effects of heat on the flavor and textures of various foods, her mind drifted to Luke Stone.

Her body warmed at the mere thought of him, everything inside her feeling light and airy. The rational part of her warned she was treading in dangerous waters with these fluffy, romantic feelings, but it felt so good to let all her darker emotions of the past year—discouragement, frustration, despair—float away on a cloud of pleasure.

A knock sounded at the door, breaking into her reverie. Hoping it was a surprise visit from CEO Stone, who could certainly help her study the *effects of heat*, Polly hurried to peer through the security-installed peephole in the door. A slender woman with long, straight brown hair stood on the landing.

Polly's heart slammed against her ribs. She pulled the chain off the door lock and yanked it open.

"Hannah," she breathed in shock.

Her sister smiled. "Hey, Polliwog."

A familiar rush of both pleasure and resentment flooded Polly as Hannah stepped forward to embrace her. She hadn't seen her sister since Jessie's funeral, and the faint smell of sandalwood drifting from Hannah brought back a sharp reminder of their mother. A lump of emotion rose to her throat.

"Good to see you, sis." Hannah detached herself, her gaze going over Polly. "You look great."

"So do you." Polly blinked back the sudden tears stinging her eyes and stepped aside. "Come in. Do you have a suitcase?"

"Just this." Hannah indicated the canvas backpack she was carrying as she entered and flopped down on the sofa. "Nice place. Looks the same."

"It is."

Had Hannah expected anything different? She knew Polly was the one who craved familiarity, whereas Hannah needed constant change.

She closed the door, unable to stop looking her sister. Dressed in a cotton skirt and tank top that displayed the tattoo on her shoulder, Hannah looked both young and also somehow jaded. With her bow-shaped lips and aquamarine eyes, she had always been beautiful, but her seemingly endless traveling had given her a sharp, restless energy.

"I can't believe you're here," Polly said. "I had no idea you were even coming into town."

"I was in LA for about a week. Thought I'd stop in and see if I could stay with you for a while."

"Of course." She went into the kitchen. "Are you hungry? I have another pot pie if you want."

"Sure." Hannah picked up *The Art of French Pastry* book on the coffee table and leafed through it. "You've been okay?"

"More or less."

Polly pulled the pot pie out of the oven and put another one in, punching the timer buttons. As the microwave whirred into action again, she set the cooked pie on a plate with a fork. She pushed her textbooks and papers to the side, creating a space at the kitchen table as Hannah came to sit down.

"With school and the bakery, I haven't had a chance to keep up with your blog as much as I'd like." Polly set the plate in front of her sister. "Last I read you were in Brazil."

"For *Dia dos Namorados*." Hannah picked up the fork. "It's like Valentine's Day, with gifts and date nights. Celebrated because of St. Anthony, who blessed couples with prosperous marriages."

"Are you ever worried you'll run out of love traditions to write about?"

"Astonishingly, people around the world seem to think love has no end." Hannah rolled her eyes slightly. "That's good for me, though. I've picked up enough readers that I've started running ads on my blog now."

"Really? That's great."

"And not all my posts are about love because that would be boring." Hannah broke the crust on her pie and scooped up a portion. "So how are things at Wild Child?"

"Not great," Polly admitted. "We're in debt and business sucks. But believe it or not, I'm getting help from the CEO of The Sugar Rush Candy Company."

"Really? You're going corporate?"

"No, no. Luke Stone is a friend of mine. He's helping me with a business strategy."

"A friend?" Hannah arched an enquiring eyebrow.

"Well, he's a little more than a friend." Polly's cheeks heated. "But it'll never be anything serious."

Saying the words aloud dissipated the fluffy feeling that had surrounded her heart earlier. "Nothing serious" was what she'd been looking for the night she first saw Luke at the Troll's House. So why did it feel like a punch in the gut to actually say that out loud to her sister, who blogged about *love*?

"How long are you staying in town?" she asked in an effort to change both the subject and her train of thought.

"A friend is heading to Portland, and he's going to let me know when he passes through here. I'm going to hitch a ride with him."

"What's in Portland?"

"The Tulip Festival. I went to the one in the Netherlands last year, so I thought I'd do another tulip post."

They ate in silence for a few minutes. Polly still couldn't fathom how her sister could be on the move so much, in Spain one week and China the next, though part of her did envy Hannah's sense of adventure and her outright bravery. Certainly Polly would have liked to visit just a fraction of the countries Hannah had been, but she also liked the idea of having a home to return to.

After they finished eating, Polly got clean towels and a wash-cloth for her sister, then changed the bedsheets while Hannah showered and changed.

"We'll have to share the bed," she said when Hannah emerged from the bathroom. "The sofa isn't big enough to sleep on."

"That's fine. I've slept on concrete floors, so a bed is a luxury."

Polly sat on the bed and watched as Hannah brushed her wet hair. She had always been slender, with narrow hips and long legs that gave her a feline kind of grace. She was thinner now than she'd been a year ago, and her hair fell past her shoulder blades in a straight, thick curtain.

Hannah's eyes were the same, though. Polly couldn't remember a time when her sister hadn't had those striking, thick-lashed eyes that sometimes unnerved people with their perceptiveness. Even with subtle changes, Hannah was still beau-tiful in an otherworldly way, like a forest elf.

"So where else have you been?" she asked.

"Oh, everywhere." Hannah waved her hand, as if it were easy

to go *everywhere*. "I went to Greece for a few months, but I've mostly been in South America. Mexico, Peru, Chile."

"Did you see Machu Picchu?"

"Not this time." Hannah worked at a tangle in her hair. "After Oregon, I thought I'd go up to Alaska and work for a while. I met a woman whose brother owns a restaurant up there, so I can wait tables."

Polly brought her knees to her chest and wrapped her arms around them. Hannah fastened her long hair into a ponytail. Her sister had always had a natural elegance about her, like a dancer or a gymnast.

"If you need money, you can always work at Wild Child," Polly said. "We might have to close soon to do some remodeling, but Clementine is the only employee I still have. I can't pay you much, but we could use help at the counter while we're still open."

"Doesn't Clementine work the counter?"

"She can't always be there. Besides, it's your bakery too."

Hannah shook her head. "It's not mine. It's always been yours."

"Mom left it to both of us."

"I know, but Wild Child is your thing. You were always the one hanging out there with Mom, not me. I've never even been much of a dessert person anyway." She sat beside Polly on the bed, a crease appearing between her eyebrows. "Why don't you just buy me out and keep the whole thing for yourself?"

Because if I do that, then there really will be nothing tying you to Rainsville. Not even me.

"I can't afford to buy you out," Polly said. "And besides, Mom wouldn't want that."

"Mom isn't here."

"I know. I'm aware of that fact every time I walk through the front door of Wild Child."

"Maybe you should let it go then." Hannah motioned for her

to move over so she could climb under the covers. "Don't hold on to Wild Child just because you think it's keeping Mom close."

Irritation scraped Polly's insides. "That's not why I'm doing it. I love the bakery. I practically grew up there, especially after you left."

"I left because I didn't want to be stuck in this town for the rest of my life. But unless you make a change, that's exactly what's going to happen to you."

"Being responsible is not the same thing as being *stuck*."

"Polly, if you want to stay here and run Mom's bakery, that's your choice." Hannah turned to fluff up the pillow. "It's just never been mine."

"Well, I'd really like it if you at least stayed longer than a few days." Polly's heart thumped with sudden anxiety. "Even if you don't want to work at Wild Child, it would be nice to have you here. There's a new outlet shopping mall near Gilroy we could go to."

Hannah's expression softened, and she reached out to stroke a lock of hair away from Polly's forehead. "Sure. That would be fun."

Polly climbed off the bed, unable to help feeling as if her sister was just indulging her.

"All right," she said, heading back to the kitchen table. "Get a good night's sleep."

She turned off the light switch on the wall and sat down again. She'd always known Hannah had a penchant for adventure and travel—when they were kids, Hannah's pretend games were always about being on the crew of a sailing ship or explorers on uncharted territory. Polly, on the other hand, tended to want to play house or school.

Still, that didn't explain why Hannah had bailed without either an explanation or a plan two days after her high school graduation. Polly had been baffled by her sister's departure, but she hadn't been angry—at first. The longer Hannah had been away and the less she seemed to care about Jessie or Wild Child, the more Polly had resented her.

Jessie hadn't, though. Their mother had been happy that Hannah was off seeing the world, and she'd read her lively blog updates as if they were letters written just for her.

And despite her resentment, the posts always incited envy in Polly that she couldn't ignore. Reading Hannah's descriptions of the ice-blue waters of Silfra, eating curry on a beach in Goa, hiking to a Buddhist temple in Vietnam, all sparked a latent wanderlust that Polly hadn't even known she possessed. Sometimes she wished she had even a fraction of Hannah's bravery.

But she didn't want her sister's nomadic, uncertain life. She didn't want whatever darkness came along with it—uncertainty, no home base, risk-taking, leaving friends behind, fear. Polly wanted to live and have fun, but with people she loved and with a home to return to. Hannah, of course, wanted a different kind of life.

And as their mother had always said, "Live *your* life." Though Polly and Hannah were both doing exactly that, she wished their lives weren't so separate.

CHAPTER 17

"**M**r. Stone? Mr. Stone."

Luke jerked his attention away from staring out his office window. He turned in his chair, forcing himself to focus. Kate stood by his desk, holding a folder and watching him with a furrowed brow.

"Are you all right, sir?" She put the folder on his desk. "Do you need anything?"

"No."

What he *needed* was Polly to stay at his house, security system or not. But even more than that, what he *needed* was to stop thinking about her and concentrate on his work. He hadn't contacted her all morning, and he hated himself for checking his email more often than he usually did in the hopes of finding a message from her.

She'd told him her sister had shown up unexpectedly, and he couldn't tell whether or not she was glad about that. Polly missed Hannah, but their relationship was strained.

And he sure as hell knew something about strained sibling relationships.

"Perhaps a protein drink?" Kate asked.

"No, thanks."

It would take a lot more than a protein drink to straighten him out. He didn't enjoy that realization one bit. In less than three weeks, Polly Lockhart had infiltrated his mind to the point that she was clouding his usually razor-sharp concentration on the business. Hell, he'd make a stupid mistake on the Switzerland project analysis this morning because he couldn't stop thinking about sinking into her warm, tight—

"...the corporate social responsibility report," Kate was saying.

Luke shook his head slightly, as if that would somehow get thoughts of Polly out of his mind. "Okay, thanks."

"And I've confirmed your travel plans to Bern, so everything is settled."

Travel plans. Bern.

Shit.

"Did you still want to take a few extra days at the end of the trip to go to Brussels?" Kate asked.

Luke dragged a hand down his face. A month ago, a three-week-long business trip to Switzerland would have been just a regular part of his work. Typical. Ordinary. But since the instant he'd looked up from the pool table to see a curly-haired angel watching him from across the room, nothing in his life had been ordinary.

He rubbed his palm, still feeling Polly's light touch as she examined his heart line.

"Sir?" Kate prompted. "Would you like me to reserve a room for you in Brussels for a few nights?"

"No." Luke didn't want to be away from Polly for three hours, much less three weeks. He sure as hell wouldn't extend his trip any longer than necessary. "I'll come back after Bern. Is Evan in yet?"

"I believe so, sir. Shall I summon him for you?"

"No, I'll go see him." Luke shrugged into his suit jacket and headed down the hall to his brother's office.

Evan stood at the table in the corner, looking over a bunch of graphics. He glanced up when Luke entered.

Tension tightened the air.

"Did you talk to Sam about the Fair Trade Foundation?" Luke closed the door behind him. "He had a marketing idea about a fair trade challenge to get other companies on board."

"Yeah, he mentioned it. He didn't know where to start, though." Evan rubbed his jaw. "I got the website up and running, and I started drafting a charter of standards and principles."

Despite Evan's frustration with not having control of the foundation, his brother would never stall a Sugar Rush initiative out of spite. Just the opposite—he'd still do everything he could to help.

Luke had a stab of regret over his decision to turn the foundation over to Sam, even if he still couldn't justify letting his brother travel extensively to remote locations. He doubted Evan's cardiologist would sign off on the idea either. At the same time, he did need to do more to get his brother involved in Sugar Rush…or risk losing him in a different way.

What would Polly read in Evan's heart line? Luke had almost believed her when she'd talked about all the qualities she could see in his palm. Just like he'd almost believed her when she'd told him the crystal around her neck had fallen from the Northern Lights. And when she'd talked about love being something you couldn't explain through science or reason…

Stop.

"Hey, you want to grab a beer or something this weekend?" he asked.

Evan glanced at him in faint surprise. "With you?"

"Yeah, with me. Even though you ratted me out to Julia about Polly, I might even pay."

"I didn't rat you out, man. I was trying to save you."

"From what?"

"Julia gave me a list of the women she'd invited to her

museum fundraiser, and she said she was reserving a few of them for you. So I told her you were already dating someone and didn't need to be set up."

"Oh. Well, thanks for the save."

"No problem." Evan straightened, resting his hands on his hips. "For the record, you owe me big because Julia is now seating me between two single ladies in an arrangement she's calling the *spinster sandwich*."

Luke shook his head in both resignation and amusement. "Who else has she recruited?"

"Dad, of course, and maybe Spencer if she bribes him enough. Are you bringing Polly?"

"I was planning to." He was no longer sure. Not because of Polly, but because he still didn't want to share her with anyone.

Pushing aside that unsettling thought, Luke grabbed his phone when it buzzed with another text.

POLLY: There is a very scary woman here who claims to be related to you.

"Shit." Luke hit the call button. It rang once before Polly answered.

"She just told me it looks like a hippie threw up in here," she said indignantly. "What the hell is going on, Luke?"

"Put her on the phone."

A second later, Aunt Julia said dryly, "Really, Luke? This is your latest investment? You're going to make pot brownies under the Sugar Rush label?"

Luke heard Polly's incensed screech in the background. His jaw clenched as fresh anger filled his chest.

"Julia, what are you doing there?" he asked. "How did you find it?"

"There aren't that many Hartford culinary students named Polly who own a bakery," she replied. "And I remembered your father told me some students had visited the offices recently, so a little digging and...voilà. I find out you're a victim of reefer madness. This is where you plan to sink your money?"

"It's none of your goddamned business, Julia. Leave Polly alone."

"Not likely. If this place is going to be associated with Sugar Rush, you'd better believe I'm giving you my opinion. We have a brand to protect, and roach clips don't go well with lollipops."

Polly snapped something again, and there were muffled noises. Were they tussling for control of the phone?

"Julia!" Luke shouted.

"Luke, I'm calling the cops if she doesn't leave right this instant," Polly said into the phone.

A Julia-ache pounded at his skull. "Don't call the cops. I'm on my way."

"You'd better get here soon before I throw chocolate ganache on her stupid designer suit."

The line went silent. Evan was staring at him.

"Julia is having it out with Polly?" he asked. "Why?"

"I'll explain later. I gotta go." Luke headed toward the door. "Tell Kate to cancel my meetings for the next couple of hours."

He was halfway out the door when he heard Evan's muttered, "Man, you must have it worse than I thought."

Luke ran down the hall to the elevator and stabbed the button impatiently. When it opened, Evan called for him to hold the door. His brother followed him into the elevator.

"I'd better go with you," Evan said. "We might have to kill one Julia with two Stones."

Five minutes later, they were in the car, careening down the interstate and wondering if they'd make it in time to prevent homicide-by-baked-goods. Luke parked illegally in front of the warehouse, and he and Evan ran across the street to Wild Child.

The air inside crackled with hostility. Julia stood by the window, arms crossed and stilettoed foot tapping impatiently.

Polly swept the floor vigorously while casting lethal glares in Julia's direction.

"What the hell is going on?" Luke snapped at Julia.

Both his aunt and Polly swung around to glower at him.

"Luke," Polly said, her voice icy and controlled. "Please remind Poison Ivy here that this is *my* bakery."

"It's also his, if he invested in it," Julia scoffed.

"He didn't invest in it! He's helping me with a business strategy."

"You can't afford to pay him for his consulting services," Julia replied. "Which means he's had to take a percentage of your equity to make it worth his while to do business with you."

"You don't know anything about what Luke's done," Evan put in.

"And he hasn't taken a percentage of anything," Polly said angrily. "We have another agreement that is none of your damned business."

Julia narrowed her eyes. "Oh, do you? What kind of *agreement?*"

"Stop." A wave of protectiveness toward Polly flooded Luke. "Julia, Polly is right. It's none of your damned business. This is her bakery."

"Bakery?" Julia arched an eyebrow so high it almost reached her hairline. "This is an old hippie's wet dream, not a *bakery.*"

"Julia, shut up." Evan started toward the door, but Polly got there first and yanked it open.

"Get out." She leveled an icy stare at Julia." This was my mother's bakery, and I'll be damned if I'm going to let someone like *you* insult her."

"And *this*," Julia swept her hand out to indicate Luke, "is my nephew who has worked his fingers to the bone for his family's company. I will see you in hell, little girl, before I let you gold-dig your way into his life."

Luke stalked across the room and grabbed his aunt's arm. "And I'll see *you* in hell before I let you talk to Polly like that."

"Oh, for God's sake, Luke, wake up." She yanked her arm from him. "Look at this place. You think *consulting* is all she wants from you? I hope you have the lawyers involved and plenty of condoms on hand, or you're going to end up with another paternity suit and a serious case of really bad press."

Polly's mouth dropped open. Luke's heart pounded.

"Julia," he said through clenched teeth. "Get the fuck out of here."

Evan grabbed Julia's handbag and thrust it toward her. She stalked toward him, her heels clicking sharply on the wooden floor.

"Luke, Evan," she said. "You'd both better come along."

"And you'd better walk out that door right now." Luke's hand shook with fury as he pointed to the door. "I'll speak with you later, Julia."

She opened her mouth to protest, but when their eyes clashed in challenge, Julia backed down. She gave Polly a condescending sniff and walked out.

"I'll go back with her." Evan threw Luke an *I've got this* look before he followed Julia out to the street. He stepped in her path and delivered what looked like a harsh lecture before directing her to her car.

"Oh my God." Polly pressed her hands to the sides of her head. "What godforsaken swamp did *she* crawl out of?"

Luke forced his fists to unclench.

"I'm really sorry." New anger filled his throat. "For what she said."

"How did she know about me?" Polly asked. "I didn't think you were the kind of man to kiss and tell."

"I'm not." He sighed, rubbing the back of his tight neck. "Julia is a head case about my dating life, and she was mad because I dumped her friend's daughter. So I told her I was seeing a culinary student who owns a bakery. Obviously she found it necessary to seek you out."

"You mean *hunt me down*," Polly said bitterly.

"Her bark is worse than her bite," Luke offered.

"Oh, please. Her bark gave me shell shock. And what was that business about Wild Child having anything to do with the Sugar Rush brand?"

"Nothing. I told Julia I was helping you out, and she thought that meant I was cutting a deal or a merger. Because she knows I don't do anything without work in mind. Usually," he added. "And I told her just to get her off my case."

"Well, she jumped right onto mine," Polly said with an irritated sniff. "Roach clips, indeed."

"She won't come back. I'll make sure of it."

Polly didn't look terribly convinced of his ability to keep Julia under control. She went back behind the counter and started rearranging the doughnut baskets.

"What was she talking about?" She moved a basket of chocolate doughnuts to another shelf. "You had a paternity lawsuit?"

Resentment clawed at his chest. He hadn't intentionally kept it a secret from Polly, but he hated that Julia had been the one to tell her.

"About a year ago," he admitted. "A woman claimed I was the father of her two-year-old kid and sued me for child support and other expenses."

Polly looked at him warily. "What happened?"

"Her lawyer stalled on the DNA test because he wanted to pressure me into acknowledging I was the father. He thought I'd agree to a hefty payoff to avoid court."

"Did you?"

"No. I wanted the truth, but it turned out that was a mistake."

"Wanting the truth is a mistake?"

"In this case it was." Luke smothered a rush of old anger. "We ended up in a court case that went on too long. The press was all over it because of the Stone legacy and the immorality of the claim. They even dug up the reports about my mother's death. Reporters started hounding my brothers and my little sister, friends, anyone who knew us. Finally the DNA test cleared me, but the damage had already been done."

"To your family?"

"And the company," Luke said. "Sugar Rush profits took a nosedive. Three of our top executives jumped ship. And the board considered forcing me to resign for my fiscal performance and violation of the company's code of conduct."

"They could do that?"

"No one in the company is exempt from termination."

"But you didn't resign."

He shook his head. "I seriously considered it since I was the reason the company had taken such a hit. But I wanted to stay and repair the damage. My father stepped in to negotiate on my behalf."

"And have you repaired the damage?"

"I'm trying."

Polly was quiet for a long minute, studying him with those brown eyes that looked as if they could see right to his core.

"Is that also why you're usually so strict about the women you date?" she asked.

He nodded. "A few other women tried making similar claims, but my lawyers were able to shut them down quickly with DNA proof. I've had to be careful ever since."

"I'm so sorry you had to go through that."

Her concern and sympathy hit a soft spot inside him. She watched him with a gentle expression, her dark eyebrows drawn slightly together.

"No wonder you work so hard," she murmured, gesturing to a table. "Sit down, and I'll bring you some tea."

Luke sat and checked his phone as Polly poured a cup of tea

and set two pastries on a plate. She brought the plate to the table and put it in front of him.

"This is the new creation I told you about," she said. "Declairs, a hybrid doughnut and éclair. Gavin Knight and his team are my new fans, and they've been instrumental in bringing in new customers."

Luke picked up one of the round, chocolate-covered pastries and took a bite. His teeth sank through layers of crispy pastry and creamy chocolate custard that filled his taste buds with enjoyment.

"Wow," he remarked around the mouthful.

"Right?" Polly grinned as she sat down opposite him. "I fried the wrong dough by mistake, and after tweaking the recipe, I came up with the Declair. As Ramona said, it was a happy accident."

Kind of like us.

Some of Luke's anger drained as he finished the Declair. He remembered that night at the Troll's House when he'd been ready to take a shot at pool but stopped because he'd *felt* something. He'd turned and looked toward the bar, only to find this curly-haired young woman staring at him with an open, unabashed fascination that flooded him with responding heat. Like a magnet, his gaze had locked to hers. He hadn't wanted to look away.

He still didn't. He was beginning to think he'd never want to —a thought that was as unsettling as it was pleasurable. Because the idea of looking at Polly every day for the rest of his life—

He concentrated on picking the crumbs off the plate. "So where are we going on our next date?"

"Oh, it's a good one, but I have a few conditions."

She lifted her eyebrows at him, and she was so damned adorable with her hair falling in ringlets around her face and her brown eyes all bright with anticipation and eagerness. He wanted to wrap her up and keep her in the breast pocket of his shirt, right next to his heart.

Christ. What the hell is wrong with me?

Apparently he was not only an idiot, he was a sap too. His brothers would give him hell if they knew he was thinking things like that. He was about to give himself hell.

He shook his head and forced himself to focus on what Polly was saying.

"...just about an hour south," she continued. "And I really want to be *alone* with you. Thirty-six hours straight. We'll leave Saturday morning at six a.m. and return Sunday evening."

Luke had a feeling he'd missed something while he was thinking his sappy thoughts.

"Okay," he said warily.

"So you agree?" Polly asked.

His CEO brain kicked in. "What are the conditions?"

"You leave your cell phone, laptop, tablet, and all other communicative devices at home," Polly said. "You don't call, text, or email anyone at any time. Even if you wanted to, you probably couldn't since connections there aren't good at all. In other words, for a full weekend, Mr. Stone, you are completely off the grid."

"I can't do that, Peach."

She blinked and sat back, a crestfallen look descending over her features.

Shit.

"I'm sorry," he said. "I can't be out of reach for that long."

"A weekend isn't that long," Polly urged. "I want you alone. Just you and me. No one and nothing else to interfere. And I guarantee we'll have fun."

He didn't doubt that last part. Turned out that every minute he spent in Polly's company was *fun*.

But though the thought of having her all to himself for thirty-six hours straight was a nearly irresistible pull, Luke had been immersed in Sugar Rush for so long that he couldn't wrap his brain around the idea of being *off the grid*.

"Hannah's still here, and Clementine said she'll ask her to help at the bakery," Polly explained. "And Mia promised to work at the front counter on Sunday. All you need to do is say yes."

There she went with the bright-eyed expectation again. If he wasn't careful, she'd have him believing in leprechauns and elves.

"I'll try," he said.

"Promise?"

"I can't promise anything." A knot tangled in his chest. He wished he could make her promises that he could keep. She was the kind of girl who deserved promises. She *believed* in them.

Polly nodded, faint resignation appearing in her eyes as if she'd been expecting that very response.

"Okay," she said. "But will you say yes?"

"Peach." Luke dragged a hand through his hair. "I don't think I can ever say *no* to you."

"Well." She leaned across the table and pressed her lips gently against his. "That's a start."

CHAPTER 18

"You're sure Codswallop won't scare him away?" Hannah pushed her messy hair off her forehead. She was curled up on the sofa with a cup of coffee, wearing an overlarge T-shirt and a pair of Polly's knee socks.

"I'm sure." Polly sighed. The only thing that could scare Luke was a threat to his family.

And a long-lasting relationship.

And making promises.

She put her toiletries kit in her travel bag. While her discovery of Luke's paternity suit had explained a great deal about both his workaholic nature and his approach to relationships, she felt sad rather than enlightened.

Sad that Luke had had to go through such pain when he'd already worked so hard to protect Sugar Rush after his mother's death. Sad that one vindictive woman had scarred him so deeply. Sad that he'd thrown himself back into the company with such force that everything else was obliterated.

Except...

He'd agreed to go with her this weekend. Even though Polly didn't like leaving while her sister was in town, Codswallop only happened once a year and she wasn't about to miss the chance to take CEO Stone.

"Do you know yet when you're leaving?" she asked Hannah.

"I'm still waiting to hear from Dave. He's in Arizona now, I think."

"Is he your boyfriend?"

"No." Hannah grimaced slightly. "I've found out that it's easier in general not to have boyfriends."

"Kind of an odd philosophy coming from a woman who writes about *love*," Polly remarked.

"Tell me about it." Hannah took another sip of coffee and looked at Polly speculatively. "But writing about love has also made me a realist. And I know you like Luke, but I hope you don't think he's going to whisk you off to his castle on the cliff to live happily ever after."

Polly's heart clenched. She turned away to fold a couple pairs of panties, stuffing them beneath the rolled blanket in her travel bag.

"Of course I don't think that," she said, hoping she sounded as if she were scoffing a little. "Luke and I are just having a good time. Besides, what business is it of yours anyway?"

Hannah shrugged. "None. Just making sure you know that men like him have their futures already figured out."

"Please." Polly shoved two pairs of socks into her bag. "This isn't the eighteenth century. Luke's family hasn't arranged some marriage to a wealthy heiress for him."

But the words rang hollow in her ears as she remembered her encounter with Luke's Aunt Julia who, even if she didn't have her sights set on a wealthy heiress, had some very definite ideas about the type of woman her nephew deserved to be with.

Polly shook her head. None of that mattered anyway because even though her *emotions* were getting involved, both she and Luke had established that neither one of them was in this for the long-term.

"We're having a good time," she repeated, which was certainly the truth. "After four years of helping Mom and trying to save Wild Child, I deserve to have a good time."

"Of course you do." Hannah set her cup on the coffee table. "And you've already put so much energy into running the bakery. Are you sure you want to keep doing it for the rest of your life?"

"Why wouldn't I?" Polly zipped her bag and set it on the floor. "Mom worked so hard for Wild Child. Remember how she was the town baker at Twelve Oaks? She baked something for every meal—bread, muffins, biscuits, and of course tons of desserts. She once told me she'd wanted to open a bakery since she was a teenager, but never had the chance. So when we moved to Rainsville, she was finally able to make her dream come true."

"Exactly," Hannah said. "*Her* dream."

"What does that mean?"

"Just what I said. Wild Child was *Mom's* dream. Not yours or mine."

"So?" Polly spread her hands out, suppressing a crack threading through her heart. "I promised her I wouldn't let Wild Child fail."

Hannah's brow furrowed. "Polly, your loyalty is one of your best qualities. But honestly, do you think Mom expected you to dedicate the rest of your life to a struggling bakery that was never your dream in the first place?"

Polly pressed a hand to her aching chest. Though she and Hannah had once been close, she'd never thought her sister knew she had dreams that were bigger than the bakery.

Dreams that would mean going back on her promise.

"What do you care if I want to run Wild Child for the rest of my life?" she asked, her voice sharpening. "It's not as if you were ever around to help out."

"Because I wanted to follow a different path." Hannah's expression gentled. "And following our own paths is exactly what both Mom and Dad wanted for us."

"And you didn't once stop to think I might need you? That maybe it was hard for me to read about all your travels on your blog while I was here the whole time, taking care of Mom and the bakery the best I could?"

For a moment, Hannah didn't respond, though her eyes darkened with remorse. "I didn't ask you to do that."

"You didn't have to. I wanted to be with Mom, but it was so hard to watch her dying while knowing Wild Child was failing at the same time. That bakery was her favorite thing in the world, and I couldn't save it for her."

"The bakery was not her favorite thing," Hannah said. "*You* were. And she's gone, Polly. You don't have to save the bakery for her anymore."

"Yes, I do." Polly's heart cracked deeper. "Even though things are improving, I have such a long way to go. I still feel like a failure for not being able to do what Mom did."

"And she would hate knowing you feel that way." Hannah unfolded herself from the sofa and pushed to her feet. "You don't have to live the rest of your life on a promise. You can be free too."

"Free to do *what*?" Polly wiped at a stray tear trickling down her cheek. "Wander the world aimlessly like you've been doing for the past ten years?"

"Do whatever you want." Hannah approached and took hold of Polly's arms, her expression intent. "Go work for Sugar Rush. Go back to college and finish your degree. Hell, go work on an Alaskan fishing boat. Just don't pigeonhole yourself into a life only because you think you can't do or *be* anything else."

"How am I supposed to do any of that and run the bakery at the same time?"

"Sell the bakery."

"You know I can't do that."

"Why not?" Hannah tightened her grip on Polly's arms. "It's

not as if Wild Child is making all your dreams come true. You don't have to play it safe anymore."

"I'm not playing it safe. I'm being responsible."

"Really? When was the last time you took a chance?"

I'm taking one right now by letting myself feel too much for Luke Stone.

Polly couldn't admit that to her sister. As she straightened, her gaze fell on Pierre Lacroix's *Art of French Pastry* book on the coffee table.

"I applied for a French pastry-making course in Paris." She gestured to the book. "Getting accepted would be like winning the lottery. But it's still taking a chance."

Hannah moved away and reached for the book. "Didn't you and Mom used to watch this guy's show all the time?"

Polly nodded. "That's his latest book. I even sent in my own original recipe with my application."

"That's great, Polliwog." Hannah sat back on the sofa and leafed through the glossy pages. "Wild Child isn't the only place in the world you can be."

But what if it was the only place Polly wanted to be? Not the shabby place on the verge of bankruptcy, but the lively, vibrant haven of creativity and friendship that her mother had created? What was so wrong with wanting to *nest* and take care of people?

"I think your CEO is here." Hannah nodded toward the window.

Polly glanced outside just as a sleek Porsche pulled to a stop in front of Wild Child.

Fun, she told herself firmly. This was all about having fun, getting herself back into the world again, and learning how to run her business so she could take control of her life.

And it was perfectly fine that her heart did a little jump at the sight of Luke's tall figure getting out of the car and walking around the side of the building with that easy, long-legged stride of his.

It was okie-doke that anticipation filled her veins when the doorbell rang. And it was *no problemo* that she got all soft and mushy inside when she opened the door and saw him standing there, utterly beautiful and masculine in cargo shorts and a faded San Francisco Giants T-shirt that stretched over his shoulders and the expanse of his chest. Even the morning sun got in on the act, gleaming off his thick, dark hair and lighting it with strands of gold.

"Hey, Peach." His gaze moved appreciatively over her Indian print, cotton skirt and purple tank top. "Ready to go?"

"Almost." She leaned toward him, breathing in his scent of soap and shaving cream as he bent to kiss her cheek. "Come in."

She closed the door behind him and gestured to Hannah. "Luke, this is my sister Hannah. Hannah, Luke Stone."

Hannah extended a hand, though a faint gleam of suspicion lit in her eyes. "Good to meet you."

"You too. Polly's told me a lot about you." After shaking her hand, Luke held out a green paper bag that Polly hadn't even realized he was carrying. "I brought this for you."

Hannah glanced at Polly before taking the bag. She peered inside and took out a clear cellophane package filled with multi-colored, round candies and tied with a red ribbon.

"What..."

"Polly told me the Sugar Rush Jelly Rolls were your favorite," Luke explained. "I thought you might like some."

An emotion rose in Polly that she couldn't name, one that seemed both disproportional and a perfect reaction to the fact that Luke had brought her sister her favorite candy. It was like walking from a frigid day into a warm, cinnamon-scented house and feeling every part of her body thawing and melting. It was like making a perfect meringue or tasting a buttery madeleine for the first time.

It was like realizing she might be falling in love.

"Oh." Though Hannah still appeared a bit baffled, a pleased smile curved her lips. "Well, thank you."

"My pleasure."

Polly crossed the room and put her hand on Luke's arm. Her palm tingled at the sensation of his taut, hair-roughened skin and hard muscles.

"We should get going," she said. "Hannah, are you sure you don't want to come with us?"

"No, I told Clementine I'd help at Wild Child, if she needs me." Hannah was already opening the bag of Jelly Rolls. "Thanks again for these. Have a good time."

That was exactly what they had whenever they were together, Polly thought. Luke picked up her bags, and they went down to his car.

"Thank you," she said, still feeling all warm and melty inside. "I can't believe you even remember I'd told you the Jelly Rolls were her favorite."

"I pay attention to you." He unlocked the trunk and loaded her bags inside. "Has it been okay with her here?"

"More or less. It's always a little tense just because I know she's going to leave again. So there's that."

"How long is she staying?"

"I don't know. I never know. I don't think she does either, honestly. That's just one of the things that's always made her both brave and irresponsible." Polly shook off a twinge of sadness, reminding herself of the reason she'd planned this weekend. "So we're ready?"

"I'm always ready, baby." Luke let his gaze slide over her body again. "And you look edible."

She eyed him in a pleasurable return assessment. "So do you."

"Then we could just stay here and…" he raised an eyebrow, "… eat each other."

"Oh, no, Mr. Stone." Tempting as the idea was, Polly shook her finger at him. "You don't get off that easy."

"Actually with you, I do." He winked at her and opened the passenger side door. "Are you going to tell me yet where we're going?"

"Still a surprise." She eyed him with mild suspicion. "Are there any electronic devices on your person?"

"No, but you're welcome to give me a pat-down to be sure." Luke turned toward her, extending his arms to the sides.

Not about to deny herself the opportunity of touching him, Polly patted her hands all over his chest and back, down the length of his legs, and—just to make extra certain—over his groin and incredibly firm rear.

"Okay," she said, rather breathless after having discovered nothing but warm, solid muscles. "You're clean."

"I can be dirty too."

"Oh, I know."

They exchanged smiles as Luke gestured her into the car. After Polly had given him the address, which he inputted into his GPS, they started south away from Indigo Bay. He drove along the Pacific Coast Highway, the Porsche handling the winding roads with ease. Cliffs swept majestically down to the ocean, and the water splashed and sprayed against the rocky shoreline.

They drove for an hour, having easy conversations about movies, Luke's extensive travels, and Polly's life at Twelve Oaks. Eventually he turned away from the coast toward the flat, dry landscape of the Central Valley, where miles of farmland stretched out in all directions. As they exited Interstate 5 and headed east, parked cars began appearing along a two-lane road, and the faint sound of music filled the air.

Luke peered out the front windshield as they neared their destination. A banner proclaiming *Codswallop Festival* hung between two trees, beyond which was a vast field dotted with cars, tents, and RVs. People wearing heavy-looking backpacks and carrying bags and camping gear streamed toward the entrance gates.

A man wearing an orange safety vest waved them to the right, where a sea of cars sat in another field. Luke pulled into the lot, maneuvering the Porsche over the rutted dirt to an empty space by a ditch.

"Have you ever been to a music festival before?" Polly asked.

"Back when I was younger, yeah. But it's been awhile."

"Have you ever been to a hippie music festival?"

"Not that I can recall."

She smiled. "Then welcome to Codswallop."

CHAPTER 19

*I*t was the most beatnik scene Luke had ever experienced, including those of his wilder college days. The field was awash in tents, shacks, teepees, and stages where bluegrass, jazz, and rock bands played, and the throb of music resounded for miles.

Enough pot smoke hung in the air to give non-users— meaning no one—a contact high. There was henna painting, hard liquor, fortune tellers, tattoos, hula-hooping, body odor, dread-locks, porta-johns, bikinis, drum circles, food tents, fire-eaters, and more tie-dye than was needed to outfit everyone during the Summer of Love.

Polly seemed right at home here, pausing to greet or hug someone every now and then, always introducing him as "my friend Luke." Because his cooperation would make her happy— and because he increasingly wanted nothing but happiness for her—Luke told himself that no one here had any idea who he was and that it would be fine if he just rolled with it.

So he did. Polly insisted he buy—and wear—a rainbow Grateful Dead T-shirt. They ate burritos and drank cider in the hot sun while listening to a bluegrass band, beat the bongos in a drum circle, signed petitions to protect the environment, people-watched, danced, played hacky sack and ping-pong, socialized with a motley crew of friendly folk, and tried as many foods as they could, including blueberry lemonade and chili-flavored cotton candy.

The only activity Luke declined was hula-hooping, but only because he wanted to watch his girl without any distractions. The decision yielded amazing results, as he sat in the shade with a cold beer, listening to the beat of reggae steel drums and watching Polly's curvy body shaking and shimmying with such gusto that he eventually had to look away or risk a hard-on. Though he suspected this crowd would probably approve.

After she'd gotten him worked up with the hula-hooping, Polly grabbed his hand and tugged him over to a grove behind a camping site. Latched between two trees in the shade was a wide cloth hammock layered with Indian-print pillows.

"As much as I love your bed," Polly climbed into it, "hammocks have their own special qualities that you won't find anywhere else. They're known for great health benefits."

She reclined and tugged him down beside her. Luke settled in, and she tucked herself against his side. Their combined weight rocked the hammock, the motion pressing their bodies closer together.

Ahh...

He closed his eyes as the breeze cooled his hot skin and the oranges-and-cloves scent of Polly filled his nose. As he sank into a light doze, he had the vague thought that he could quite happily lie here with her for the rest of the weekend, rocking gently as music played in the distance and the sun filtered through the trees...

"Wake up." Polly's lips pressed against his cheek. "We've been asleep for an hour, and we'll miss the blues concert if we don't head over there now."

As Luke pulled himself reluctantly out of sleep, he couldn't remember the last time he'd taken a nap. And waking from one in a hammock...he was beginning to think this hippie lifestyle had a lot going for it.

He and Polly returned to the festival activities with renewed energy. By the time the sun began to sink on the other side of the sky, they were both sun-burned, sweaty, tired, and dirty. Campfires began to light up around the tents, though most people streamed toward the main stage where the headliners were playing. Polly's friend Tom, along with his wife and another fellow who went by the name Wolf, lounged beside a campfire.

Luke looked to where Polly sat on the other side of the fire. Her hair was falling out of its knot, loose tendrils drifting around her face, and a warm contentment filled her brown eyes. With the firelight glowing on her skin, she looked almost other-worldly, like she really was a pagan witch who'd cast a spell on him.

She met his gaze across the flames. Her lovely mouth curved with a smile.

He didn't return her smile, only kept staring at her. An emotion flickered inside him that he didn't recognize. If Polly really had bewitched him, what would it take to be free of her? He didn't know if he wanted to be.

The thought unsettled him, like a crack in his armor. Not once since he'd picked Polly up at Wild Child sixteen hours ago had he reached for his non-existent phone. Not once had he wondered if anyone in his family or at Sugar Rush was trying to contact him. Not once had he thought about market shares or net sales.

That alone was a measure of the power Polly had secured over him in only a few short weeks.

What would happen if he let this affair go on for another week? Or a month? Or two months?

"Hey." Her soft voice filtered into his ears, and he felt the movement of her body as she sat beside him. "There's no scowling at Codswallop."

He pulled himself from the morass of his thoughts and turned toward her. "There's a lot of fun, though."

Polly smiled again. He wished he could be responsible for keeping that smile on her face forever.

"My parents used to come here every year," she said. "Though my mom didn't bring me along until I was a teenager. She missed a couple of years when she got sick, but last year she insisted on coming even though she was still right in the middle of chemo. So Clementine and Tom loaded up a van, and we went along with them. Stayed all three days, visiting old friends, listening to music, eating and drinking. I think my mother knew the end was getting close and she wanted to have one last really good time with her friends."

Sorrow passed across her face as she looked at the fire. Luke settled his hand on her knee.

"Sounds like she did," he said.

She nodded. The band on a nearby stage started playing an acoustic cover of the Stones' "Wild Horses," the strains of the guitar accompanied by the crackle and pop of the campfire.

Luke stood and took Polly's hand, tugging her to her feet. He pulled her to him and slid one arm around her waist before starting to move to the music. She eased closer, her body pressing to his as she rested her cheek against his chest.

He let go of her hand and wrapped both arms around her. Something always settled inside him when she was tucked in his arms like this, her curves fitting perfectly against the planes of his body like she was made for him alone.

They danced slowly for another few minutes. He pressed his lips to the top of her head and lowered his mouth closer to her ear.

"By the way," he murmured, "where are we sleeping?"

She grinned, turning her face toward his. "You mean you're not going to ask me if we can go home yet?"

"Actually I'm starting to wish you'd wanted to get me alone for longer than a weekend."

She eased away from him, twining her fingers with his before leading him toward a small blue tent that was set up a short distance away.

"Tom and Anne bring an extra one in case someone needs a place to sleep." She unzipped the flap. "Tonight, that's us."

As she bent over to enter the tent, her skirt stretched across her round ass. They were about to do a hell of a lot more than *sleep*.

Luke followed her inside, crouching to zip the flap closed behind him. Firelight and passing shadows flashed over the thin nylon walls, which did nothing to block out the sound of music and voices drifting over the field.

Their bags were already inside, and Polly switched on a flashlight attached to the edge of the tent. She unzipped her large bag and pulled out a tightly rolled cotton blanket.

"I figured we wouldn't need much because it's so warm." She unfastened the blanket. "I brought pillows too."

Luke sat back on his haunches since the tent was too small to even sit up comfortably and watched her work. She knelt by the air mattress, reaching over it to spread the blanket, her bent position giving him a tempting display of her cleavage. Even though he'd been sneaking looks at her breasts all day—and what a sight they were when she was hula-hooping—now he could stare at them all he wanted.

"I brought extra water too, so we don't have to trek to the water station in the dark." Polly pulled water bottles out of her bag. "And if you...oh."

Luke had crawled forward and crouched on his hands and knees, his face only inches from hers. She looked up, her eyes widening. The scent of her—sweat, sun, smoke—fired him with a bolt of lust.

In less than a second, he grabbed her by the back of the head and pulled her toward him, his mouth crashing down on hers. Her lips parted on a soft moan, and then he was inside her, his tongue seeking hers, his lust burning hotter.

"Come on," he murmured, moving them both to sitting positions without breaking the contact of their mouths. "Let's fuck."

She drew in a breath and lifted her head. Shock darkened her eyes.

"Really?" she whispered. "You want to...here?"

"Hell, yeah." Luke grabbed her hand and pressed it to the front of his shorts, forcing her to feel the hard ridge of his cock. "I've wanted it all goddamned day."

"But...I mean, there are people right outside." Polly gestured to the tent flap. "I didn't think you'd want..."

"Oh, I want," Luke growled in the instant before he brought his mouth down on hers again.

He kissed her hard and deep, tasting blueberries and cotton candy, feeling her surrender as she lowered herself to the air mattress, her arms coming up to twine around his neck. He found the edge of her tank top and yanked it down, making a noise of frustration when his fingers encountered the cotton barrier of her bra.

"Wait, I'll take it off." Polly pushed him away, giving a breathless little laugh as she pulled off the tank top and reached around to unfasten her bra.

And then her warm, bare breasts were in his hands, her nipples so hard and tight he couldn't resist lowering his head to suck on one of them. Polly gasped, fisting her hand in his hair and arching toward him. He pressed his lips over the half-circles of sunburn reddening her breasts, heat still clinging to her skin.

Christ. Already his cock was throbbing, as if he'd been in a state of suspended lust all day and was now, finally, able to unleash it. He tugged Polly's skirt off her hips, running his hands over the curves of her torso and thighs.

He pulled back only long enough to look at her, his breath scorching his lungs at the sight of her spread out in front of him wearing nothing but a pair of polka-dot panties. She was all curvy, inviting warmth, the filtered light casting shadows on her skin.

She squirmed, curling her hands around his biceps and drawing him to her.

"I think you'd better hurry," she murmured, pushing her lower body against his. "Because I'm so wet and ready for you…"

Luke swore softly under his breath. He tangled his fingers into the elastic of her panties and pushed them down to find the heat of her pussy. Ah, shit, she was more than ready…one flick of his finger on her clit, and she'd arch up against him with a cry of pleasure. He slipped his fingers into her, working her gently until she started writhing underneath him.

"Oh my God, Luke, I feel it already…harder, please…I'm…*oh!*"

He covered her mouth with his the instant she came, her body convulsing and trembling as he continued stroking her to draw out the last sensations. Polly fell back, her chest heaving. She tugged at the buttons of his shorts.

"Take them off," she urged.

Luke hitched his T-shirt over his head and tossed it aside, then pulled off his shorts and boxers. He was so hard it hurt, and when Polly curled her hand around his shaft he almost came right then and there.

"Wait," he ordered, his voice thick. "I'm going to fuck you."

She released him and shimmied out of her panties. And then he wanted nothing more than to be buried deep inside her, to feel her enclosing him, gripping him…

He clutched her hips. "Turn around."

Polly's breath caught. For an instant, he didn't think she'd do it, but then she turned, getting to her hands and knees and presenting him with the fucking incredible sight of her round ass and parted thighs.

"Jesus, Peach, you're so goddamned perfect," he muttered, stroking his finger right down the opening of her slit. "I could bury myself inside you for days."

She quivered in reaction to his touch, turning to look at him over her shoulder. Her brown eyes were wide and luminous in the dim light.

"Do it," she whispered.

He fumbled to put a condom on, then got to his knees behind her. He gripped Polly's ass with one hand and tortured himself by rubbing his cock over her damp folds, slipping it partway into her before pulling back out again.

"Luke," Polly groaned, lowering her head onto her folded arms, a movement that caused her back to arch. She shifted her hips, as if she were trying to impale herself onto his erection.

He couldn't hold back any longer. Heat coursed through him as he grabbed her hips and pushed deep in one, hard motion. She cried out, grabbing one of the tent poles to brace herself.

Blinding lust descended over him. He started to thrust, driving into her as far as he could. His world distilled to the grip of her tight heat, the feel of her ass hitting his stomach with every surge, the sound of her cries. The raging fire inside him drowned out the crash of music.

He stroked his hands around to her breasts, fondling them as they bounced in rhythm with his thrusts. He moved back to press his fingers between her legs again, bringing her to another orgasm that had her shrieking anew. Only when her body tensed, as if the position were starting to hurt, did he pull out of her.

She turned and eased onto her back, her hair a tangle of curls around her flushed face. He pulled her in for another kiss as she parted her legs. And then she was wrapping herself around him as he pushed into her again and again. Their skin rubbed together, sweaty, grimy, and hot with sunburn, the friction heating Luke's blood with a thousand flames.

"Ah, my little Polly." He gripped the sides of her head, pressing his forehead to hers. "Take me."

"Yes," she gasped, winding her legs around his hips. "God, yes…I feel you so deep…"

She bit down on his shoulder, the mild pain of her sharp teeth jolting him to the edge. With a groan, he thrust again and shot deep inside her, the sensation tearing like an explosion through his body. He braced his hands on the sides of Polly's head, barely managing to restrain himself from collapsing on top of her.

He fell to the side with another groan and flung his arm over his eyes. Beside him, Polly's breath rasped through the air. Slowly the world came back into focus, the sounds of music and conversation drifting into the tent.

He sat up, turning to Polly and letting his gaze move over her naked, glossy body. He reached out to rub her breasts, liking the way she arched into him as if anticipating his touch. They looked at each other, faint tension suddenly stretching through the air.

Then Luke broke eye contact and rolled onto his back. He stared at the stretched canvas above him, unnerved by the emotions crowding his chest, the growing feeling that he didn't want to leave the haven of Polly and return to his normal, workaholic life.

She shifted closer to him and tucked her face against his chest. Trembles continued to course through her warm body.

"Peach," Luke said.

She lifted her head, wariness coloring her eyes. He stroked her hair away from her face and ran his hand over her soft cheek.

"Thanks," he said. "This whole day has been incredibly fun."

"For me too." She kissed his fingers as he touched her lips. "If you want to get more of your hippie on, there's a full moon gathering down in Laguna Beach in a couple of weeks."

"A what?"

"A celebration in honor of the full moon, and of cosmic align-
ment and spirituality. There'll be a drum circle, gypsy dancing,
performance artists. Last time I went there was even a snake
charmer."

It was a measure of her influence on him that Luke didn't find
that at all strange.

"So what do you say?" She rested her chin on her hand. "We
could take the van, camp out under the stars."

He looked at the tent above them, where the campfire light
flickered through the nylon. He wanted with a force as strong as
any he'd ever known to tell her that of course they'd drive down
to Laguna Beach, that there was nothing he'd love more than to
sleep with her under the stars, to kiss her by the light of a full
moon.

"I wish I could." He slid his hand down her back to her hip.
"But I have to go to Switzerland a week from Monday. Meetings
and stuff for the Alpine acquisition. I'll be gone for three weeks."

"Oh." Uncertainty flickered across her face. "I didn't know
you were leaving."

"I'm sorry I didn't tell you sooner. Kate reminded me the
other day. It's just a business trip."

"You must go on a lot of those."

He did, but before her, he'd never cared where he was going
or how long he'd stay there. Now he only wanted to go wherever
Polly was and to stay there forever.

He looked at her, struck by a bolt of inspiration. "Come
with me."

Polly blinked. "What?"

"To Switzerland." Relief flooded him at the idea of not having
to spend three weeks without her. "You told me you'd wanted to
travel, right? So come with me. Yeah, I have to work, but I can
still show you around, and we can take the train to Paris for a
couple of days. I know you've always wanted to go there."

"Luke." Warmth and regret mixed in her brown eyes. "I can't go with you."

"Why not?"

"I have to stay and run Wild Child. With all that's going on and the interior designers coming, I can't leave now to head off to Switzerland for three weeks."

He frowned. "You're the boss. You can do whatever you want."

Polly ran her hand over his chest. "I'm pretty sure that not even CEO Stone does *whatever* he wants. And while I would love to go with you, we both know how hard I've worked to get to this point. I can't leave Wild Child right now."

Luke bit back another argument. She was right, and as much as he selfishly wanted her with him, her dedication to her mother's bakery was just one of the many things he adored about her.

"Don't scowl." She pressed her finger between his eyebrows, smoothing out the crease. "Three weeks isn't that long. You'll be back before you know it. And we can talk and video-call, right? I mean, as long as I'm on your *schedule*."

She lifted her eyebrows pointedly. He tweaked her nose.

"You're on my schedule all the time, Peach," he assured her.

24/7. In permanent ink.

"Good." She kissed his shoulder. "I promise, your trip will fly by."

"Still." He threaded his hand into her hair, letting out his breath on a sigh. "If the moon celebration is anything like Codswallop, it sucks that we can't go."

"I'm so glad you like it here," Polly said. "Do you miss your phone?"

"What phone?"

She smiled. As she settled against him again, Luke pressed his lips to her forehead. No, he didn't miss his phone. But when he went to Switzerland, he sure as hell was going to miss Polly. Probably more than he could stand.

CHAPTER 20

A happy, dream-like fog surrounded Polly as she went down to the bakery early Monday morning. Sunday had been as magical as Saturday, if a little more fatigued. She'd thought Luke might get antsy about the lack of Wi-Fi, but it had appeared to be the last thing on his mind.

Instead he'd wandered the grounds, danced with her, played hacky sack, made treks to the food stands to buy coffee and sandwiches for everyone in their camping circle, and given her warm forehead kisses while simultaneously patting her rear.

Polly had never before had such a good time at Codswallop. Her mind filled with all the other things she wanted to do with Luke—folk festivals, rainbow gatherings, street fairs, bonfires, community gardens. He'd embraced Codswallop so easily, fitting into her world as if a place had always existed there for him. Maybe it had, just like the place in her heart.

And although his impending business trip cast a shadow over the coming month, they would find plenty of ways to breach the physical separation. Talking, texting, emailing, maybe even finding some creative things to do with video calls…

Hmm. Since CEO Stone's business trips were probably filled

with boring meetings and reports, it would be up to Polly to make certain that his downtime was especially *fun*.

Her mind began zinging with ideas as she prepped for opening the bakery. Clementine came in with the announcement that a news reporter and cameraman had stopped into Wild Child on Saturday afternoon, claiming they were working on a segment about the new interest in reality baking shows.

"I tried to call you, but your phone was down and I know the connection at Codswallop is iffy at best." Clementine stowed her bag under the counter. "Apparently the reporter is a cousin of one of the Knight Security men. She was hoping to interview you and didn't want to wait until Monday. So I gave them permission to film because I thought we could use the publicity."

"We still need all the help we can get."

Because one day, Polly would have to keep the bakery going by herself. Clementine would be gone, and though Luke hadn't given her a time limit for his business expertise, a day would likely come when he wouldn't be here to answer questions about budgeting or profit margins. And even if he was, Polly had always intended to run Wild Child independently and under her own power, exactly like her mother had.

During a mid-morning lull, she sat at a mosaic table with her laptop to continue putting vendors into the new accounting software.

"These are different." Hannah sat at a table by the window, a book open in her lap. She waved a cookie in Polly's direction. "What did you do to them?"

"Cheaper ingredients," Polly replied. "Mom always used the best ingredients, but I couldn't afford them anymore and had to downscale."

"Well, that sucks."

"Believe me, I know." Polly glanced up at the sound of the wind chimes jingling above the door.

Luke's brother Evan was holding the door open. A dark-haired woman wearing a stylish wrap dress, gold-rimmed eyeglasses, and dangling earrings entered, sweeping her gaze over the display cases. She was accompanied by a slender, blond man decked out in a suit and bow tie, holding a large carrying case.

A memory of her encounter with Julia spread over Polly like a bad rash, but she reminded herself to give these people a chance. Luke had been kind enough to set up a meeting with interior design firm partners about remodeling Wild Child, and Polly couldn't be churlish enough to refuse.

"Hey, Polly." With a smile, Evan approached her table and lowered his head next to her ear. "I'm here as a peacekeeping force, in case these two give you flashbacks to Julia."

Polly narrowed her eyes at the couple who were wandering around the bakery, looking at everything with a critical eye.

"As long as they don't use the phrases *roach clips* or *reefer madness*, we'll be fine," she muttered to Evan.

"Miss Lockhart?" The woman approached. "I'm Eleanor Pendergrass. My partner Simon Peabody. Pendergrass and Peabody Designs. We'll just have a look around, if you don't mind."

"By all means."

Polly went around the counter to get a few of her éclair-doughnut pastries from the cold case. She set the plate in front of Evan before sitting beside him. Still wary, she watched the two designers strolling around the bakery, examining the worn, mismatched furnishings and mandala tapestries.

"What are they going to do?" Hannah paused beside Polly.

"Nothing yet. They're here to consult about remodeling the interior."

An odd tension radiated from Hannah. "You're remodeling?"

"We have to."

"Why?"

"Because it's part of improving the business." *If you'd been around, you'd know that.*

Polly clamped down on the remark and gestured to Evan. "Hannah, this is Luke's brother Evan. Evan, my sister Hannah."

"Pleasure." Evan rose and extended his hand.

Hannah nodded and shook his hand, pulling away more quickly than was polite.

"These are amazing." Apparently unoffended, Evan sat back down and held up one of the pastries. "I've never had anything like this before."

"It's called a Declair," Polly said, pleased by his praise. "My new creation. I'll get you some more."

She took his empty plate and went to pile it with fresh Declairs.

"Not even grunge chic." Eleanor Pendergrass turned a paper lantern around in her hand. "Just *grunge.*"

Simon peered with faint distaste at an upholstered chair so well-loved the fabric was worn down to the threads in places.

"Retro-tech might work here," he said, "or perhaps French Rococo with fringed curtains and gilt molding."

Polly and Hannah exchanged glances.

"That's not really what Wild Child is about," Polly told Simon gently.

"Perhaps a minimalist approach then." Eleanor retrieved a drawing pad from the carrying case. "It creates a very soothing environment. The primary materials would be steel, glass, and concrete—very in vogue with corporate retail design at the moment—and black backgrounds with spotlighting to showcase the products."

"This isn't a corporate—" Polly began.

"Excellent." Simon nodded at Eleanor with approval. "We'll get rid of all this stuff on the walls so we can have a chic, mono-chromatic palette. Black tables, silver chairs, a sleek new logo."

"I'm sorry," Polly said. "But Wild Child really isn't about chic or sleek."

The two designers looked at her. Simon arched an elegantly plucked eyebrow.

"So what are *you* thinking, doll?" he asked.

"Well, sort of what we already have, but upgraded?" Polly ventured.

Eleanor and Simon exchanged glances.

"Darling, there's really no such thing as *upgraded* grunge," Eleanor said. "That's the point of grunge. It's dirty and messy."

After her encounter with Julia the other day, Polly was in no mood to have more criticism being hurled in her direction by people who thought they were better than her.

"My bakery," she said, her voice icy, "is neither dirty nor messy."

"I didn't mean to imply that it was," Eleanor assured her. "But it's definitely outdated, moth-eaten and, frankly, a bit depressing."

Okay, Polly could concede that point. The Wild Child décor was over fifteen years old, and aside from the rotating, consignment artwork on one wall, none of it had ever changed. Even she could see that it was looking rather shabby.

"That macramé is yellowing." Eleanor waved her hand at a plant hanger in the corner that held a limp spider lily. "Not to mention...it's *macramé*."

"So get a new one," Hannah said crisply. "And go with bohemian."

Eleanor and Simon stared at her. Hannah was leaning against a table, winding a strand of hair around one finger, her eyes narrowed on the two designers with faint hostility.

"Excuse me?" Eleanor pursed her lips.

"Boho." Hannah waved her hand in the air. "Plants, multitonal prints, a couple of hammock chairs in the corners, globe lights. Take out one of the display cases and add some rough-hewn tables and chairs for more seating, maybe a couple of repurposed coffee-tables. You know." She shrugged. "Boho *chic.*"

In a turnaround so fast it made her dizzy, Polly was suddenly filled with delight. Eleanor and Simon looked at each other, then back at Hannah.

"You sure you don't want to go with the minimalist?" Eleanor asked Polly.

"Very sure. Boho chic all the way."

"We could hit up the flea markets," Simon told Eleanor, with a lift of his shoulder. "Antique shops. It might be fun."

"I am on a strict budget," Polly said. "And I don't know what Luke told you, but I can't afford too many design fees either."

"That's all right, darling." Eleanor settled into a chair. "Simon and I love a challenge."

Within seconds, she and Simon had their heads bent over a drawing tablet and were deep in a discussion about rustic tables and color palettes.

"That's a great idea," Polly told Hannah. "Thank you."

"Just seemed obvious. I mean, you don't want to change the atmosphere of the place, right? Mom wouldn't have liked that at all."

Polly nodded. She and Hannah looked at each other, and a current of tenderness passed between them.

Then Hannah broke eye contact and returned to her seat by the window. Polly picked up Evan's empty coffee mug and went to refill it.

The warm feeling lingered, as if her sister had hugged her heart.

After setting Evan's cup in front of him, she sat back down at her laptop and pulled up her email. Her gaze settled on a message bearing the subject line *Art of French Pastry Course Application.*

Her heart did a slow, strange roll. She'd convinced herself she wouldn't hear anything about her application.

Her hand shook as she clicked on the message. She scanned the letter, first written in French and then duplicated in English.

Dear Mme Lockhart,

We are pleased to accept and welcome you to The Art of French Pastry course, held at the kitchens of Le Cordon Bleu in Paris. The course first taught by M. Pierre Lacroix begins on 6 September.

We are impressed with both your application and the innovation you have shown in your creation of the "Declair." Our six-month course is followed by a three-month internship at one of several patisseries or hotels, with the option of further training at the recommendation of one of the chefs pâtissiers.

Polly stopped reading and sat back in her chair. Exhilaration flared inside her, and before she did something silly, like run around the bakery screaming with disbelief and excitement, she grabbed her laptop and hurried over to Hannah.

"Come here," she whispered, tugging at her sister's arm. "I need to talk to you."

Hannah gave her a puzzled look, but followed her back to the kitchen. Polly turned, her heart hammering so hard she could hear it inside her head.

"Remember when I told you I'd applied to that Art of French Pastry course?" she asked. "I just got an email that they accepted me."

Hannah's eyes widened. "Really?"

Jittery with elation, her nerves fizzing like champagne

bubbles, Polly set the laptop on the table and turned the screen toward her sister. "I had to submit an original recipe, so I first sent in Mom's éclair recipe. Then I felt bad for passing it off as my own, so when I came up with the Declair, I sent that in instead. And they accepted me."

They accepted me.

"Polly, that's incredible! Congratulations." Hannah threw her arms around Polly in a hard embrace. "You'll love Paris. I have some friends there I can contact so you won't feel like you're alone. And Pierre Lacroix...Mom would be thrilled."

Polly nodded, a rush of emotion tightening her throat.

Mom.

"What about Wild Child?" she asked, some of her excitement ebbing. "I can't leave the bakery. Not right when I'm getting everything back on track."

"Well, you can't let the bakery stop you from an opportunity like this," Hannah said. "If I were you, I'd close the place down. But since I know you won't, you can turn Wild Child over to Clementine."

"Clementine is leaving soon," Polly said. "She's going up to Humboldt County to live with her daughter."

"So hire a new manager."

"What about all the products? The doughnuts and éclairs? The Declairs?"

"You have all the recipes," Hannah said. "Hire new bakers and train them how to make stuff. September is over two months away. I'll help. You have time to get things organized."

Polly tried to picture it...and couldn't. She couldn't picture herself standing in a shiny, industrial kitchen with students from other countries, learning about the proper way to make puff pastry dough, icings, baguettes, and *viennoiseries*. She couldn't imagine actually talking to Pierre Lacroix, much less taking instruction from him.

She couldn't see herself sitting in French language classes, walking down the Place de la Madeleine and stopping at Fauchon to sample their macaroons and truffles. She couldn't imagine seeing a lost hope become a reality unlike any she could have dreamed on her own.

Except that maybe she could.

She turned her attention back to the acceptance letter and read the attached documents detailing the program and requirements. If her mother were still here—happy, healthy, alive—Polly wouldn't hesitate to send in her acceptance.

But Jessie wasn't here. And not only could Polly not leave Wild Child, there was also the matter of Luke Stone, the hot rich candyman who had eased his way right into her heart.

She pressed a hand to her chest, staring at the laptop screen through tear-blurred eyes. She'd made a promise to her mother that she was still trying to fulfill. But she knew very well that Jessie would be overjoyed at the idea of her going off to study the art of pastry-making in Paris.

Polly had no idea if it was possible to keep a promise and follow a lost dream at the same time. But it appeared the universe was telling her to find out.

CHAPTER 21

he posters of Paris that lined Polly's apartment walls, the French novels on her bookshelves, and especially her copy of *The Art of French Pastry* all took on a sudden heightened significance. She had until the end of the month to either accept or reject the course offer, and it wasn't an opportunity that would come around again. She also would never forgive herself for abandoning Wild Child after all the work she—and Luke—had done to make it solvent again.

For the next few days, a combination of exhilaration and anxiety sizzled through her. She tried to focus on the bakery and her classes, and she spent evenings writing up lists of things she would need to do if she went to Paris. Everything about the possibility was both exciting and scary at the same time.

On the one hand, she would have a life-changing experience. On the other, she couldn't shake the sense of insecurity that she might never measure up. Yes, she'd invented the Declair, but that had been a mistake. What if she wasn't able to create another pastry like that again? What if she couldn't display the kind of innovation and creativity that chefs of Pierre Lacroix's caliber would demand?

Then there was the overwhelming matter of Luke Stone. What would her moving to Paris for nine months or longer mean for them? Three weeks apart was one thing, but this was close to a year.

Hannah was still the only one who knew about the acceptance letter, though her sister seemed to think the decision was a no-brainer. But considering Hannah had made a job out of traveling, Polly wasn't surprised. Just as she wasn't surprised by her own practical, methodical approach.

As she wrestled with what to do and how to do it, Pender-grass and Peabody Designs took on the *boho chic* remodeling of Wild Child with gusto.

Eleanor came by every day for a week with color samples, light fixtures, and various types of drawer handles and door-knobs for Polly to choose from. When Polly mentioned she liked *this* one, Eleanor would sigh, shake her head, and assure her *that* one was a much better choice.

Polly was always relieved when Hannah happened to be around, since it was easier to turn the decision-making over to her sister. Hannah seemed to have a knack for knowing the difference between "light cream" and "beige," and which one would work better with the rest of the décor.

Per Eleanor's instructions, Polly took down all the decorations and prints in preparation for painting. She spent one morning clearing out the rainbow streamers and mandala tapestries from the front windows to make room for a lighted, garden-themed display.

The following Saturday night, she and Luke were scheduled to attend the Fine Arts Museum exhibition opening and fundraiser dinner. Though they talked often, she hadn't seen much of him this week—they texted and exchanged emails about the business, but he was immersed in work and the new Sugar Rush project in Switzerland.

With all his experience, he would be able to give her excellent advice and insights into the Paris opportunity, so Polly wanted to talk with him at a time when they could be alone and focused.

As the weekend drew closer, she became increasingly nervous about the museum event. It was the first time she would be in Luke's arena, and she had no idea what to expect or what would be expected of her, despite Mia's assurance that all she had to do was *"be yourself, but God in heaven, please don't do any shots."*

Well, as long as she was with Luke, it would be fine. Probably all she'd have to do was smile and make small talk and hope no one asked her about mergers or stock options.

She climbed back into the window display and unpinned a tapestry from a clothesline. A movement outside caught her eye. She glanced out the window just as a tall, blond woman crossed the street from a parked Mercedes.

Polly's hackles, dander, and guard all shot up at the same time. She dropped the tapestry as she steeled her spine and got ready for a throwdown. This time, she wasn't going to call Luke for help either.

Julia Bennett strode into the bakery as if she owned the place, dressed to perfection in an (admittedly gorgeous) camelhair wrap, a beige sheath dress that looked as if it had been made for her, and matching suede pumps.

Polly clambered out of the window display and stepped in her path.

"You're not welcome here," she said icily.

Julia held up a perfectly manicured hand. "I come in peace."

Polly suspected the other woman's definition of "peace" was quite different from her own.

Julia's cool gaze swept over the rather bare interior. "I understand you're getting a facelift."

"I hope it turns out as well as yours."

Julia gave a little sniff that might have been either offense or amusement. She walked past, her heels clicking on the worn wooden floor.

"What do you want?" Polly asked.

"My brother-in-law told me that somehow you managed to convince Luke to take a weekend off."

It was such an out-of-left-field comment that Polly was caught off-guard. "So?"

"And apparently it was a short but *real* vacation," Julia continued, swiveling on her heel to look at Polly again, "because for at least forty-eight hours, Luke didn't answer any phone calls or emails."

"How did you know that?"

"Luke told Warren he was going off the grid, as he put it, and not to call. Warren tested him several times by calling and asked other Sugar Rush execs to do the same. No one heard back from Luke until Monday morning. Some people even got a bit worried."

Monday morning? Polly's assumption that Luke would jump right on his computer and phone late Sunday night had been wrong.

"We had a good time," she said warily. "And why are you bringing this up anyway?"

"Because not once in twelve years has Luke taken a vacation and been unreachable," Julia replied. "In fact, he's never really taken a vacation at all. If he has, he's still always called and directed things from afar. It's insane."

"His hard work has paid off," Polly said. "If it weren't for him, Sugar Rush wouldn't be such a success."

"I realize that. However, Sugar Rush also started as a family-run business, and Luke hasn't forgotten that either. In fact, he feels so responsible for his siblings that Sugar Rush is even the reason he's not married. He doesn't have *time*. Warren and I have never been able to convince him to slow down, and he's only gotten worse over the past year."

After the paternity suit. That was the final lock slamming into the wall Luke had built around his family and his heart. Though Polly had discovered a few weak spots in that wall.

"So what does this have to do with me?" she asked.

Julia's gaze slid over her from head to toe, taking in her flour-dusted apron and messy hair.

"Clearly you're a good influence on him," Julia remarked, "despite this *penniless Victorian orphan and the wealthy duke* romance you've got going on."

Polly looked her up and down in a return assessment.

"You're a Scorpio, aren't you?" she asked.

Julia blinked.

"Mercury in Scorpio, I'll bet," Polly continued. "Moon too. It's why you're naturally suspicious. Expecting the worst in people. That's how you form your strategies...you think all your suspicions are right and then plot accordingly. Mercury in Scorpio is also why you're fearless. Except when engaged in a showdown with a bakery girl, in which case you turn tail and run."

A very faint smile cracked Julia's perfect face.

"And *you*," she said, "are a Sagittarius. Moon in Scorpio. You possess an excess of emotional energy. And though you're quick and self-reliant, you're overly sensitive and defensive. Which is why you took me on, even though you know I can crush you like a bug."

"Fixed sign." Polly narrowed her eyes. "You think you're always right."

"Mutable sign," Julia replied. "You have trouble finishing what you start."

They locked gazes. A weird feeling rippled in the air between them—mutual irritation and grudging admiration. Julia scrutinized Polly again from head to toe.

"You're scrappy," she allowed. "I'll give you that."

"You're snooty. I'll give you that."

Julia's smile glinted again, sharp and white. She folded her arms and tapped her painted fingernails against her sleeves.

"Luke told me you haven't taken any money from him," she said.

Polly's guard went up again. "I'm not a gold digger. And frankly, even if I were, do you really think Luke would be stupid enough not to see it?"

"So why are you with him?"

For a second, all the breath escaped Polly's lungs. She couldn't speak. It was a question she thought she'd known the answer to, but the more time she spent with Luke, the more she realized it wasn't just about her having a new, exciting experience and fulfilling lost years. Every minute of every day, the answer revolved more and more around *him.*

"We...have a good time together," she managed to get out. "That's it."

Julia studied her with a stare as penetrating as a laser. "Are you going to the opening of the Manet exhibit with him this Saturday night?"

"He invited me, yes."

"Good." Julia paused and cleared her throat. "I can help you get ready for it."

"Get ready how?"

"With your clothes, makeup, and hair." She reached into her Prada handbag and removed a slim leather case. "I'm a fashion stylist and consultant. And I'm very good at what I do."

She opened the case and pushed a business card across the counter toward Polly.

"You're a pretty girl," Julia continued, "but the way you dress, and with your freckles and that mop-top hair, you've got a real Raggedy Ann vibe. I'd consider it a personal challenge to help you look presentable to Luke's circle."

"That's hardly a flattering offer."

"No charge." Julia strode toward the door, her heels clicking sharply. "Call me for an appointment. You know you want to."

"Are you this bitchy with all your clients?"

"You're not my client," Julia replied. "And this is me being nice."

"Compared to who?" Polly asked. "The Wicked Witch of the West?"

"Please. Flying monkeys and a terrible sense of fashion?" Julia flicked a smile over her shoulder. "That witch was an amateur."

CHAPTER 22

$\mathcal{I}$t took one sleepless night for Polly to come to the conclusion that if she was revamping Wild Child, she shouldn't be afraid of revamping herself. Especially for a high-society museum gala.

And though the thought of being at the mercy of Julia Bennett was rather terrifying, there was no question Julia knew how to rock "personal style," whatever that was, and high-class fashion. Polly, on the other hand, was happy when she found a shirt in her drawer that didn't have chocolate stains.

And she was pretty sure that Pierre Lacroix maintained an impeccable appearance, even when he was making *religieuses au chocolat* and champagne truffles.

So Polly called Julia (grudgingly) and told her (pointedly) that she wasn't about to pay for any of her pricy consulting or hair-styles or whatever else Julia had planned.

"That's what *no charge* means, dear," Julia replied coolly over the phone. "What time is Luke picking you up?"

"He's not. He has a business call with China or whatever, so I'm meeting him at the museum."

"God forbid he should put China on hold," Julia muttered.

"However, this will give us more time to work on you. The event starts at six, so you'd better be here at two. On second thought, make it one. We'll need that extra hour."

"For your voodoo curses, right?"

"*Art* takes time, Polly."

"I'm not art."

"You will be, as long as you wear what I tell you to wear and look how I want you to look. And for God's sake, lay off the doughnuts and muffins. *Bloat* is never stylish."

Polly didn't tell Luke she was letting his aunt style her up, just in case she ended up on the lam for melting Julia with a bucket of water, but she showed up at the studio at one sharp on Saturday afternoon. A hair salon, boutique, offices, and spa comprised the entire first floor of a private, refurbished building near downtown Indigo Bay.

Polly was greeted not only by Julia but by a team of male assistants whose names all ended in O—Marco, Antonio, Stefano—and women whose names ended in A—Anisa, Dawna, Isabella. First the women made her strip down to her skivvies before coming at her with enough tools and products to fill a warehouse.

Polly was waxed all over, including places where she didn't even know she had hair, then her skin was exfoliated, conditioned, moisturized, massaged, and plucked. Julia walked around issuing orders like a general, commanding her to try on at least a dozen gowns—"*The latest*," she informed Polly—and designer shoes.

Polly modeled clothes that were probably more expensive than her debt and savings combined, while Julia and the assistants circled her with comments and critiques.

"*The mermaid style doesn't flatter her hips.*" "*Nice around the bust.*" "*Orange isn't her color.*" "*With her figure, she needs an A line.*"

They decided on a black-and-gray gown that hugged her breasts and torso before flaring around her hips into a soft waterfall of silk and lace. Polly had barely had time to admire herself in the mirror before Julia sent the gown off to be altered to her figure.

Then Julia led her over to a chair in front of a lighted mirror, where another small army of stylists waited. Julia and a hair-stylist named Enzo walked around her, flicking at her hair and discussing the "split ends," "frizz," and "heavy length" of her locks while a cosmetologist recommended certain color choices for eye shadow and blush.

Polly silently congratulated herself for not saying a word as she read *Vogue* magazine and let Julia and her cohorts have their way with her.

And when she finally stood in front of the full-length mirror, polished to a shine, she couldn't believe she was looking at herself.

"So." Julia stood behind her, her hands on her hips and her lips pursed as she raked a final, critical eye over Polly's figure. "I told you I was good."

She'd been right. Polly looked…amazing. They'd cut, shaped, and straightened her hair, so it fell in a thick, shimmering curtain to her shoulders, and added sun-streaked blond highlights. The cosmetologist had beautified her face with subtle colors that brought out the dark brown of her eyes, the angles of her cheek-bones, and made her lips look as if she had just been kissed.

And the gown! It hugged her in all the right places, with the V neckline displaying a perfect amount of cleavage. Diamond earrings glittered against her hair, and a gold diamond necklace made her neck look swan-like. Her shoes were satin flats embell-ished with a crystal ("Manolo, though I don't trust you to wear heels gracefully," Julia had remarked), and they complemented the gown perfectly.

Everything about her glowed—her hair, her skin, her eyes, even her French-manicured fingernails.

"Wow," she finally said.

"To be sure." Julia smiled, this time actually displaying her perfect teeth.

Polly couldn't take her eyes off her reflection. This version of Polly Lockhart looked like a princess. A woman who could sail through Paris with self-assurance and not be intimidated by famous chefs or learning a new language.

"My mother would have loved what you did with my hair," she told Julia. "She was always telling me I should take better care of my hair."

"Mothers are often right."

As Polly gazed at herself in the mirror, a weird emotion tightened her throat. She blinked.

"Don't you dare ruin your mascara." Julia snapped her fingers at Anna, who hurried over with a tissue and a beaded handbag that matched Polly's gown.

"Twirl," Antonio said.

"Twirl?"

He nodded and smiled, making a circling gesture with his forefinger. Polly didn't think she had ever twirled in her life, but she did then. She stood on her tiptoes and spun in a circle, her gown flaring out like a cloud. She wanted to dance like Cinderella at the ball—all she needed was Prince Charming to guide her. Or Luke Stone.

That strange feeling filled her chest again. She stepped away from the mirror.

"I don't know how I'm going to drive in this," she remarked.

Dawna and Enzo chuckled.

"She's not joking," Julia told them dryly.

"Why would I be joking?" Polly asked, though she secretly dreaded the thought of driving her old VW van while wearing this. She would be a pearl inside a cranky old oyster.

"My dear, Luke sent a car to take you to the museum," Julia replied. "I told the driver to pick you up here rather than your apartment."

"Don't forget to hold up your gown on the stairs," Marco advised.

"Have a wonderful time, darling!" Enzo added. "You look magnificent."

All the assistants cheered and clapped as Polly sashayed to the door, making her feel like she was walking the red carpet. She stopped to thank them before Julia guided her outside to where a sleek, black Bentley town car waited, the driver standing beside the open door.

"Enjoy yourself." Julia narrowed her eyes and adjusted Polly's décolletage. "Just try not to destroy the illusion that you're glamorous and sophisticated. In other words, don't open your mouth."

Polly looked up to make a smart retort, only to find Julia watching her with amusement. Very faint, but there nonetheless.

"At the risk of sounding sappy," Polly said, "thank you."

"I told you I was good." Julia tilted her head to the car. "I'll be there a bit later, so I'll keep an eye on you. Go."

Before Polly did something embarrassing, like hug the other woman, she got into the car and settled against the plush leather seats. Through the tinted window, she saw the group of assistants waving as the car pulled away from the curb.

Better be home by midnight. This car will turn back into a VW van, and I'll be Raggedy Ann again.

Limos and town cars crowded the front of the Fine Arts Museum. Spotlights glowed on the huge banners advertising the opening of the Manet exhibition, and women in glittering evening gowns and men in tuxedos walked up the wide, marble steps to the entrance.

Nervousness tightened Polly's stomach. She thanked the driver and followed the stream of guests up the stairs. Halfway there, she stopped. Luke stood next to one of the Roman columns lining the front of the classical building.

Wearing a tuxedo that stretched to perfection across his powerful chest and shoulders, his dark hair glowing and the lights casting shadows on his strong features, he was nothing short of beautiful.

Polly's heart ignited, filling her blood with warmth and quickening excitement. For tonight at least, she would revel in the fact that this particular handsome prince, in all his masculine strength and beauty, was hers.

Carefully holding her skirt, she continued up the steps. Luke scanned the approaching guests. Polly waited in breathless anticipation for the moment when he'd see her, his eyes widening in surprise before filling with heat and love…

Well, wait a minute. Let's not get carried away here.

…before filling with heat and admiration…

His gaze passed right over her to the parked cars. Polly faltered for a second before realizing that he hadn't recognized her. A bubble of laughter rose. Well, she had hardly recognized herself in the mirror, so she shouldn't be surprised.

She climbed the rest of the steps, admiring him all over again. He was everything she adored—buttery almond cream, lemon zest, royal icing. She stopped beside him, her whole being reacting to his nearness, the air charged with energy. A radiant happiness filled her, and she thought she'd never before felt something so powerful, a pull so strong it almost hurt.

Luke turned toward her. He blinked and went very still. Electric silence crackled between them. For an instant, the rest of the world disappeared and it was just the two of them again—kissing at the Troll's House, rolling candy in the kitchen, making love on his beautiful bed.

"Polly." He stepped back, disbelief flashing in his eyes.

"From bakery girl to glamor girl," she said with a smile, spreading her arms out.

He shook his head as he looked her over. "I didn't recognize you."

"I know. I hardly recognized myself."

"How did…"

"Aunt Julia got her claws into me," Polly said, holding up a hand when he frowned. "No, it's okay. She offered to help me get ready for tonight, and I decided to let her. Designer gowns and exfoliation aren't exactly in my wheelhouse."

"What did you do to your hair?"

"Straightened, styled, highlighted. All sorts of fancy things." Polly gestured to her dress. "And much as it pains me to admit this, Julia does know what she's doing."

"You look…" He let his gaze rake over her again, lingering on the modest valley of cleavage exposed by the gown's neckline before sweeping back up to her face.

She expected a thousand compliments. A man like him had a treasure trove stored away. *You're beautiful. You take my breath away. You're the most incredible woman I've ever seen. Not even the stars can outshine you.*

"Um…" Luke said. "Wow."

A smile curved Polly's mouth. She'd reduced the eloquent, powerful CEO Luke Stone to *"um, wow."* It might have been the best compliment she'd ever received.

"Um, wow to you too," she said, indicating his tuxedo.

He returned her smile and extended his arm. "May I have the honor?"

"Of course."

She slipped her arm through his as they entered the great hall, which was filled with linen-draped tablecloths and bouquets of flowers. A string quartet played in a corner of the hall, and several people glided up to greet Luke as they entered. He graciously introduced her to everyone who approached, stepping back as if to let her glow in the limelight.

Though Polly was nervous about being among the *bon vivant* crowd, she soon found herself rather enjoying the looks of blatant admiration men tossed in her direction, not to mention the curiosity of the women who'd seen her come in with Luke.

"Before dinner, I have to talk to a few people about the Foundation, then speak to one of our investors about acquisition tax issues." Luke grimaced as he handed Polly a flute of champagne. "It's going to be really boring."

"Go ahead without me." She nodded toward where his brother and father stood near the exhibition entrance. "I'll say hello to Evan and your father."

"It'll just take a few minutes. I'll find you as soon as I can get away."

"If you're getting desperate, scratch your ear as a signal," Polly said. "I'll come rescue you."

"You already have, Peach."

He winked at her, brushed his lips across her cheek, and walked away.

CHAPTER 23

A warm, happy feeling surrounded Polly as she wandered among the crowd. She watched Luke cross the room, remembering when she'd seen him assessing the Sugar Rush test kitchen with the same regal command. People stopped him as he passed, extending their hands and smiling. He paused to speak with everyone before approaching the bar where a portly man sat.

Polly made her way to where Evan and Warren had been standing, but they'd both already disappeared into the mass of people. Surprisingly, she didn't mind being by herself. Her nervousness had shifted into excitement over a night of dining, dancing with a certain handsome man, and strolling through the museum galleries, gazing at priceless works of art. A month ago, she never would have imagined such an evening.

"Is that an Elie Saab?" An elegant woman who had introduced herself as Gabrielle, one of the museum donors, stopped and eyed Polly's gown.

"Why, yes." Polly was pleased that she knew the answer. "It's from his spring collection." She extended her foot to show off her black satin flat. "And Manolos, of course."

"Of course." Gabrielle smiled. "I went to his show in Paris last year. Incredible, really. His shoes are works of art."

Considering they were in the middle of an Impressionist exhibit, Polly hardly thought there was a comparison, but she nodded in agreement anyway.

"I suppose Julia was your stylist?" Gabrielle sipped her champagne. "I see her handiwork. I wouldn't be surprised if she finds a designer apron for you."

Er...what now?

"Designer apron?" Polly repeated.

"For your bakery." Gabrielle lifted an eyebrow. "Luke told me you own a little bakery over in...where is it? Fordham?"

"Rainsville."

"Yes." The other woman gave her an arch smile. "He says you're working to remodel and upgrade to some sort of bohemian theme. Very industrious of you."

Well, didn't that adjective make her sound like an ant?

Polly excused herself and went to refill her champagne flute. A thread of unease twisted through her, which didn't make much sense. After all, Luke had just told Gabrielle the truth. Polly did own a little bakery that she was upgrading. But the fact that he'd brought it up while talking about her with a museum donor at a fancy dinner and art exhibition opening, felt...strange.

She didn't want it to feel strange. But she also wanted to enjoy being this beautiful, princess version of herself for one evening without being reminded of her real-life struggles.

"I always wonder how many people show up for the art and how many show up for the free booze." A tall man whose bow-tie was askew stopped beside Polly and extended his empty glass to the bartender. "Scotch."

As the bartender refilled the glass, the man glanced at Polly.

"Haven't seen you at one of these shindigs before," he said.

"I'm Polly Lockhart. I'm here with Luke Stone."

"Ah." His demeanor shifted, and he took a step away from her.

"Sam Walker. I'm the head of Sugar Rush's new Fair Trade Foundation. I've heard about you."

Polly eyed him warily. "What have you heard?"

"You're a baker, right? Luke's giving you a hand. Taking classes at a community college?"

"That's correct."

Her unease intensified. She shouldn't be ashamed of attending community college any more than she should be ashamed of owning Wild Child. But knowing that Luke was telling all his fancy friends and coworkers about her comparably modest life, she began to feel like little pins were poking into her perfect, fluffy soufflé of happiness.

She glanced over to where Luke was still talking to the portly man. Except now a statuesque redhead had joined the conversation, and she was standing intimately close to him.

Jealousy flickered in Polly. She had a sudden flashback to that night at the Troll's House when another redhead had made a move on Luke.

"I don't remember any redhead," he'd told her. *"I only remember you."*

How drastically her life had changed since that night. She'd changed too—not only in the sense of being a more skilled businesswoman, but she'd also become so much more self-confident and hopeful. She'd started to believe that she could do anything.

Polly straightened her spine with sudden determination. Since Luke was telling everyone about Wild Child anyway, she might as well drum up some business.

"Wild Child is in Rainsville," she told Sam Walker. "We're in the middle of a major renovation and are launching a number of new French pastries, all handmade with organic ingredients. Eclairs, croissants, brioche. Baked fresh every morning and served with dark roast, French press coffee. You should stop by and give us a try."

"I certainly will." Interest flashed in his expression, but before he could continue, Polly excused herself and slipped into the crowd again.

She spoke with several other people who either caught her eye or stopped her in passing, but she didn't give them a chance to bring up either Wild Child or Hartford. Instead she introduced herself first as, "Polly Lockhart, Luke's date and owner of Wild Child Bakery in Rainsville" before launching into details about the bakery's renovation and new pastries.

Unfortunately, preempting the other guests didn't ease the tension in her shoulders or the feeling that she was being judged.

"You must be Polly." An older woman approached, her gaze sliding over Polly's figure. "I hear you're Luke's new little project."

"Actually, I'm his hot little sidepiece, but I suppose it's just a matter of semantics, isn't it?" The retort flew out of Polly's mouth before she could stop it.

The woman widened her eyes just as an elegant laugh sounded from nearby. They both turned to see Julia Bennett approaching, looking magnificent in a gold dress that skimmed her slender figure like water.

"Semantics, indeed." She eyed the older woman narrowly. "And really, Barb, you mustn't be catty simply because Luke decided your daughter was far too desperate and clingy for his tastes. Or any man's, I imagine. Is Cindy at home in front of the TV tonight, wearing sweatpants and eating ice cream?"

The woman pressed her lips together tightly, then gave a little huff and walked away. Polly tried to deflect her vindictive pleasure—meanness had never made her feel good—but it was hard to deny the satisfaction of being on the winning side of a well-deserved cut.

"Well." Julia looked Polly over, as if assessing that her handiwork was still in place. "At least everyone is talking about you. Just don't spill anything on your dress during dinner."

"I'm twenty-five, not five," Polly muttered.

Julia arched an eyebrow. "You're twenty-five?"

"Is that a problem?"

"Not for me," Julia replied. "It's just that Luke's women tend to be closer to his age. Shared interests and all."

"He didn't seem to mind when..." *he was fucking me from behind in a tent* "...we were dancing at the Codswallop Music Festival."

Julia blinked. "You took him to Codswallop?"

"You *know* about Codswallop?"

"My dear..." Julia's lovely mouth curved into a smile as she leaned toward Polly and lowered her voice. "I lost my virginity at Codswallop."

She turned and walked away, her stride like that of a runway model. Vaguely impressed, Polly watched her go. She had the odd thought that her mother might have liked Julia Bennett. Or at least said something like, *"There's a woman with some stories to tell."*

Polly shifted her gaze from Julia to Luke, who was standing with a cluster of people, his expression serious as he nodded at something another man said. The redheaded woman was now so close her breasts pressed against his arm.

Polly was suddenly glad she and Luke had come in separate cars. At least she could leave whenever she wanted. She even had a flash of envy toward Cindy, sitting at home with her TV, sweatpants, and ice cream.

Maybe visiting the Impressionist exhibition would make her feel better. In the main galleries, the paintings glowed like lighted windows—water lilies, haystacks, railroads, cathedrals, boating parties.

She stopped in front of a Manet painting called *The Railway*. A woman with long, red hair and a blue coat sat in front of an iron fence, the steam and smoke of the railroad billowing in the air.

A little girl stood next to the woman, wearing a white dress tied with a shiny blue bow. The girl's back was to the viewer, and she was gripping the fence as she looked at the passing trains.

Like she wished she could climb aboard one of them and ride...somewhere.

"Did you notice the puppy?"

Polly turned at the sound of the male voice. Warren Stone approached her, handsome and regal in his tuxedo. Luke would probably look like his father one day—his dark hair streaked with silver, his strong features creased with lines that made him look distinguished rather than old.

"The puppy?" she said.

Warren stopped beside her and looked at the painting. He gestured to the sleeping puppy lying in the woman's lap.

"Sometimes it takes a second look to see it," he remarked. "I'm sure there's some deep symbolic meaning to it, but I just like the fact that it's so cute."

She smiled. "Nothing wrong with cute."

He glanced at her. "If you don't mind my saying so, you look beautiful tonight."

"Thank you." A glow of pleasure lit in her heart. "Does any woman ever mind hearing that she looks beautiful?"

Warren chuckled. "No woman that I know. Are you having a good time?"

"I'm enjoying the exhibit," Polly said evasively. "I love museums. Whenever my mother and I traveled, she always made a point of visiting local museums. We used to talk about seeing the famous museums of the world one day."

"The big museums are impressive, no question," Warren said. "But the smaller ones are sometimes more personal and memorable. There's a little museum in Aix-en-Provence that used to be Cezanne's atelier. Walk in and you almost expect to see him there, still painting."

A burst of music came from the great hall. Warren extended his hand to the door.

"Care to dance?" he asked. "I'd like to be able to brag that I danced with the most beautiful woman at the ball."

Amused and flattered, Polly took his proffered arm as they walked back out to the great hall.

"My sister-in-law tells me you've been dating Luke for several weeks now," Warren said. "Thank you for getting him away from work."

"I don't know that I've done that too much," she admitted. "But he's been a great help with getting my bakery back on track."

"Yes, I heard him talking about it. You'll likely have some new customers tomorrow."

That would be good, even though Polly still didn't like the idea that all the posh guests here thought of her as Luke's little bakery girl "project."

She let Warren lead her onto the floor and was happy to discover that he was an excellent dancer who easily compensated for her lack of experience. He led well, didn't mind when she stepped on his toes, and guided her in time with the music.

After Polly danced three songs with Warren, Evan Stone appeared at her side and guided her into a waltz. She had never danced a waltz in her life, but with him it was easy. Apparently rhythm and grace ran in the Stone genes as powerfully as handsomeness did.

"How's the redecorating going?" Evan asked. "Are Pendergrass and Peabody asking you to shell out for Italian marble?"

"No, but Hannah and Eleanor almost had a throwdown over these crystal wall sconces Eleanor was pushing for. Hannah said they looked like they belonged in a bordello."

Amusement lit Evan's blue eyes. "And what did Hannah want instead?"

"Moroccan-inspired lanterns."

"I don't need to ask who won the battle."

"Hannah has literally climbed mountains in the Himalayas. Eleanor isn't much of a challenge for her in comparison. The lanterns are arriving early next week."

Evan smiled. "So is Hannah planning to help finish the remodeling?"

"I don't know." Polly bit her lip, unease rising to her chest. "I hope so. But she's never been one for staying in town longer than a couple of weeks. So I expect she'll take off again as soon as she can."

Something flashed in Evan's expression that looked remarkably like disappointment. Polly's curiosity sparked. She hadn't noticed anything going on between Evan and her sister, but then she hadn't been looking.

She wouldn't, however, be surprised if Evan was interested in Hannah—men had always been attracted to both Hannah's beauty and the wild restlessness that was such an intrinsic part of her. The bigger question was if Hannah was attracted to Evan in return. And if so…?

Before Polly could probe for more information, Evan spun her again. She let go of his hand and twirled in two circles. She reached the edge of the dance floor and suddenly bumped against a hard male body. She turned, her heart leaping at the sight of Luke standing behind her, his expression a mixture of frustration and relief.

"There you are," he said. "I couldn't find you."

The distress Polly had experienced earlier in the evening returned, underscored by a longing for the happiness she'd felt when she'd first seen Luke waiting for her on the museum steps. But now, the sight of him only intensified her sense that she didn't belong here, even all dolled up in her designer gown.

"I thought you'd forgotten about me." She couldn't keep the cool note from her voice. "You were gone for over an hour."

"I know." A scowl creased his forehead. "I'm sorry. I couldn't get away."

"Or did you not want to get away from important company business?"

Luke frowned, his gaze shifting as Evan came to a stop beside them.

"Hope you don't mind me borrowing your date for a while," he told Luke. "If you leave a woman like Polly alone, she won't stay alone for long."

Luke glowered at his brother. "I'll take it from here, man."

"Sure." Evan turned to her with a smile. "Thank you, Polly. I enjoyed dancing with you."

"Go," Luke growled.

Evan held up his hands in surrender and strolled back across the dance floor, pausing to speak to Gabrielle, the woman who'd made the "designer apron" remark.

Polly sighed. She might have appreciated Evan's pointed comments to his brother if a weight weren't pressing down on her heart. Luke moved closer, his gaze on hers.

"For what it's worth," he said, "I am sorry. I only meant to take fifteen minutes, but Rich Monroe has some issue with my brother Tyler, who's kind of a fuck-up to begin with. I can't have him causing problems when we're on the verge of an acquisition. Hell. I can't have him causing problems at all."

A pang of remorse hit her at the realization he'd been dealing with family difficulties. "Is Tyler here?"

"He doesn't come to these things." Luke shook his head, as if wanting to rid himself of thoughts of his brother. He extended his hand to her. "Look, I want to make it up to you, and I'm all yours for the rest of the night. Will you dance with me?"

Polly wanted to. Of course she did. As much as she'd enjoyed dancing with Warren and Evan, she'd been dreaming of twirling around the dance floor in Luke's arms, her feet barely touching the ground.

But.

"Actually, I...I think I should head home," she said.

"Home?" His forehead creased. "They haven't even served dinner yet."

"I know, but it's...well, I have to open Wild Child tomorrow morning, and I should get some sleep."

Luke studied her face, his frown deepening. "What's going on?"

She looked past his shoulder to avoid having to make eye contact. She didn't want to hash things out with him right in the middle of such a glamorous event, but she couldn't fake her way through the rest of the evening or get that happy feeling back again.

"I really need to go," she said.

He closed his hand around her arm. "Come with me."

"Luke, I don't want to do this here."

"Too bad, because I do." His mouth tightened with irritation, his fingers digging into her arm.

To avoid a scene, Polly gave in and let him lead her off the dance floor. All right, then. She'd been getting a few too many flights of fancy lately, and maybe it was time she was brought sharply back to earth where she belonged.

Better now than later. If she kept going on this path and *really* fell for Luke, a reality hit reminding her of their differences would hurt even more.

But she hadn't fallen for him. Much.

Luke cut a swathe through the crowd, leading her outside to the museum's portico where the outside air cooled Polly's heated skin. He turned to face her, his eyes dark with frustration.

"Polly." His tone was measured and controlled. "I'm so sorry for having left you, but I had no idea it would take as long as it did. And then I went through all the galleries looking for you because I couldn't find you in the crowd near the bar, and you didn't pick up when I called your cell, so—"

"Luke." She put her hand up to stop him. "It's not that."

"Then what is it?" He searched her face, a sudden anger rising to his expression. "Did someone say or do something to you? Who was it?"

"No. Well, not really."

"What does that mean?"

Polly moved away from him, hating that she was letting other people make her feel inferior.

"Everyone I talked to brought up the fact that I own a floundering bakery," she explained. "They said you told them about it. And my classes at Hartford."

"So?" He spread his hands out in bafflement. "What's wrong with that?"

"They weren't telling me because they were impressed," Polly said. "Just the opposite, in fact. Why is that the first thing you tell people when you talk about me?"

"Because it's the truth. Why *wouldn't* I tell them?"

"Because they're used to seeing you with wealthy, glamorous women." She turned to face him, her throat tight. "And because this isn't the right place for you to bring a struggling bakery girl who's playing dress up for one night. I mean, I know that's who I am, but I was hoping to forget for a few hours. Like Cinderella. Which I realize is stupid."

Luke shook his head, his expression hardening. "Polly, if anyone in that room made you feel bad about who you are, then give me their names right now. I'll have it out with them so fast they'll regret ever having come here."

"I don't want you to do that. It just made me remember how different we are."

"*We* are not different," Luke snapped. He stalked toward her and grabbed her by the shoulders. "Yeah, we had different lives, but you and I are two peas in a fucking pod. You said it yourself. We both know what it's like lose our mothers and to leave college for the sake of our families. We know how to take charge, to be responsible, to work our asses off to save our businesses. We'd both do anything for the people we love. Hell, we both like cherry-vanilla Jelly Rolls the best. We're the *same*, you and me. And if you think for one second I'm not going to brag about your accomplishments to everyone I meet, then you've got me all wrong."

Polly stared at him, curling her hands into her skirt. "Brag? That's what you were doing?"

"Of course that's what I was doing." Luke tightened his grip on her, his dark eyes flaring. "Did you think I was putting you down?"

"No, but it felt like they were."

"Well, fuck them." He took a breath, visibly suppressing his anger. He flexed his hands on her shoulders. "Polly, whenever I talk about you, the first thing I do is tell people how smart and savvy you are, how you've worked so hard to save your mother's bakery. *Your* bakery. I tell them you enrolled in classes for the sole purpose of improving the bakery, that Wild Child is more to you than just a business. It's your heritage, your…"

His voice trailed off. Polly's throat was so tight she struggled to pull in a breath. Tears stung her eyes. Luke locked his gaze to hers, understanding dawning in his expression. He rested his palm against the side of her face.

"Peach." His voice was hoarse. "I'm so fucking proud of you I could burst. That's why I tell everyone about Wild Child and Hartford. And if those dickheads are twisting that around and making you feel somehow *less*, then they can go to hell. Never be ashamed of who you are and all you've done. You're amazing. I tell people that every single chance I get."

Polly's heart rose like a multicolored balloon, breaking through the clouds that had gathered above it. She curled her hand around Luke's wrist, not caring that her tears were probably ruining her artfully applied makeup.

"Thank you," she said. "I feel the exact same way about you. And I'm sorry I let other people affect *us*. Maybe I'm not as thick-skinned as I'd like to believe."

He wrapped his arms around her, enclosing her in a protective circle where everything steadied back into perfection.

"Your sensitivity isn't a flaw," he said. "It's just one of the things that makes you *you*. But if anyone makes you feel bad, I want you to tell me. I'll do everything I can to make it right for you, but I need to know what the problem is. Okay?"

"Okay." Polly tightened her arms around his waist, breathed in his delicious scent, and thought surely there was no place in the world she would rather be than in Luke's arms.

Not even Paris.

CHAPTER 24

*L*uke reluctantly disengaged himself from Polly when a burst of conversation and laughter flooded from the museum atrium. He wanted to go back to the gala for only one reason—to make sure every last person knew he wouldn't stand for anyone making his girl feel inferior. By the time he was done, the guests would be wondering how they could have gotten it so wrong. Hell, they'd be groveling to gain Polly's favor.

But he didn't want to be with anyone but her right now. Sure as hell didn't want to talk to anyone else—about acquisitions, his reckless younger brother, or anything to do with Sugar Rush. All he wanted was Polly.

His chest tightened. He'd seen it the instant he'd turned to face her on the front steps of the museum. The second he realized that the shining beauty walking toward him was his Peach. Because even though she looked a world away from the tousled girl who'd smashed her mouth against his at the Troll's House, Polly hadn't changed. All of her emotions still shone through those thick-lashed brown eyes. She still couldn't hide what she was feeling.

And when his gaze collided with hers...his heart had turned into a falcon—flying, swooping, and gliding over a blue sky.

Love.

It was there in her eyes, clear as glass, brilliant as a painting. No woman had ever looked at him with such blatantly pure emotion.

Christ. It felt like he'd first seen her a lifetime ago, when in reality it had only been a couple of months. And yet she'd filled him so completely, her presence so softening and soothing, that somehow without his even realizing it, she'd become part of him.

"Luke?"

Her soft voice broke into his thoughts. She was standing by the doors, the light glowing off her thick hair.

"We should go back in," she said.

"Do you want to?"

She hesitated. "We have to, don't we?"

"We don't have to do anything." Luke headed to the doors. "Wait here. I'll be right back."

He strode inside to collect Polly's wrap and handbag. He found Julia and apologized for leaving, then escaped before she could rip him a new one. He returned to Polly and took her hand.

"Let's go," he said.

"Where?" She hurried after him as he descended the steps and handed his ticket to the valet.

"Anywhere but here."

"But they haven't even served dinner yet." She glanced back at the museum. "Julia won't like it if we leave."

"She'll get over it."

Amusement flashed in Polly's eyes. "You'll risk unleashing her flying monkeys?"

"I'll risk anything for you." He winked at her as the valet pulled the Porsche up to the curb. "And I'm used to battling Julia's flying monkeys."

Luke texted Polly's town car driver that she was with him before he guided the Porsche away from the museum. The tension lingering in his shoulders eased as soon as they were alone again.

He drove back to his house and instructed Polly to stay in the car while he went in to grab a couple of blankets. He put them in the trunk, then headed to a strip-mall pizza joint on the outskirts of Indigo Bay.

"Dinner?" Polly asked, lifting her eyebrow.

"Tyler can be an ass, but the kid knows his pizza like no one else." Luke got out of the car. "He claims this is the best pizza place in a twenty-mile radius. I'll get one for takeout."

He ordered the pizza and a couple of sodas, storing them in the backseat before driving toward the beach. The ocean fog had just started to descend on the coastline, but the setting sun cast a brilliant reddish-orange glow on the horizon.

Luke spread the blanket onto the sand and pulled off his tuxedo jacket. He wrapped it around Polly's shoulders as they settled down. Draping her skirt over her legs, she hugged her knees to her chest and smiled at him.

"This is way better than a fancy dinner," she said.

"Couldn't agree more."

They ate pizza and watched the sun set, as low waves rolled onto the beach and the salty sea air grew colder. The dampness made Polly's hair curly again, just the way Luke liked it. Most of her makeup had worn off, and she had a smear of pizza sauce on her chin. She couldn't have been more perfect.

He turned to look out over the ocean, rivers of red and gold cast by the sunset. Where would he be without Polly? *What* would he be?

His life would be everything it was before—work, meetings, negotiations.

No explosive sex. No ridiculously overcrowded clubs. No midnight skinny-dipping. No flirtatious texting. No palm reading, aura cleansing, or beatnik music festivals ending with them naked and sweaty in a tent.

There would be no *fun.*

What if he changed? He'd spent so much of his life being like this that he didn't know if he was even capable of change. He was old and hardened. Burned. And suddenly scared that he couldn't offer Polly everything she deserved.

"I'm going to miss you when you go to Switzerland." She wiped her fingers on a napkin and closed the pizza box. "But we'll be completely finished with the remodel by the time you get back, so you'll have a nice surprise waiting for you."

"After you've hired more employees and can leave the bakery in someone else's hands, I want to take you to Paris. Maybe this fall."

She went still, as if he'd said something untenable. Cold prickled his skin. He frowned.

"Polly?"

For the first time ever he couldn't read her expression, couldn't see past the invisible veil that had descended over her eyes.

What the...?

"Luke." She turned to face him, wrapping his tuxedo jacket around her body. "Do you remember when I told you I'd once wanted to go to a pastry school in Paris?"

He nodded, his apprehension intensifying.

"The day after my birthday, I found out there's a special pastry-making course being offered in Paris," Polly explained. "It's being taught by several renowned chefs, including Pierre Lacroix. I applied for the course on kind of a whim, not thinking I stood a chance, but I got an email a few days ago telling me I'd been accepted. Part of the reason was that they liked the innovation I showed in the creation of the Declairs."

Luke heard what she'd said but for a second, he couldn't process it.

"The course starts in September but they recommend arriving earlier to settle in." Wariness appeared in her eyes. "It's a six-month series of classes followed by a three-month internship, with the possibility of a longer position."

"That's..." He should congratulate her, but he couldn't get the words out.

"That's great," he finally said. "So what...what did you tell them?"

"Nothing yet. I wanted to tell you first. I have until the end of the month to send in my response."

Silence fell. Luke could only look at her, stunned by the depth of his pride in her. When he'd approached her about helping with Wild Child, he'd thought he would be the teacher. Turned out he'd been the student all along because she'd been the one to teach him about true determination, loyalty, never giving up, and believing in yourself and your dreams.

But the thought of her leaving for almost a year, maybe even longer, made his chest knot like an old fishing line.

"Congratulations, Peach," he said. "You deserve this."

"Thank you." She still looked wary. "Do you think I should go?"

"You're questioning whether or not you should?"

"Wild Child is just starting to take off," Polly said. "How can I leave right when it's finally turning a profit?"

"Because..." The words died.

Because this is your dream, the one you put on hold years ago. Because it will open more doors than you can imagine. Because you'll learn so much. Because you'll do so well and be the star student. Because it's a once-in-a-lifetime chance. Because it's what you were meant to do.

"Because you can't turn down an opportunity like this," he finally said. "Who else knows?"

"Just Hannah."

"What did she say?"

"She thinks I should go."

"Will she stay in town and help with the bakery?"

"I don't think so." A shadow passed across her face, and she fiddled with a button on the tuxedo jacket. "I'd love for her to stay, to finally realize that the bakery belongs to her too. But I don't think she will. Honestly, Luke, I don't see how I can possibly go."

An intense combination of despair and relief filled him. Because as much as he knew she *had to* go, he couldn't stand the thought of being without her for that long.

It wasn't supposed to happen this way. He had no idea how it was supposed to happen, or even what *it* was, but Polly heading off to live in Paris while he stayed here and immersed himself again in the cold business of Sugar Rush without her warm presence to give him everything he didn't have...

No. That wasn't *it* at all.

He took a breath and tried to think logically, but all he could see was a Polly-shaped hole in his life that would never be filled by another woman. Ever.

And yet he couldn't—wouldn't—convince her to stay. He knew what this kind of opportunity meant for her career, her *life*. He'd once had the same kind of dream about one day making it to the big leagues, and though it was far too late for him, her dream—the one she'd put on hold four years ago—was now right in front of her. Waiting.

"You have to go." The words hurt as he spoke. "Your mother would want you to."

She looked at him. Jesus God, he hoped that glint in her eyes was a trick of the light and not tears. It took everything he had not to haul her into his arms and beg her to stay.

"What about us?" Polly picked up a fistful of sand and let the grains run through her fingers. "A year is a lot longer than three weeks."

"Yes, it is."

"You think emails and Skyping will get us through?"

His jaw tightened. The darkest scenario of all rose in front of him. The one where a hardened corporate CEO did the right thing and let a lovely young woman go so she'd be free to experience all that her new life could offer.

"Peach," he said slowly. "You need to go without any...attachments."

Polly blinked. "What does that mean?"

"You're twenty-five." Luke pushed to his feet, his heart hammering. "You haven't even had much chance to be young. You left college for your mother. You spent four years caring for her and trying to keep her bakery afloat. And you put your dream of Paris on hold for longer than you should have. You have to go. But you need to be on your own."

"You mean without you tying me down?" Irritation flashed in her eyes as she stood and bent to shake out the blanket. "Will you break up with me if I go to Paris?"

"Of course not. But I want you to have a good time. To have *fun*. Not to be thinking about a heartsick CEO over here drowning himself in Cocoa Nibblers."

Polly didn't smile. She straightened, her features set as she leveled her gaze on him.

"Luke," she said. "I love you."

Her words poured through him like hot syrup, warming every corner of his soul. He shut his eyes and dragged in a breath.

"Even when you're acting like a misguided ass who thinks you're doing something right when you're not," she continued. "I love you."

I love you too. The confession lodged in his throat. Of course he loved her. So hard that the thought of her leaving was a physical ache. He'd fallen in love with her the instant he'd turned from the pool table at the Troll's House and caught her staring at him.

And now he wanted a lifetime with her—one in which he would wake up every morning to find her curled up against his side. One in which she'd insist he go "off the grid" so she could take him to hippie music festivals. He wanted her hybrid pastries, teasing smiles, and her unending belief that life is meant to be lived with joy.

He wanted a lifetime of Polly.

But.

He wouldn't take anything about Paris away from her. And even with all they had together, he doubted his ability to sustain his commitment to Sugar Rush and make her happy at the same time. To give her the fairy tale she both wanted and deserved. At least, not for years to come. And he'd sooner live his workaholic life for an eternity than ever...*ever*...be responsible for Polly Lockhart's unhappiness.

"This is what I meant when I said I was proud of you," he said. "You don't just talk about doing things. You *do* them. And who knows what else will open up for you in Paris? I wouldn't be surprised if Pierre Lacroix himself offers you at job at one of his patisseries."

"And because of that, we can't be together?"

"Polly, I've spent twelve years immersed in Sugar Rush business. 24/7. My father and aunt have constantly been on my case about taking a vacation. And not for one minute do I regret putting everything I have into the business, but *you* opened a whole new world for me. You made me wonder what I might have done if I'd looked up from my damned computer once in a while. But Sugar Rush is still my life. I'll always be the CEO who puts the company first."

"Even before us?"

Pain cut through him. He put Polly before, above, and beyond anything else in the world—especially himself and Sugar Rush. That was exactly why she had to go.

Her gaze shifted away from him, a shadow crossing her face. "Well, maybe you're right then. Maybe I should go without *attachments*. Without you."

"Polly—"

"I know we can make this work," she interrupted, hugging the blanket to her chest. "I *want* to make it work. I want everything—you, Paris, Wild Child. I want museum galas and full moon festivals. I want to sleep in your fancy bed and make deliveries in my bakery van. But if you really believe we're the *same*, then you need to want all that too. You need to meet me halfway. And if you won't, then it will never work."

"Polly, I want everything you do." Frustration tensed his shoulders. "But I don't want you to miss out on anything either. Look, you need to send in your response and make plans. Once you get settled in Paris, we'll set up a schedule around your classes and—"

"Oh, for God's sake." Polly stalked toward him and poked him in the chest. "I will not be on your schedule, Luke Stone. I *love* you. And I'm pretty sure you love me too, because what you said about being proud of me was the most extraordinary poetry I've ever heard.

"But if you want me, then you need to be *all in*. Full force. One hundred percent. None of this *scheduling* or *wait and see* crap. You give me everything you are, everything you have, because we don't deserve less. Certainly not a half-baked, once-a-day schedule. And if you want this as much as I do, you'll put *us* first and prove that not even the Atlantic Ocean is big enough to separate us. Nothing is."

He couldn't respond past the tightness in his chest. Tension thickened the air. Polly's brown eyes filled with sorrow.

"Luke," she said. "You just told me to tell you if something makes me feel bad. You said you'd do everything you can to make it right. Well, this is your chance. Because I feel pretty crappy right now."

And yet he couldn't make this right, not for both of them. He could only do the right thing for her.

"Peach." Something stuck in his throat. He suppressed the

desperate urge to confess he loved her too, that she'd put together all the pieces of his heart and made it whole again.

"Go to Paris," he finally managed to say. "Have fun."

She gazed at him, her eyes still bright, and then she turned and walked away. The ocean wind swept in from the water, turning his blood to ice.

CHAPTER 25

Life goes on.

Polly expected to mope around after last night's deba-cle, nursing her wounds and feeling sorry for herself. Maybe even indulging in a jumbo-sized bag of Cheetos. But being a business owner meant that you couldn't close for the day just because the man you loved was being a stubborn ass. If you could, female-owned businesses across the globe would probably shut down for good.

So after a sleepless, tearful night on her lumpy mattress, she hauled herself downstairs at dawn on Sunday to prep for open-ing. Pale light filtered through the layer of fog covering the sky as she let herself into Wild Child and locked the door behind her. Hannah had texted that she was up in San Jose for the weekend, the message reminding Polly that both her sister and Clementine would be leaving for good soon.

She set her bag on the counter. An air of desolation hung over the bakery, though she supposed that might be partly due to her mood. The tables and chairs were stacked to one side, and all the wall hangings had already been taken down and stored.

Tomorrow they'd close for a week so Eleanor Pendergrass's crew could come in and get the renovations work done.

Polly walked into the kitchen, focusing on getting things ready. She turned on the deep fryer and retrieved various batters from the walk-in refrigerator. She put tins of muffins into the oven and fried the *pâte à choux* for the Declairs. As she started making the chocolate custard, a knock sounded at the front door.

She went to answer it, surprised at the sight of Hannah on the other side of the glass. She unlocked the door to let her sister in.

"I thought you weren't getting back until this evening," she said.

"I caught a ride with a girl who's going down to LA." Hannah followed Polly back to the kitchen. "How was your museum event?"

Polly was tempted to lie, not wanting to relive it, but she didn't have the energy.

"Not great." She checked the timer on the oven. "I looked good, though. I looked *beautiful.*"

"So what happened?"

"Nothing. That was the problem."

Hannah plucked a muffin from the tray and lifted her eyebrows. Polly turned back to making custard and started spooning it into a pastry bag.

"You might have been right," she mumbled.

"About what?"

"About me thinking there might have been some fairy tale between me and Luke."

Embarrassment rose in her throat. Hannah travelled and blogged about love traditions throughout the world, but as far as Polly could tell, her sister didn't have any romantic notions about love. Maybe Polly should envy that about her too.

"There's never a fairy tale," Hannah finally said.

Polly glanced at her sister. Hannah was staring down at the broken muffin, her forehead creased.

"Why did you leave?" Polly asked.

"I never fit in here."

"But that didn't mean you had to leave me and Mom."

Regret darkened Hannah's eyes. "You were fine without me. You were so close, always happy at the bakery and watching movies together. I was just more comfortable with Dad. And there was nothing for me to do when we moved to Rainsville. I wanted to see what else there was."

Maybe it was time for Polly to do that too. She took paper liners from a shelf and handed them to her sister. Hannah started layering paper onto the display baskets.

"Did you tell Luke about Paris?" she asked.

"Yes. He has some silly notion that I should go without anything tying me to Indigo Bay. Especially him."

"Was it a break up?"

"No." Polly bit her lip. "Not really. I mean, I don't think so. He just seems to think he'd be stifling me or whatever, when he's never done anything of the sort."

"Well, it sounds good of him to want you to go freely. Honestly, that's the best way to travel."

The problem was Polly didn't want to be free—not from Luke, at least. But she wouldn't cling to him either.

Maybe Hannah was right. Maybe it was time to let the bakery go and pursue her life abroad. To reinvent herself as a woman of sophistication and worldliness, queen of the culinary arts. Few people had a chance to take such a step.

And as painful as it would be to close her mother's legacy, especially after all that she and Luke had done to save the bakery, maybe sometimes you had to let things go. If she closed Wild Child, she wouldn't have anything to come back home to, or a business where she could apply all the things she'd learn in Paris, but she could start over by herself. Somewhere. She just wished that thought made her heart feel whole and soft, not cracked like brittle, hard caramel.

A loud knock sounded at the front door. Polly glanced at the clock. Who could be at the door so early? Hannah went to peer through the kitchen doors.

"Polly."

She looked up at the surprised note in her sister's voice. "What?"

"You have customers waiting," Hannah said.

"What are you talking about?" Polly set down the pastry bag and walked to look out at the front.

At least two dozen people were outside the door—men and women, young, old, middle-aged—and they stood in a line that snaked halfway down to the bail bondsman's office.

Polly's stomach jumped.

"I don't get it," she said. "There must be a mistake."

"Considering Wild Child is on the window, I doubt that." Hannah strode across the room and unlocked the door.

The crowd rustled with excitement as they saw her approach. She opened the door and held up a hand to indicate they weren't opening yet.

"Good morning," Hannah said. "Are you waiting for muffins?"

"No, ma'am." The college-aged kid who was first in line peered past her into the bakery. "We wanted to get one of the Declairs."

"We heard about them on the news," his friend added. "Are they ready yet?"

"We'll try to open a little early." Hannah glanced at the rest of the crowd. "Are you all here for the Declairs?"

Good-natured shouts of "Of course!" and "Hurry it up!" filtered through the air.

"Not much longer," Hannah said. "I'll be right back."

She closed and locked the door, amidst a rise of impatient groans from the crowd. She returned to Polly, anticipation suddenly lighting on her face.

"You're on the map, Polliwog. Get the Declairs out for your customers."

Emotion tightened Polly's throat. She couldn't wrap her brain around the fact that not only did Wild Child have a line of customers, they were actually waiting for a pastry that had been a mistake. Or a happy accident, just as she'd once thought about her and Luke. Something that was meant to happen.

"I can't believe it," she finally said.

"You'd better." Hannah steered her back into the kitchen. "We have a crowd to satisfy and less than an hour to finish getting ready. Tell me what to do."

Emboldened by her sister's take-charge attitude, Polly took a breath and snapped into action. She showed Hannah how to fill the pastries with the chocolate cream, then fried up more dough. They worked quickly, glazing the Declairs with ganache while the dough cooled. Hannah took over frying another batch while Polly mixed more chocolate custard.

As the clock inched toward their seven o'clock opening, they had three dozen Declairs ready with another six in progress. Polly pushed a lock of hair away from her forehead, nervous excitement rising inside her as they set the Declairs into baskets.

"We need to open in twenty minutes." She looked out at the crowd again. "Oh my God, I think there are more people out there. We won't have enough for everyone."

"You keep making them." Hannah moved past her with one of the baskets and set it on the counter. "I'll sell. If we run out, we'll give rain checks to the remaining people in line. In fact, we *should* run out to get people to come back and keep them talking."

When Polly didn't move, Hannah gave her a nudge. "Hurry. I'll get the coffee made. What else needs to go out?"

Polly jolted into action again. Together she and Hannah set out the muffins, doughnuts, éclairs, and croissants. Hannah organized the tables and chairs while Polly made as many Declairs as she could and tried to control the butterflies still zinging around her stomach. By the time they were ready to open, she was shaking with anxiety.

"I'll open," Hannah said. "Get ready, Polliwog. This is your show."

She went to unlock the doors.

Her show. Polly closed her eyes and took a deep breath. An image of their mother rose in her mind, the healthy, vibrant Jessie Lockhart with her warm brown eyes, ever-present pony-tail, and her serene belief that people were essentially good at heart.

I love you, Mom.

A cacophony of excited voices filled the bakery suddenly. Polly opened her eyes and picked up another batch of Declairs, heading out to join her sister at the counter.

"Line up single file, please," Hannah called, directing the crowd to the front counter. "Declairs are three-fifty a piece, limit of three per customer."

Considering Polly had been selling them for two dollars with no limit, this was news to her. But Hannah seemed to know what she was doing, so Polly let her take over the counter.

"Made less than fifteen minutes ago and filled with rich chocolate cream," Hannah announced to the college kids who eagerly hurried up to the counter. "We also have chocolate éclairs, glazed doughnuts, blueberry muffins...everything is fresh baked with the finest local ingredients. What else can I get for you?"

The boys loaded up on three Declairs each, plus doughnuts and muffins. Leaving her sister to handle the crowd, Polly returned to the kitchen to make more Declairs. Enthusiastic chatter and orgasmic moans of pleasure came from the customers who were happily eating their pastries.

She hurried out with another batch only to find that the previous three baskets were already empty. Energy and excite-ment rippled through Wild Child. Hannah rushed around behind the counter, pouring coffee, boxing up croissants, and selling Declairs faster than Polly could make them.

"What's going on?"

Polly looked up as Ramona pushed her way past the crowd—amidst grumbles and shouts of "Get in line, lady!"

Ramona came around the front counter, looking from the customers to Polly in bafflement. "Where did all these people come from?"

"They heard about the Declair," Polly replied, handing a paper-wrapped pastry to a little boy who was waiting with his mother. "Word somehow got out about it because now everyone wants one."

"We could use some help here," Hannah added.

"It was the Labradorite." Ramona pulled on an apron. "Aura healing."

Polly wasn't about to argue that point, since there was no reason it couldn't be the truth. She hurried back to the kitchen to keep production rolling.

The morning flew past, and by the time Clementine appeared to take over at noon, the Declairs were long gone and most of the other baked goods had been depleted as well. But customers continued to linger at the tables, drinking coffee, playing board games taken from the shelf in the corner, and leafing through the newspapers and magazines. Tom had arrived mid-morning for his usual chai tea, and he sat in the corner strumming his guitar.

Hannah put a sign in the window that proclaimed: *Declairs sold out today! More tomorrow at 7:00 sharp.*

After Polly explained the situation to Clementine, her friend only smiled.

"I'm not surprised, with the news report and all," Clementine said. "That kind of publicity is priceless."

"What news report?"

"The one KCBN ran last night." Clementine arranged a fresh batch of muffins in a basket. "Didn't you see it?"

Polly shook her head, her excited rush dissipating a little at the mention of *last night.*

"I wasn't home," she said. "What was it?"

"Remember I told you that cameraman and reporter came in here when you were away for the weekend?" Clementine pulled up a video on her phone. "They were doing a segment on local bakeries and bought a few of the Declairs. Turns out the reporter loved them so much they dedicated the whole segment to Wild Child."

She turned the phone to Polly. A pretty blond reporter stood in front of Wild Child's window, holding a Declair and smiling.

"If you thought there were no new pastries in the world, you'd be wrong," she announced. "Here at Wild Child Bakery on Hunter's Avenue in Rainsville, we've discovered what will surely be the Next Big Thing in pastry creation. A hybrid éclair and doughnut, this incredible creation is a deliciously airy, fried *pâte à choux* filled with a chocolate cream so rich and smooth it's almost sinful."

She talked about the history of hybrid pastries before biting into the Declair with a moan of pleasure. She held it up to the camera and smiled.

"This is without question the best pastry I've ever had," she said. "I do Declair."

Polly looked at Clementine in astonishment. "When you said the news people stopped by, I didn't realize you meant they were doing a story about *us.*"

"Neither did I," Clementine replied. "The reporter said it was something to do with the new interest in reality baking programs. I should have gotten a hint when she bought a box of Declairs to bring back to her office, but I really had no idea what their angle would be."

Polly was lucky to have gotten on the good side of the press. By all accounts, Luke hadn't had the same experience when he and his family had had all that bad publicity over the paternity lawsuit.

The thought of Luke diluted some of her elation, but because he'd been instrumental in helping her, she took out her phone and sent him a link to the news segment along with the message: *Wild Child is on the map. Just wanted to let you know. P.*

She went into the kitchen, where Hannah was sitting with a bottle of water. Strands of hair had escaped her ponytail and stuck to her damp forehead, and her apron was covered with streaks of chocolate and powdered sugar.

"You look like a real baker now." Polly hitched herself onto the stool beside her sister.

Hannah gave her a wry smile. "I guess I feel like one too, if exhaustion and at least three burns from hot pans are part of the deal."

"They are. And so is the feeling of making people happy with yummy pastries and chocolate cream."

"Too bad I've never been much of a dessert person." Hannah lifted the water bottle to take a drink.

"I couldn't have handled the rush this morning without you," Polly continued. "Thanks for your help."

"I've worked in enough bars and restaurants to know what I'm doing." Hannah glanced at her. "And you did good, Polliwog. Mom would be proud of you."

A rush of emotion filled Polly's heart.

"I'm really glad you were here," she said, hesitating for a minute before asking, "You're still planning to leave?"

Hannah nodded. "Whenever Dave gets here."

Though it was the response she'd expected, Polly's throat tightened at the idea of losing Hannah again, especially since she was already missing Luke. But he would eventually return—to his family, at least. She had no such confidence that her sister would return to *her*.

"Are you still going to Portland?" she asked.

"I don't know where I'm going," Hannah said. "I guess I'll find out when I get there."

Polly smiled faintly. "Sounds like love."

"What does?"

"Sometimes you don't know that's where you're headed. But you sure do know when you get there."

CHAPTER 26

*T*he initial surge of excitement over the Declairs lasted for a week after the news report aired, but the flow of customers remained steady, with intermittent lulls throughout the day allowing them to restock and regroup before the next rush.

Polly and Hannah both woke at three so they could go downstairs and start prepping the Declairs, and then Polly either worked through the morning or until she had a class, after which Clementine took over. Through it all, Polly hoped against hope for a call from Luke, promising he would give as much, if not more, to *them* as he did to Sugar Rush. But the call never came.

Rather than close for renovations and risk losing momentum, Pendergrass and Peabody Designs sent in a crew to work overnight, and soon the interior was freshly painted with new shelves and tables stenciled with mandala designs, bright hammock chairs, an array of earthy plants, colorful lanterns, an antique birdcage, and framed art from local artists.

Julia Bennett strode in one morning and told Polly it was imperative that she didn't succumb to "mass production" of the Declairs.

"Keep your batches small and stick to a limit of three per customer," Julia said. "Not only will that maintain consistent quality, it will let people know that they have to come back if they want more. And when a person has to work a bit for that which they desire, they will value it even more."

She gave Polly a pointed look, which made her wonder if the other woman was also talking about Luke. But she didn't ask about him, not wanting to even think about him over in Switzerland, touring a building site and burying himself in work.

He'd responded to her text with a short *Congrats—I knew you could do it*, but there was a massive distance between them now, one with little chance of meeting in the middle. Polly wasn't sure there even was a *middle*.

The Wild Child accounts began to show a significant profit, and because of the business structure Luke had helped her put in place, the bakery could maintain the momentum to the point that she could hire more employees. He was part of the reason Wild Child was able to handle the sudden influx of customers and production.

Polly set a fresh batch of doughnuts on the front counter, enjoying the conversation from the customers who were sitting at the tables, talking and eating. The strains of "Here Comes the Sun" drifted from the speakers.

After cleaning a few smudges from the glass counter, Polly looked up when a young man with a scraggly beard approached.

"Hey." He pushed his overlong hair away from his face. "I'm looking for Hannah."

Apprehension flickered through Polly. "Hold on, I'll get her for you."

She went to the kitchen, where Hannah was piping éclair dough onto a tray. "There's someone here to see you. I think it's your friend Dave."

Hannah almost dropped the pastry bag before setting it down.

She wiped her hands on her apron and followed Polly to the front.

"Hey." Dave smiled at the sight of her. "You ready to hit the road again?"

"Yeah, sure." Hannah glanced uneasily at Polly. "Um, can you give me some time to get my stuff together?"

"Sure, but I'd like to get going early tomorrow morning," Dave said. "A friend said we could crash at his place when we go through Eureka."

"I'll be ready." Hannah put a cranberry muffin into a bag and passed it across to him. "Come back here around six tomorrow morning, okay?"

Dave nodded, peering into the bag as he headed back out the door. Hannah pulled a few dollar bills out of her pocket and put them in the cash register.

"Still going to Oregon?" Polly tried to ignore the ache in her chest.

"I guess so."

Hannah hesitated, as if she wanted to say something else, then went back into the kitchen. Polly looked at the customers clustered around the tables. She listened to the lyrics of the song and breathed in the scents of coffee and chocolate.

Find your happiness.

She had done exactly that. And she'd discovered that happiness didn't have to be found in just one place. Yes, her happiness had always been right here, wrapped up in Wild Child and memories of her mother.

But Polly had also found a bright, glowing happiness with Luke. She'd found happiness in spending time with her sister after so many years of separation, in being with her friends, in watching movies and reading good books. She found happiness in baking, in learning about the culinary arts, in the idea of creating new innovative pastries.

And she'd found an intense happiness and excitement in the

discovery that she'd been accepted to an Art of French Pastry course that would be a life-changing adventure.

She turned and went back to the kitchen. Hannah straightened from taking a tray of éclairs out of the oven.

"I'll make the custard and leave it in the fridge," she said. "Do you need me to finish these?"

"I need you to stay here," Polly replied, her heart thumping against her ribs as she added, "Please."

Hannah grabbed a rag and started wiping down the counter.

"You told me I couldn't turn the chance down," Polly continued. "And of course you were right."

"I just want you to know there's more to the world."

"Do you remember when we lived at Twelve Oaks? There was a grove of trees out past the apple orchard."

Hannah shook her head, focused on putting the baked éclairs onto a cooling rack.

"It was this really nice, shaded area where we always played," Polly said. "There were old logs and stumps to climb around on, and one summer you helped me turn the place into a French restaurant. You corralled the other kids into being customers and waiters, and I was the chef sending out escargots made of acorns and muddy-water soup. We spent the whole summer running the French restaurant before the boys took it over as a fort."

Hannah pulled the parchment paper off the tray and tossed it into the trash.

"Clearly running a French café is something I've wanted to do since I was a kid." Polly rested her hand on her sister's arm. "I couldn't have run the French restaurant without you. And I can't go to Paris without you."

"Yes, you can." Hannah picked up the pastry bag again, her eyes downcast. "You've always been able to do everything without me. You and Mom."

"Mom isn't here." Polly was unable to keep the desperate note from her voice. "I need you, Hannah. I need you to take care of

Wild Child so I can go to Paris. The Declair sales have put us back on the map, and I want to take this pastry course so I can bring back everything I learn. I want to create specialty éclairs and perfect macaroons. I want to make chocolate truffles, pralines, and croquembouches, and can you even imagine what I'll learn how to do with puff pastry? When I come home, I'll have a whole repertoire of experience and ideas for Wild Child."

Her heart was beating fast with excitement and the striking realization that this was what she was *meant* to do. The Art of French Pastry course hadn't dropped into her lap out of sheer luck. She'd proven to the admissions committee that she had both the wherewithal and talent to be chosen as one of their students. She'd already measured up.

"I'm scared to go," she admitted. "But seeing how brave you've been for ten years makes me think I can be that way too."

Hannah looked almost startled. "You think I'm brave?"

"Of course. To travel the way you do, for as long as you have? That takes tremendous courage. I've always envied that about you."

Hannah blinked, her eyes darkening. "It doesn't take courage to get on a train and leave. It takes courage to stay and help your mother even though you know she might not get better. It takes courage to try and save a failing business. To *believe* the way that you do."

Tears stung the backs of Polly's eyes. "Then please do this for me, Hannah. I just need a chance."

As they looked at each other, the current of warm tenderness passed between them again, an echo of the bond they'd once shared as children. Hannah reached out and squeezed Polly's arm.

"All right, Polliwog. It's your turn to go."

CHAPTER 27

"Where's the fucking budget report?" Luke snapped.

And what the fuck was wrong with everyone? Why couldn't they do their fucking work and get him the fucking paperwork on fucking time?

"Sir, you just asked Roger for it two hours ago." Kate looked so implacably unmoved that Luke was all the more annoyed. "I'm certain he's working on it."

"What's taking him so long?"

"He's running the numbers as we speak."

Luke shoved away from the desk, his fists clenching. Why was his executive assistant so calm when there was a volcano roaring inside him, scorching his veins with lava and burning him to the core? Why were people acting as if nothing was wrong, as if the world hadn't fallen off its axis? Why the fuck was the sun still rising every morning?

Everything should have damn well stopped the second Polly Lockhart walked out of his life. No. *Flew* out of his life, on the way to live her dream in Paris.

She'd been gone by the time he returned from Switzerland. He'd dived straight back into work. Because what else was there?

Countless times he'd reached for his phone, desperate to call her, to hear her voice, but something always stopped him. The truth of his responsibilities. The knowledge that he'd been right to let her go.

Cowardice. Fear.

"I'll call Roger and get you an ETA." Kate strode to the door. "Will there be anything else?"

"Yes. Get me a coffee."

"You don't drink coffee, sir."

"I do now. Black. Not one of those fancy au laits or whatever. Nothing *French.*"

"Yes, sir." Kate pulled open the door and tossed him a glance over her shoulder. "By the way, I forgot to tell you your aunt is on her way up."

Luke ground his teeth together and shot Kate a glare that could have sliced metal.

"You forgot, huh?" he snapped.

Kate blinked, somehow managing to look innocent despite her severe, scraped-back hairstyle and crisp black suit. "It completely slipped my mind, Mr. Stone."

"See that things don't slip your mind again," he gritted.

"Yes, sir."

He could have sworn she muttered something under her breath as she stepped outside. He heard her talking to Julia, and before he could get to the door and lock it, his aunt entered his office.

"I hear you're terrorizing everyone from here to Timbuktu." Julia tossed her handbag onto a chair. "And that your employees are working beyond overtime to get shit done for you."

"I pay them well to do their work," Luke retorted. "What are you doing here?"

"Someone has to tell you you're being an asshole, and everyone else is too scared to confront you," she replied bluntly.

"Not to mention that I've gotten half a dozen calls about your association with the inventor of the Declair."

She took out her phone and scrolled through it before turning the screen toward him. Luke took the phone, his chest twisting as he stared at a photo of him and Polly standing beside each other at the museum exhibition. Although the photo was grainy and dark, his girl glowed with an iridescent, inner light.

He handed the phone back to his aunt. "There's no association. She's gone."

Polly had been gone for exactly one week and three days. Wild Child was still selling plenty of Declairs to the customers lined up outside every morning, and they had launched online orders through their website. According to Julia, Clementine had delayed her move to help Hannah settle in, and Polly's friends Mia, Tom, and Ramona were all now working at Wild Child. Everyone had rallied to help Polly fulfill her dream of going to Paris.

Everyone except him.

"She rented an apartment in the 7th arrondissement," Julia remarked. "In a building that used to be an artist's atelier. Her classes haven't started yet, but she's met her instructors and is enrolled in French lessons."

Luke glowered at his aunt. "How do you know all that?"

"We're texting. And she sent me an email last week." Julia looked at her phone. "I told her to contact my friend Marie-Laure, who can introduce her to people her own age. Not that Polly will have trouble making friends."

And having fun. She was probably already having a blast. Hell, she'd probably forgotten about him already. When a young woman went off to live a dream in Paris, why would she give a second thought to the dickhead she left behind?

Except Polly wasn't like that. She loved with everything she had, and she sure as hell didn't *forget* about the people closest to her. Just the opposite—she had a permanent place in her heart for them.

Luke shrugged into his suit jacket. "I gotta go."

"Where are you going?" Julia asked.

Anywhere that wasn't here. Anywhere that he didn't have to be reminded he would spend the rest of his life in the corporate offices of Sugar Rush.

"Just out." He grabbed his keys and went to the door.

Kate was still at her desk, and she looked up at him. "Sir, Roger is on his way up with the budget report. Lucy is fetching your coffee right now."

"Forget the report and the coffee."

"Excuse me?"

"Go home, Kate. Tell everyone else to do the same."

Luke headed for the elevator. Outside, it was already getting dark, the faint scent of fall in the air. He got into his car, flexing his hands on the wheel. He couldn't stand the thought of returning to his "space station" house, so he put the Porsche in gear and headed toward Rainsville. Twenty minutes later, he found himself pulling into the parking lot of the Troll's House.

He went inside, welcoming the loud music emanating from the jukebox, the after-work crowd of blue-collar men who didn't care who he was or where he worked. He pulled off his jacket, rolled up his sleeves, and headed for the bar. His gaze narrowed on the stool where Polly had been sitting when he'd turned and seen her watching him. A college-aged kid was sitting there now, and the sight of him in *her* seat scraped Luke's insides with irritation.

He sat at another barstool and ordered a scotch. The burn of alcohol felt good going down. He reached into his breast pocket and took out Polly's elephant charm, which he'd been carrying around with him since she left. He stared at the charm, all of her words filtering through his head.

You're a cardinal sign. Cardinal signs govern the seasons and have the power to change.

There are too many mysteries in the world. Things you can't explain by science or logic.

Your heart line is deep and clear.

I'll save you.

Tell me you believe in love.

Promise?

"You want another?" The bartender stopped in front of him.

Luke dropped the charm back into his pocket and looked at his empty glass. "You got something called a birthday cake shot?"

The bartender lifted his eyebrows. "Sure. You want one?"

"Yeah."

"Is it your birthday?"

"No."

The bartender shrugged and turned to concoct the shot. He then placed a shotglass frothy with whipped cream and lined with rainbow sprinkles in front of Luke.

"Enjoy," he said.

Luke stared at the shot. He'd first touched Polly when he'd taken a pink sprinkle off her lip.

"Man, that is the girliest looking drink I've ever seen."

Luke glanced up. Evan slid onto the stool at his right and his father got onto the stool at his left. Tension tightened Luke's chest. He knew an ambush when he saw one.

"What the hell is it?" Warren nodded at the drink.

"Birthday cake shot."

Luke lifted the glass to his father in a salute and downed it in one gulp. The sugar rush burned his chest and hit his bloodstream like an explosion. He coughed.

Evan grinned. "Guess you can't handle the girly stuff, huh?"

"The girly stuff is fucking with my head big time." Luke thunked the glass back on the bar and pushed off the stool. "Come on."

They went over to a pool table. Luke racked the balls while Evan and Warren chose their cues. They started playing. For a few minutes, Luke was able to focus on the game, despite the sweet taste in his mouth and the undying thoughts of Polly. He lined up a shot, fired, and missed.

"I got an email from Carson suggesting we ask the board to address your recent plunge into a dictatorship," his father said as they waited for Evan to take a shot.

Given the number of times he'd overridden decisions in recent weeks, Luke wasn't surprised. He was, however, surprised that he didn't much care.

"Go ahead," he said.

"Son."

Luke's heart sank. His father only called him *son* when things were getting serious.

"Morale is down," Warren continued. "After you called Carson out at the board meeting, two VPs have told me this is exactly what happened after the paternity suit. People are even scared to approach you with ideas now. Unless you want another mutiny, you can't keep doing this."

"Yeah." Luke dragged a hand down his face, defeat suddenly spiraling through him. "I know."

"You need to take some time off," Warren said.

"I can't."

"Actually, you can," Evan said. "You just don't want to."

"And it's time that you did," Warren added.

"No."

Evan and Warren exchanged glances. Luke gestured to the bartender to bring them another round of drinks. He hated the fear simmering inside him, the sense that he had no idea what he would be or do without Sugar Rush. He'd spent his adult life working for the company. What else could he do?

"Don't push me out," he warned his father and brother. "I saved the damned company, remember?"

"Yeah, we remember," Evan said. "God knows you remind us often enough."

Warren clapped a hand on Luke's shoulder. "I'll never be able to tell you how much I appreciate everything you've done. I know you wanted to fix things, and you have. Net sales are up, North American and international profits have increased, and we're regaining our market position. You've worked damned hard to get those results. But it kills me to see you living your life for the company instead of...*living your life.*"

"You mean like you are?" Luke snapped.

Warren was silent. Regret speared through Luke. He moved to line up a shot, unable to look at his brother. None of them had ever mentioned their father's self-imposed isolation after their mother's death. Even twelve years later, Warren remained focused on work and family. Not himself.

Luke stared at the pattern of balls on the pool table as if it would somehow provide him with answers to all the questions crashing through his head. He was starting to sense that his controlling nature had affected his relationships with his family more than he'd been willing to see or admit. Not for the first time, he wondered how different their lives would be if his mother were still alive.

His chest tightened. He didn't want his father to be alone any more than he wanted himself to be alone. And a future without Polly was a bleak, arid desert of *nothing*.

Surely there had to be a way to fix what he'd broken, to figure out how to run Sugar Rush and give Polly everything she deserved at the same time, to *make it work*.

He just had no idea how.

❧

She'd been standing right next to the stove. Even with her curly hair hidden under an ugly plastic cap, Luke had known exactly who she was. He'd felt her presence the instant he'd walked into the Sugar Rush test kitchen all those weeks ago. It had taken every ounce of his self-control to find a way to get rid of everyone else so he could be alone with her.

He stirred the mixture of sugar and corn syrup boiling on the stove. He added coloring and flavor, then checked the candy thermometer and carried the pot over to the counter. He was pouring the mixture into the heart-shaped molds when the kitchen door opened. His younger brother Spencer walked in, still in his lab coat despite the fact that it was past eight at night.

"Hey, man." Spencer's eyebrows lifted behind his glasses. "What're you doing here?"

"Experimenting." Luke set the pot down. "You?"

"Need a hand roller." Spencer opened a drawer and removed a stainless steel roller. He turned, eyeing the candy molds. "That's going to be grainy. See those sugar crystals? You should have wiped the excess sugar off the pot."

Luke frowned. His eyes burned with fatigue, but he wasn't about to stop now. He dumped the candy into the trash and started again. As he measured sugar back into the pot, Spencer stopped beside him.

"The pot needs to be clean and dry." He took the pot from the stove and brought it to the sink. "Otherwise it'll screw up the mixture."

After cleaning the pot, he set it back on the stove and showed Luke how to properly measure the ingredients. They were halfway done before Luke felt his brother's gaze.

"So what's this about?" Spencer asked.

Luke shrugged. "Just seeing what I can come up with."

They worked a while longer—with Spencer's expert help, the candy poured easily into the molds, a perfect ruby-red unmarred by sugar crystals.

"Evan and I are going up to the city next weekend," Spencer said. "See a concert, get some dinner. You want to come?"

"Thanks, but no. You should ask Dad."

"We did. He also said no." Spencer's mouth twisted wryly. "Then he told us to ask you."

Luke smiled faintly, even as unease simmered inside him.

"Did he give you a lecture about me taking a vacation?" he asked.

"Sure, but he knows none of us can convince you to do something you don't want to do. He said you still have months of vacation time you haven't taken."

Only a few weeks ago, Luke wouldn't have known what to do with "months" of vacation time. But now...what if he could fill it with everything Polly?

He tried to imagine it, and couldn't. Even if he did go after her, there was a good chance she'd want nothing to do with him anymore. And then what? He'd come back and spend his days doing nothing?

"I can't take all that time off," he said. "I have to handle the Alpine acquisition. Besides, who'd take over if I left?"

"You asking me or yourself?"

Luke looked at the candy. If he did take time off, he'd have to appoint an interim CEO to handle things in his absence. And there were very few people he trusted enough to deal with the business, much less close the acquisition...

Wait a minute.

He pulled the apron off, his heart suddenly kicking into gear. "Hey, is Evan still in his office?"

"Far as I know. You should add rock candy to—"

Before his brother could finish, Luke was halfway out the door. He hurried to the main building and took the stairs to Evan's office. Evan was at his desk, his attention on his computer. He looked up, frowning as his gaze scanned over Luke's wrinkled dress shirt, stained with food coloring, and his unshaven jaw.

"What the hell is wrong with you?" Evan asked.

Luke stopped in front of the desk. "You still want a better position in Sugar Rush?"

"Why else do you think I've been trying to prove myself for so long?"

"You've never had to prove anything," Luke said. "Everyone knows how good you are."

"I've always had to prove something." Evan shut down the computer and pushed to his feet, tension lining his shoulders. "I've always had to work harder and be better just to get recognized for being competent. That's why I was flattered when Crown Foods contacted me about their COO position. For once, someone was looking at what I'd done, what I *could do*, instead of what I have."

Shame nudged at Luke. He hadn't given his brother the credit he'd deserved. But now he would do that and more, if he could finally relinquish control.

For Polly, he could. He *would*. He'd do anything for her.

"Look, I get why you gave the Fair Trade Foundation to Sam, okay?" Evan continued, old irritation rising to his eyes. "I know you were worried about the traveling. Fine. But don't you tell me I shouldn't take on the stress of a higher level position or that I don't have the experience. And don't you dare tell me I don't love this company as much as you do just because I wasn't the one who saved it."

Silence fell. Luke still couldn't envision his life without Sugar Rush, but maybe he had the courage to let go so that he could find out. Polly had. She'd left Wild Child in the hands of her trusted friends in order to discover what her dream contained.

He had a flashback to when he'd been eight years old and anxious about his upcoming tryout for Little League pitcher.

"If I don't pitch, what would I do?" he'd asked his father.

"Whatever position you get, you play the best game you can," his father replied. *"That's all you can ever do."*

Luke paced to the windows and back. A current ran through his veins, electrifying him with unexpected anticipation.

"I'm going to ask you one question," he said. "Would you be Sugar Rush's interim CEO?"

Evan blinked. "Are you serious?"

"If I take a leave of absence, I need someone to step into my position," Luke explained. "Not only to handle daily operations, but also to close the Alpine deal."

"And you want me to do it?" Evan looked as if he couldn't believe what he was hearing.

"Seven years you've been wanting to do more." Luke straightened and crossed his arms, his gaze steady on his brother. "Now's your chance."

"For how long?"

"Nine months, maybe a year. Until I get back."

Wariness appeared in Evan's eyes. "Then what?"

"Then we'll talk."

"No." Evan shook his head. "I want a deal. You give me a year. I'll run the company and finish the Switzerland project. If at the end of twelve months, you come back and think I've made a mess of things, then I'll leave. If not, you give me a position I want."

Luke extended a hand. "Deal."

They shook, firm and certain. A light appeared in Evan's eyes that hadn't been there in a very long time.

"What are you going to do?" Evan asked.

Luke grinned and turned to the door. "I'm going to get my girl."

CHAPTER 28

"*Non*, Polly, too much mixing." Pierre Lacroix poked at one of the flat *macarons* Polly had just pulled out of the oven. His bushy eyebrows drew together in displeasure. "You overwork the dough. *Recommencez.*"

He strode away. Polly pushed a lock of hair away from her forehead and sighed. *Recommencez* was a refrain she'd heard multiple times in the week since classes had started. She scraped the macarons into the trash, catching the sympathetic eye of Isabelle, the student at the adjoining workstation.

At least Polly and her fellow students were all in the same boat, trying to meet the high expectations of the renowned pastry chefs by working on their recipes over and over. She was happy to keep trying as long as it took to please the chefs, but she had yet to become accustomed to their demands for perfection. However, by the end of class, she'd managed to produce a sheet of *macarons* that, if they didn't earn a Lacroix smile, didn't provoke a frown either.

She cleaned her station, said goodbye to her classmates, and headed outside. She took the long walk back to her apartment, stopping on the Pont des Arts.

The gray waters of the Seine flowed around the curve of the Île de la Citè. The bell towers of Notre Dame sat against the cloudy sky like building blocks, the banks of the river lined with elegant stone quays and buildings that resonated with beauty and history.

She slipped her hand into her satchel for her phone. She wanted—no, she *longed* to call Luke and tell him all about her first two weeks in Paris.

She wanted to talk about the challenging classes and confess that she was still finding her footing in this brilliant city. She wanted him to assure her in his deep, warm voice that it would get easier, and that he'd always be there when she was feeling homesick and needed a friend.

But he wouldn't be. And though she could find her way without him, there was no denying that she outright missed him. She was even starting to regret not agreeing to his ridiculous idea of a *schedule*.

She let go of the phone and crossed the bridge. She'd get over him…eventually.

As she walked alongside the Seine, she wondered why she'd ever wanted to be a different version of herself. She'd always been brave, resourceful, *scrappy*. The only thing she had to find was the courage to realize that she didn't have to deny her own dreams to follow ones that weren't hers to begin with. To remember that she had dreams of her own.

Outside of classes, she spent most of her days learning French and exploring the city—watching tourists and Parisians, visiting museums, local markets, restaurants, and shops. She sent emails and photos to Mia, Clementine, and Hannah, all of whom updated her regularly with assurances that Wild Child was just fine, thank you, and even had a bit of international aplomb now that they were telling everyone owner Polly Lockhart was off studying pastry-making in Paris.

Polly stopped alongside the quay when her phone buzzed with a text. She tugged it out of her satchel.

JULIA: If you fall in love with a Pierre or an Antoine, I will personally curse you.
POLLY: Your very existence upon this earth is a curse.
JULIA: True. But I mean it. No Frenchmen for you. At least, not until I'm over this breakup.
POLLY: You aren't supposed to like me, remember?
JULIA: I was starting to soften toward you until you went off to live your life instead of thinking about how it affected me. You're not wearing jeans, are you?
POLLY: Uh, no. Of course not.
JULIA: Hear that? That's me grinding my teeth. And if you're wearing tennis shoes, I am personally coming over there to shake some sense into you.
POLLY: No tennis shoes. Promise.
JULIA: Wear the blue crepe dress tonight.
POLLY: I'm not going anywhere tonight.
JULIA: Yes, you are.
POLLY: Scorpios don't have clairvoyant powers.
JULIA: This one does.

Polly shook her head with amusement, resisting the urge to ask about Luke. She'd said everything she needed to say to him, and she didn't need Julia to tell her he was holed up in his office working 24/7.

Sadness nudged at her. She put her phone away and walked toward the left bank. Her studio apartment was located just off Montparnasse Boulevard in a rickety little building that had once been an artist's workshop. She crossed the courtyard and stopped at the building's entrance.

A row of cellophane-wrapped hard candies sat lined up on the steps, a glittering pathway leading to the front door.

Polly's heart gave a wild, crazy leap.

She bent to pick up the candies one by one, putting them into her bag as she walked to the door. The trail continued up the wooden staircase to her apartment. She hurried up the stairs. Her hand trembled as she unlocked the door and pushed it open.

Oh.

Sugar Rush lollipop trees filled the small room, drenching the air with the smell of chocolate and sweet fruit. Jars of Puffles, Sweeties, Jelly Rolls, Honeybee Toffee, and Cocoa Nibblers sat on the tables and chairs, and candy bars and boxes of chocolates lined the windowsill.

Her pulse raced. She stood there, not daring to believe or hope that...

"Hello, Peach."

The deep, resonant voice flooded Polly with warmth. She spun toward the kitchen, where Luke stood in the doorway, holding a large glass jar filled with pink, blue, green, orange, and red candies.

Her breath stopped in her chest at the sight of him—tall and incredibly beautiful in dark trousers and a white shirt with the sleeves rolled up past his corded forearms. His thick hair was ruffled, his dark eyes intent and serious, and he was as warm and yummy-looking as chocolate mousse laced with rum and coffee.

"What..." Polly swallowed hard. "What are you doing here?"

"The concierge let me in after I explained that I wanted to bestow a grand romantic gesture on the love of my life."

The love of my life. A thousand sparks flew through her.

"You mean m-me?" she stammered.

Luke grinned, his eyes creasing at the corners.

"The one and only," he said as he approached her. "Polly Peach."

He extended the jar. Their fingertips brushed as she took it from him, the light touch causing a little zinging sensation. Polly lifted the lid of the jar and looked at the rainbow of rock candy inside. She took one out; it was shaped like a heart and multi-faceted, with each angle and surface capturing the light.

"I haven't seen these before." She held the candy up to the window. The sunlight shone through, making the crystal sparkle like a jewel. "Are they new?"

Luke nodded. "They're called Polly Promises."

She lowered her hand and stared at him. "Seriously?"

"Seriously." Amusement gleamed in his eyes. "Marketing is working right now on packaging and a launch campaign. We're planning a big push for Valentine's Day."

"But how did you...?"

"I spent a few days in the test kitchen, making candy and trying to decide if I fell in love with you when I saw you at the Troll's House or when I realized the fates had put you back in my life, or when you told me I was a control-freak Capricorn. At some point, with Spencer's help, I came up with Polly Promises. And I realized it didn't matter when I fell in love with you...the fact was that I just loved you. I *love* you."

He took the candy jar from her and set in on the table, then placed his hands on either side of her neck. The warm, focused look in his eyes as he gazed at her—as if she were the only person who existed in the world—made Polly's soul want to sing all the songs.

"I love everything about you." Luke stroked his thumb gently over her collarbone. "I love your openness, your trusting nature, the way you do everything with your whole heart. I love how your eyes give away everything you're feeling, even when you try to hide it. I love the interesting ways your hair sticks up in the morning. I love your scent, the sound of your laugh, and that look you give me when I'm being an idiot. I love your body to the point of obsession, and I could spend an eternity learning all the facets of your mind. In other words, you are the glaze on my doughnut, the sugar on my cookie, and the chocolate on my éclair."

"Oh my," Polly breathed, placing her hand on his chest. "That was the most delicious speech I've ever heard in my life."

"I meant every word. I need you to be mine."

"I'm yours. Of course I'm yours." She let her eyes track over his face, his strong features that were indelibly imprinted on her mind. "But…"

"I'm here to stay," Luke said.

"For how long?"

"For as long as you'll have me."

Hope rose anew into her heart. "Really?"

"Yes." He cupped her cheek, faint uncertainty flickering in his eyes. "I know you're busy, but I want to be here with you. To make it work."

"What about Sugar Rush?"

"I took a leave of absence for the next year. I delegated all my projects, turned my office over to Evan, shut down my company email accounts, and threw away my business cards."

"You're kidding."

"I'm a man of leisure now, baby," he said. "I have nothing to do except follow you around Paris while you gaze at old buildings and I gaze at your mighty fine ass."

A laugh bubbled into Polly's throat. Luke smiled, the warmth in his expression flooding her with happiness.

He was hers.

"I want us to be together," Luke said, his voice threaded with urgency. "I want us to have *fun*, but not just for a few dates. I want us to have fun forever. I want us to live a fairy tale. I want to take you everywhere you want to go."

"No."

He blinked. "No?"

"I don't want you to take me places," Polly said. "And I don't want you to follow me. I want you to go *with me*."

"Peach," he murmured, lifting his hands to the sides of her head. "I'll go with you anywhere. I promise."

Their lips met in a kiss that sent her into a cascade of love, spilling like hot butterscotch through her whole body. She slid her fingers into his hair as their kiss grew deeper and hotter. He moved his hands to her hips and backed her up toward the bed situated against the wall.

She gripped the front of his shirt, bringing him down with her as she fell against the mattress, which enveloped her in a soft, fluffy cloud of—

Polly jerked away from him, her breath fast as she stared at him in shock. She put her hand on the bed.

"Is this…"

"A custom-made Savoir mattress?" Luke pressed his lips across her neck, his touch igniting little fires in her blood. "It might be."

"I can't believe you did this."

"That's not all I did." He flicked his tongue into the hollow of her throat. "I also cancelled the service on my company phone."

"Oh my God." Polly laughed and stroked her hands down his muscular back. "What have I done with CEO Stone?"

"You saved him." Luke lifted his head to gaze at her. "Remember when you told me to find my happiness?"

She nodded.

"I did," he said. "She's a beautiful, curly-haired pastry chef who changed my life and filled it with everything good. You're my happiness, Polly Peach."

And he kissed her again. Full force.

ABOUT THE AUTHOR

New York Times & USA Today bestselling author Nina Lane writes hot, sexy romances about professors, bad boys, candy makers, and protective alpha males who find themselves consumed with love for one woman alone. Originally from California, Nina holds a PhD in Art History and an MA in Library and Information Studies, which means she loves both research and organization. She also enjoys traveling and thinks St. Petersburg, Russia is a city everyone should visit at least once. Although Nina would go back to college for another degree because she's that much of a bookworm and a perpetual student, she now lives the happy life of a full-time writer.

www.ninalane.com

ALSO BY NINA LANE

THE SUGAR RUSH SERIES
Sweet is the new sexy.

From the Stone family patriarch down to the youngest
bad boy, follow the lives and loves of the Sugar Rush men and the
women who bring them to their knees.

THE SPIRAL OF BLISS SERIES

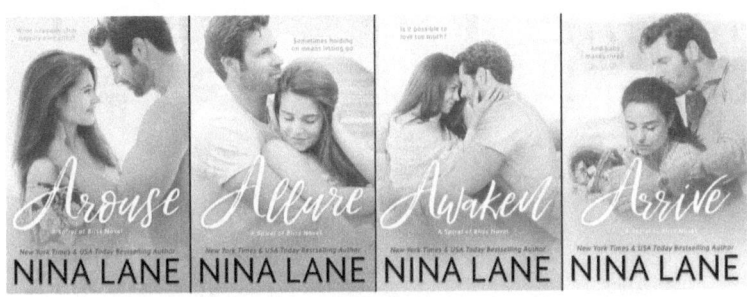

"Give me a kiss, beauty."

From an exhilarating crush to the intensities of marriage, Liv and Dean West embark on a passionate lifelong journey together. As the medieval history professor and his beloved wife face both personal challenges and painful battles, they never lose sight of the hope, humor, and devotion that belong only to them.

Liv and Dean's everlasting romance will melt your heart, turn you on, and enchant you with the power of a love to end all loves.

First we fell in love. Then we fell apart.

Shattered by tragedy a decade ago, two lovers fight the secrets that could destroy them.

"This book is a work of art."

A woman fleeing scandal. A town's mysterious recluse.

Lust and secrets collide in this provocative romance.